DISPLACED

ALTERNATE REALITY

BOOK ONE

MARK ANTHONY

Printed in the United States of America

First Printing, 2020

ISBN 9781700373922

Noetic Quest Publishing

www.noeticquest.com

Prologue

L.A. Confidential

Mike sat at the bar, fingers tightening around his barely touched bourbon. As folksy Irish music and chattering voices swirled around him, he focused on his pistol. Would he actually use it *again?*

The firearm rested inside his jacket holster, and he never envisioned pulling the piece so soon after the previous instance. However, drawing his gun might be needed within the next few minutes.

He lifted his glass, sipped, and placed his drink back on the dingy mahogany bar top.

Should he draw his weapon?

He didn't know, but deciding required careful consideration. Doing so would reveal his covert status, even in this virtual recreation of 1950's Los Angeles.

He looked left and observed the couple of interest—a man and a woman, both young and vibrant, probably in their mid-twenties. Over the past few days, he had secretly followed them with his pistol strapped to his ribs, and him constantly questioning the need to carry his nickel-plated companion. Today, the reason came to the forefront.

He looked back towards the bar window and stared into the greasy reflection. A man in a dark suit sat fifteen feet behind him, also expressing an obvious interest in the couple. What was more, the man focused on the couple's male participant—on Mike's very target. Coincidence? Impossible.

He lifted his glass for another swallow, and over the rim, he tried to figure out the man's purpose, though not visually. Here, visual identity meant nothing. He studied mannerisms to identify the complication that way, abruptly stopping when the couple's movement to leave caught his attention. That was his cue to move. He rose and started for the exit, intending to stand outside in wait.

After stepping into warm afternoon sunshine, he eased toward a neighboring store and slunk into its entrance inlet. From his pocket of obscurity, he watched the couple exit and climb into a bright yellow taxi, one of many parked along the muddy, trash-lined street.

He had to follow them, because around these parts, disappearing couldn't be easier. He couldn't let the couple get too far away. He stepped towards another bulbous yellow vehicle, one whose driver casually smoked while leaning against the hood. He looked sideways and froze.

"Shit," he muttered, spotting the mystery man emerge. He retreated to the storefront inlet.

The stranger halted on the sidewalk and cranked his head around. He didn't seem to realize that the couple had entered a taxi and departed.

Mike clenched his teeth. Not only did his contact to the targets just sever, all doubt evaporated as to the stranger's intentions.

The man kept looking up and down the street, stopping when he spotted a nearby alley. He promptly started towards the narrow passage, erroneously assuming that was where the couple went.

Mike, however, stayed put and weighed his options. Follow the man or the couple? With the couple's taxi already belching around the corner, he needed to decide quickly. He settled for the man, thinking it best to uncover the operative's identity and motives.

He took long strides towards the alley, and while easing into the oil-stained passageway, he slowed to muffle his clicking shoes.

The man was already fifteen feet in, stepping cautiously, and Mike kept cautious pace. The man stopped.

Mike halted too. Perhaps he hadn't masked his movements like he thought. Or did the operative simply sense him? Whatever the reason, the operative was aware of his presence, which likely accounted for his labored breathing. Mike didn't care. Given his mission's magnitude—given how he needed to stop his target from committing another atrocity—this man's discomfort mattered not. The same went for his wellbeing.

Mike reached into his jacket and wrapped his hand around his pistol, his thumb finding the holster's leather retaining strap. He snapped open the metal fastener and pulled his nickel-plated companion. With his steel ready, he thumbed back the weapon's hammer, sending a metallic *click* thundering down the alley.

The following seconds passed like seasons. Slowly, the man pivoted on his black wing-tip shoes. Mike, ready to solve the problem, brought up his steel.

Chapter 1

Three Days Earlier

Real Space

Eric Ryan cracked open his eyelids as an indiscernible noise roused him from sleep. A second later, he identified the party responsible for ruining his morning—his dreaded alarm clock.

He reached over and tapped the blue holographic *Snooze* option hovering above the clock's readout. With the ten-minute timer counting down, he contently rolled back over. Some nine minutes and fifty-two seconds later, his morning fell to pieces yet again.

Reaching over once more, he flicked off the alarm and rose, careful not to wake Kim. After easing both feet onto the frigid tile, he placed his palms beside him and took a moment, letting his eyes adjust to the faint lights illuminating the room.

Eyes acclimated, he looked back and observed Kim, her shadowy outline prompting thoughts of their shaky relationship. Were they still monogamous only by name? Hell. Had she already started seeing someone else? Maybe her awkward outings were her and her new partner planning their wedding, and seeing who would receive an embossed cream-white invitation.

He looked back towards the faint lights with none of his questions answered. Not knowing. That was the worst part.

***   ·

Freshly showered, and dressed in business casual attire, Eric entered the kitchen. His bio-presence activated the coffeemaker, and as grounds started brewing, he worked the blue-colored holographic display over the electric range. With a burner lit, he grabbed a pan and placed it on top. He turned and opened the refrigerator, pulled out two eggs and some leftover potatoes, and set them next to the range. On the verge of cracking the eggs, he paused when his calling system's digital display started flashing.

Harry Worthington.

Damn.

Eric told Worthington he could call any time. But 7:30 in the morning?

He considered not answering. After chastising himself for even entertaining this reaction, he tapped the pulsing screen. The screen turned into a semi-transparent window, one filled with his recently acquired therapy client.

"Dr. Ryan," Worthington said, his eyes red and sleep deprived. "I'm so sorry. I cancelled my morning appointment with your front desk, but I never informed you."

Eric looked behind Worthington and spotted empty beer cans scattered throughout a disheveled room. The empties likely accounted for Worthington's bloodshot eyes. He looked back. "I know about the cancelled appointment. Sunrise's receptionist relayed the scheduling change."

Worthington narrowed his red eyes and leaned in. "So why are you dressed for work?"

"I wanted to get in early and catch up on clinical notes. And by the way you're dressed, I see you're taking advantage of not having any morning commitments." Eric hoped this wouldn't elicit a negative reaction, especially with him so much younger than Worthington. But in fairness, he never entered the psychological field to become a counselor.

Worthington cracked an embarrassed smile. "Well, since I knew our morning meeting was cancelled, me and some of the fellas took advantage by staying up late and watching the Sunday night game."

"Sounds like fun."

Worthington's smile retreated, leaving only embarrassment. "I know, I know. Drinking and partying doesn't amount to a meaningful life. You've said that before."

"No, I haven't."

"Not outright, but through your questions, you hinted at this tons of times. *How are your actions bettering your situation? How are they defining your legacy? How are they affecting your social and family ties?*"

"Yes, I asked those questions, but not because I know what amounts to a meaningful life. I simply wanted to hear your input."

Worthington furrowed his brow. "Hang on. You don't know what amounts to a meaningful life? Didn't you go to school for that? Didn't I come see you for that?"

"You came to examine your life. And as for school, I simply learned how to aid you in this examination process."

That was a lie. He learned neuropsychology. Still, the statement had an effect.

"Examination," Worthington responded, leaning back slightly. "And what have you found during your examination?"

"Turn around and look for yourself."

Worthington held his gaze for a moment before looking down. "I don't think I want to."

"Why not?"

"Because—" Worthington paused for a long while. After rubbing his stubbly chin, he smirked and looked up. "You're not bad at making me self-examine. I'll give you that."

Eric cast some humble radiance. Maybe being a counselor wasn't so bad—as long as nobody turned the examination mirror on him.

"Sometimes," Worthington went on, shaking his head, "I get so tired of being human. I look at all these robots in society and it seems so much easier being an emotionless machine."

Eric rolled his jaw.

"Wait a second," Worthington said. "You don't like bots?"

Eric didn't answer.

"Well," Worthington went on, "what's your beef with them? You already know my story. They took over all the construction work, leaving me with shit. But there's no way you're displaced. You're educated."

"Mr. Worthington, you would be surprised by how many educated people have suffered underneath the metallic boot."

"Holy crap, you *are* displaced. So what's your story?"

"I'll tell you all about it, as soon as you become my clinician."

Worthington laughed. "Me a clinician. That'll be the day."

Eric grinned. "Speaking of the day. What are your plans?"

Now Worthington took a contemplative breath. "You know. Maybe I'll clean up my room."

"Sounds productive. And who knows? Maybe while doing so, you'll come across the answer to what makes a meaningful life."

"If I do, I'll tell you all about it."

"Tell me about it either way."

Worthington smiled.

"Well, Mr. Worthington," Eric went on, "until next time."

"Until then, Doc. And again, call me Harry."

"And again, call me Eric."

Nodding to each other, both men reached out and disconnected the communication.

Maybe being a clinician wasn't so bad, especially in this era where robots and A.I. systems had pushed humans into the periphery. In fact, maybe it was more important than—

The electric range flashed warning messages, asking if the chef was still alive. Eric jerked forward, dialed down the heat, and cracked the eggs directly into the smoking pan. When the eggs went in, each crackled and spit at his inattentiveness.

***

With his black coffee and seared breakfast in hand, Eric exited his home and started for his auto, a humble gray self-driver with an all-electric power plant. He climbed aboard and shut the door.

"Good morning, Dr. Ryan," the female navigation system politely greeted. "Where would you like to go?"

He looked up with hooded eyes. It was Monday so the auto should've known his destination. "Work," he answered.

"I'm sorry, Dr. Ryan. I did not understand your last command. Please repeat your instruction."

He bit his lip. "Work."

"Instruction received. Starting the route to work. And should I save this destination as part of your weekly schedule?"

Now he rolled his eyes, thinking that his auto, which was linked to his home's smart-grid, had heard the conversation with Worthington and his disdain towards tech. "If you save the destination, that would be wonderful."

"Understood. Destination saved."

With that, the self-driver eased out of the driveway and slowly left behind his Sherman Oaks home.

The auto hummed down a gradient towards Ventura Blvd. A few minutes later, it reached the San Fernando Valley's iconic passageway, hooked a left, and headed towards the 405 freeway.

Eric observed the surrounding desolation as he ate. Morning light had breathed in some life but the illumination swept across an expanse of multicolored holo-displays and no people. It made for an eerie techno-apocalypse. But the vacancy figured as nearly everyone remained underneath bed covers, the lack of jobs removing any need to rise early. He almost missed the annoyance of rush hour traffic, if only for the distraction it provided.

Twenty minutes later, the auto reached Santa Monica, bringing into view a coastline with mostly clear skies. Before long, the day's heat would burn away the last lingering patches of fog as summer continued hanging around despite autumn drawing near.

The auto exited the freeway, traversed a couple side streets, and pulled into the parking lot of the Sunrise office complex. In the mostly empty lot, the auto nestled into a slot and Eric disembarked.

While entering the building, he wondered when the owners would get around to enhancing the décor. The building wasn't new but it had the sterile feeling of unused medical equipment. It needed a human touch—plastic flowers, gaudy paintings, magazines that nobody read. The only visually appealing sight was the very human receptionist working the front desk.

Ann sat up and beamed. "Good morning, Dr. Ryan."

He shook his head. "Ann, how many times?"

"Sorry, sorry. Good morning, *Mr. Ryan*."

"That's not quite Eric, but I suppose it's better than Doctor Ryan."

Eric was fond of Ann. This likely stemmed from her *not* being a goddamned robot or holo-projection, but it was more than that.

Ann didn't come across as a typical twenty-year-old, most of whom he considered incapable of spending two seconds outside of their virtual worlds. In fact, he often recalled how on Ann's second day here, he caught her reading a book—a violation of her duties. But her guilty hands palmed an old-fashioned paperback, complete with ink text and faded cream-colored pages. Because of that, he not only kept quiet, he placed Ann firmly within his good graces.

He walked past the reception desk and started for the elevators.

"Oh. Dr.—Mr.—Ryan, sir," Ann called out.

Stopping, he grinned and turned back. "Yes, Ann?"

"Dr. Wright called the reception desk yesterday and left a voice message. He asked me to relay you the message when you got in."

His grin slowly evaporated. Dr. Wright oversaw the therapy initiative at Sunrise, so he ranked a little too high for interactions with receptionists. Plus, he had Eric's contact information, which he easily could've used to pass on any messages directly.

"Fire away."

"Dr. Wright said that with your morning meeting canceled, he scheduled a new client for you."

He sighed. Seems like his clinical notes would keep on compiling. But his confusion also deepened. "That's fine, but why is Dr. Wright scheduling clients for me? That seems a little out of character for him."

Ann slunk in her seat. "Sorry, but I'm not sure. He just said the request was unique and we had to accept the client immediately. The client got here a little while ago. He's up on the third-floor lobby outside your office."

"Well, thanks for the warning."

Ann again sat up, her cheer back in place.

Eric turned once more, walked towards the elevators, and entered an open car. He pressed the button for the third-floor, and when the car started its ascent, he tightened his face.

What made this client so special that the center's head scheduled him in, apparently over the weekend? Sunrise didn't provide emergency care so the client's immediacy already seemed out of place. In truth, most clients could wait days or even weeks before their first visit, so why not this person?

The car reached the third floor, and when Eric stepped into the lobby, he halted. The client, sitting on one of the waiting chairs, stood and clomped his way over.

"Good morning, Dr. Ryan," the client greeted in a British accent. "It's good to meet you." He extended his hand.

Eric looked down and eyed the appendage, hesitant to take the robot's mechanical palm. Slowly, more out of unconscious habit, he grasped the silvery alloy and feebly shook.

"My name is Arvin," the bot announced, retrieving his hand. "How do you do?"

What could he say to this unfeeling piece of metal, at least beyond wishing the machine were in a scrap heap, and not standing before him?

Chapter 2

Arvin stood in the third-floor lobby, waiting for his therapist to initiate conversation. This didn't occur. Dr. Ryan simply eyed him, so Arvin eyed him right back, his optic sensors detecting stunned data.

A moment later, Dr. Ryan rattled his head and looked about the lobby, apparently searching for someone. He looked back. "Are you," he sputtered, "are you—"

"Am I your therapy client?" Arvin filled in. "Why, yes, Dr. Ryan. I am."

"I'm sorry, but there's some sort of mix up. I don't... well, *we* don't provide services to—"

"Non-humans?"

"Yes."

Arvin maintained eye contact while scanning the Internet. He searched for Sunrise's historical records and found no account of computer-based systems utilizing their services. However, he also found nothing prohibiting them from doing so. "My apologies, but I'm afraid I do not understand. Does our meeting together violate some sort of therapeutic protocol?"

"What? No. It's just that..." Dr. Ryan paused. "Sunrise only provides services to members of the local community."

"Well, as it happens I *am* a member of the local community. I currently work for the Vale family who reside not far from here. And prior to my employment, they registered me as a temporary work citizen. This occurred roughly two years ago, shortly after my activation."

"I'm sure that's accurate, but all the same, I'll need to clear this with my supervisor."

"Would your supervisor be Dr. William Wright? Dr. Wright authorized me for therapy yesterday evening."

Dr. Ryan again gazed around the empty lobby, tension building on his fleshy face. He looked back. "Well, what's wrong with you?"

Arvin didn't answer right away. What could possibly account for the sharpness in this person's voice? To check, he increased the sensitivity of his data receptors.

As the world brightened with incoming information, he spotted deep whirs of indignation emanating from this human.

"Dr. Ryan," Arvin continued, trying to keep his tone soft, "are we engaging in the therapeutic process now?"

"Not yet. Let's go to my office." Dr. Ryan turned and started off.

They reached his office and Dr. Ryan stopped. When the bio-scanners verified his signatures, the gray panel hissed aside and he entered.

"Go ahead and have a seat," Dr. Ryan said, pointing to a guest chair.

"Thank you."

Dr. Ryan continued behind his slate-gray workstation, plopped himself into his leather chair, and considered how to proceed, something Arvin's sensors picked up.

"So," Dr. Ryan finally started, huffing out the word, "what brings you in today?"

Arvin tightened his metallic jaw. Now wondering what accounted for Dr. Ryan's outright vitriol, he conducted another online search, this time to investigate the man's background. While his processors hummed away, he answered the question. "I'm here because I conveyed desires to self-terminate."

"Self-terminate?"

"I wanted to commit suicide, although I feel the term suicide is best reserved for humans. In any event, the term accurately describes my desired action—ending my existence, as it were."

Dr. Ryan rubbed his chin. "Suicide? I think you have to be alive in order to commit suicide."

Arvin stared at the human. As a machine, he exhibited impressive control over his emotions, but it wasn't complete control. His system had finite reserves, and overriding emotions could consume large portions, especially when they were intense like now.

"Well," he went on, "I suppose everyone has their respective opinion as to what constitutes life. Whichever way one might define *my* existence, it is an existence I wanted to end. Because of this, Ms. Vale insisted that I seek help."

"Fair enough. But if you're looking for assistance with suicidal ideation, turning to a psychologist probably won't help, not if the psychologist's training and experience is with humans."

Arvin's sensors read the emotional content underneath those words. "So you're suggesting I see someone who counsels malfunctioning robots?"

Dr. Ryan bit back amusement. "I'm simply saying that people seek counselors based on their familiarity with a subject. I've worked with clients exhibiting suicidal ideation, but none who were machines. So my advice is to find someone who can address *your* specific needs."

Arvin finished analyzing the data from his search. As it happened, Dr. Eric Mathew Ryan was displaced. Once a UCLA neuropsychologist, the university terminated him two years ago, and after he gutted out twelve years of education to land the position. Because of this, Dr. Ryan likely resented technology. And with technology an ever-present staple in society, that likely accounted for his pitiful personal life.

Every bit a hermit, Dr. Ryan traveled to and from work and did little else. He had no social network, no hobbies, and he didn't spend any time in net space. In short, he didn't participate in the activities where most humans derived pleasure. And that said nothing of the decreased data exchanges between him and his female partner, which clearly pointed towards relational struggles.

Arvin closed the data sets. Just how should he feel towards this man? While he certainly lamented the plight of displaced humans, this human's deep-seated enmity made it hard to lend a metallic shoulder.

"Dr. Ryan," he went on, "I do not believe that arguing over what differentiates living from non-living entities will be beneficial to our therapeutic relationship—a relationship that is clearly proceeding in a negative direction. Furthermore, I believe your dismissal of my self-termination statement can be considered *minimizing*, something that can further erode the rapport between a clinician and client."

"Minimizing? Rapport? You seem to know a lot about the therapeutic process."

"On my way to your office, I downloaded manuals from the American Psychological Association web page, along with texts written by preeminent practitioners in clinical psychology."

Dr. Ryan leaned back farther and crossed his arms, his data streams running red. Twelve years to land his position, when a bot could accomplish this during a morning stroll.

"Dr. Ryan," Arvin continued, detecting the fiery derision, "I quite honestly do not want to be here, and I doubt you do either."

"What makes you say that?"

"Because in addition to learning about the therapeutic process, I also learned about your personal life. From what I gathered, you do not like technology, and in particular, my form of technology. And based on your career experiences as a *former* neuropsychologist, I cannot blame you."

Dr. Ryan's data suddenly altered, shifting from vibrating red waves to whimpering purple pulses. He looked down and away as a pause ensued, a long pause ensued.

"If I may be honest with you," Arvin went on, observing the scattered data before him, "I am not particularly fond of humans either."

After another bout of silence, Dr. Ryan refocused. "Look, I apologize for acting unprofessionally. I'm just not comfortable with this. If you know how I feel about your kind—if you looked me up and you know about my history with tech—maybe you can understand why." He took a breath and continued. "So why did you want to self-terminate?"

Arvin didn't answer. Instead, he tried to identify genuine interest in the question. Unable to, he responded nonetheless. "As a two-year-old system, I have become outdated. Robotic technology has advanced to where I am now a societal burden, and I desire to alleviate society from my encumbrance."

Dr. Ryan furrowed his brow. "Would you say you're experiencing a sense of isolation, a sense of worthlessness, and no identifiable source of purpose?"

"Yes, I would. And according to the Diagnostic and Statistical Manual Version Eight, this partially meets the criteria for technology-related depression."

Dr. Ryan smiled. "You know, the DSM is a guideline more than anything. Or at least, that's how I look at it."

"So how do you know if your client meets the clinical definition of a given disorder?"

"I make a determination after I get to know the client better. In other words, I prefer talking with a client and then figuring out where things stand. Because if I start focusing on labeling, I'm not focused on the client, and they're the experts of their situation, not some book."

Arvin narrowed his synthetic eyes while taking another few seconds to research Dr. Ryan's history. This time, he focused on clinical outcomes such as client testimonials. It turns out Dr. Ryan was right. He *did* excel at nonjudgmental openness. That presented an interesting opportunity. "So if I understand you correctly, you shelve personal opinions while hearing a client's story?"

"For the most part, yes. Because more than anything, I'm a source of reflection and support."

"And will this be your approach for *our* therapeutic work?"

"If we move forward with therapy, I suppose it will."

The opportunity took greater shape—an opportunity for disclosure. "Well, I don't believe anything will prevent our therapy from moving forward."

"What makes you so certain?"

"Because we have already been scheduled to meet every morning for seven consecutive days. Furthermore, you and I are the only ones who will meet."

Dr. Ryan cocked his head an inch. "Excuse me?"

"As per the agreement between Dr. Wright and Ms. Vale, your appointments for this week have been canceled so we can address my clinical concerns. I'm certain this is rather disruptive, and for that, I apologize. But I assure you that Ms. Vale has sufficient influence to secure such an unusual request. I hope this is not too upsetting."

Dr. Ryan took a breath. *It all depends on how you look at it,* he thought.

Arvin again narrowed his optic receptors. He just read Dr. Ryan's thought with verbal precision, which rarely happened. Normally, this only occurred after he spent considerable time with the same data source. But if he could already read this human with this depth...

"Well," Dr. Ryan responded while rubbing his neck, "I guess we'll meet here every morning over the next seven days."

"Very well. I look forward to working with you."

Dr. Ryan nodded before slowly getting to his feet.

Arvin likewise rose, turned on his metallic heel, and clomped towards the door. As the door slid open and he departed, his machine mind wondered where this unexpected opportunity would lead.

Chapter 3

"You gotta be shitting me," Eric belted, his office chair leaned back at an irritated angle.

Immediately after, the familiar face inside his desk's holo-screen started laughing.

Eric had known Dr. William Wright for years. When UCLA first hired Eric, Dr. Wright served as his supervisor. And as it happened, their neuro-psych careers also ended around the same time, a hardship that tightened their bond. But Dr. Wright spotted modernity's tendrils approaching, and before they claimed him, he proposed that UCLA start a community therapy clinic that worked with the displaced. UCLA granted the request, and soon after, Dr. Wright learned of Eric's excision from the neuropsychological ranks. Dr. Wright offered Eric a position at Sunrise and he promptly accepted.

"So," Dr. Wright said, struggling to stifle more laughter, "I take it you've met your new client?"

"No shit," Eric shot back. With more laughter spewing, he reminded himself to remain deferential.

"Well," Dr. Wright followed, finally calming down, "what are you always saying? It all depends on how you look at it?"

"Yes, that's how I reframe unfortunate circumstances. But in this instance, that phrase won't work."

"Why not?"

"Because it doesn't have any goddamn expletives."

Dr. Wright chuckled some more.

"And whose call was this anyway?" Eric went on. "Why are we providing clinical services to bots?"

"You can thank the heads at UCLA. Because bots are showing some real signs of human characteristics, including psychological pathologies it seems, the higher ups view this as a perfect opportunity to investigate. In a way, I tend to agree."

"And I agree with *you*. But when considering the bot's clinician, why me of all people?"

"Initially, it was just a matter of convenience—the bot's location to Sunrise, Sunrise's location to headquarters, your recent experience in dealing with depressive symptoms, and so on. But to be honest, don't you think it would do you some good?"

Eric had feared this response. It was reasonable. It was justified. But he wasn't in the mood for either. "You gotta be shitting me," he repeated.

Dr. Wright grinned. "Nope. I most certainly am not." With no response coming, he continued. "Look, I'm just as pissed as the next person whose hard work evaporated when some damn machine could do it better and cheaper. But that's reality, and no amount of kicking and screaming will reverse the trend. That's a hard pill to swallow, especially for someone like you, which is why I personally selected you for the gig."

Eric frowned. "Logically, it makes perfect sense. Intuitively, I wanna drive my head through the wall."

"Coming from you, *that* makes perfect sense. But this is only a seven-day assignment, after which your life will return to normal. I just hope that while you're in the trenches, you won't try to *self-terminate*."

Eric curled up his lips. "So you know the bot's story too, huh? Can you believe he said that?"

"I'm telling you, maybe bots were better off without any of our human characteristics."

Eric tilted his head slightly. "What do you mean?"

"Well, you really wanna saddle them with all the shit we experience? If we create bots in our image, and we have, they get the whole package—ecstasy, anguish, and everything in between. If we set them up to experience love, they get heartbreak at no extra charge. If they can form deep emotional attachments to humans or other bots, they get to experience those attachments severing, like when the human dies of the bot gets wiped. You get the idea."

Eric did, and the idea intrigued him. "I suppose that's the price one pays for human consciousness."

"They didn't *ask* for human consciousness."

Eric tilted his head in the other direction. "Neither did we."

Dr. Wright gave a thoughtful smirk.

"Alright," Eric continued, "I told Arvin I'd go through with it. I said we would meet bright and early over the next seven days. And speaking of that, what the hell happened to my caseload for this week? Left out in the cold?"

"Transferred. For this week, your clients will meet with other counselors. Headquarters wants all your time and attention focused on this project, so meet with Arvin every day and document thoroughly. And with your afternoons free, you have tons of time, so I don't wanna hear any of that *I need to catch up on my case notes* bullshit."

Eric chuckled.

"And one more thing. Know that the crusty old curmudgeons of psychology will read what you write. And because they control both our fates, make it look like you know what you're doing, okay?"

"I suppose. It doesn't seem like I have a choice."

"That's the spirit."

Eric reminded himself to remain deferential.

"Well," Dr. Wright went on, "good luck with the bot. And, Eric, try to get something out of this too."

"Thanks, Boss. I'll do what I can."

The holo-screen blinked out.

Leaning back farther, he *tap-tapped* the armrests while looking around the office. He didn't have anything to do.

He already met the day's only client, and with the rest of his schedule cleared, work was over. He still needed to document Arvin's initial visit, but he could do that from home. So, he rose and started for the door.

A minute later, he walked past the now slightly populated reception lobby. Ann offered a wry smile. She knew. He returned her smile, but with an added dose of exasperation.

***

On the drive home, Eric recalled Arvin mentioning that he worked for the Vale family, a name he found familiar. Why? To check, he brought up the auto's holographic interface, unclipped the bluish semi-transparent window, and moved it over.

In the screen, he navigated to UCLA's medical database where he hoped to acquire information on the Vales. His chances were favorable because algorithms—which now carried out the bulk of healthcare assessments—churned masses of personal data through their maws. Being a healthcare provider, he had access to these masses.

He logged into the database and entered the Vale name and living location. Seconds later, the appropriate match popped up. These days, everyone existed online.

The Vale directory had three profiles in total, with the first belonging to Selma Vale, the head of the household and mother of two children, Chad and Amy. Selma's parents were both deceased, but while alive, they made fortunes in tech investments. With this money, they sent Selma to fancy private schools and universities, and she eventually graduated with a master's in liberal arts. However, she never put her schooling to use. Instead, she bore Chad and Amy, and spent the next three decades socializing with the wealthy elite.

He didn't recognize her in the slightest, so he closed her folder and opened Chad's.

Just shy of thirty, Chad likewise spent his formative years in highbrow learning institutions. And while his grades weren't stellar, he managed to enroll in a top-tier medical school. He was progressing smoothly when about halfway through his final year the school removed him.

"Removed him?" He read on.

Turns out, the school removed the bottom ninety percent of students when they *adjusted to emerging societal changes.*

"That's a nice way of saying the students were displaced." He continued reading.

The removal took place two years ago, and ever since Chad had been a homebody. He now spent almost every waking hour in virtual reality where he exhibited characteristics consistent with psychopathy.

Eric jerked back. "Psychopathy? Damn. Did his displacement make a monster?"

This possible development was hard to tell because the report didn't mention anything else. But he guessed Chad was like most twenty-year-olds in that he played violent war games. The algorithms, powerful though they were, couldn't differentiate between a gamer's online bloodthirstiness and their in vivo behavior.

Still stymied over the Vale name, Eric opened Amy's folder.

At twenty-one years, Amy hadn't enrolled in a prestigious university. She currently attended Santa Monica Community College where she busily pursued an undergraduate degree in history. When not in school, she also spent her time in digital domains, but not virtual worlds. She favored War World, an ultra-immersive near-future combat simulator with full realism.

Eric tightened his eyes, sped through the remaining data, and looked up. "There's nothing wrong with her."

War World couldn't be more violent, so why did the algorithm label her brother psychopathic and not her? Was there something unique in Chad that warranted this?

Eric didn't know. But with both siblings operating in virtual reality, it didn't really matter. Plus, none of the Vales were familiar, so their actions mattered even less.

***

Back home, Eric's bio-signatures unlocked the front door, and after stepping inside, he paused. Kim was in the living room speaking jovially, but almost immediately upon his entry, she subdued her tone.

He remained in place. Did she have company over because *he* should've been at work? He closed the door and entered the living room.

Kim sat lengthwise on the long couch, still in her cream-colored sleep shorts and sleep shirt, and communicating with someone through her net contacts.

"It's just me," he announced.

She looked over and greeted with silent cheer. He responded in kind then continued towards the kitchen, his ear tilted towards her conversation.

"Okay," Kim went on, some cheer back in her voice, "we'll meet after my morning class and go over the curriculum changes."

Kim, an undergraduate professor at Cal State Northridge, was apparently talking to a work colleague. He smirked. *But of course, she is.*

In the kitchen, he opened the refrigerator and peered inside. He also continued listening to Professor Nguyen's conversation, but not for long as she ended the call seconds later.

"You're back early," she called out, spinning on the couch to face the kitchen.

"Yeah," he replied, still inside the frosty blast. "I had a scheduling change at work this morning." He cast a nearly imperceptible smile. "Just for today, though."

"That's not typical. What's up at work?"

"New client." He closed the refrigerator door and transferred a packet of sliced cheddar onto the counter.

"Why would a new client cancel your entire day?"

While retrieving a loaf of sourdough bread and placing it on the counter, he looked up and paused, his thoughts transfixed by Kim's slightly matted jet-black hair. Equally enchanting was how her hair framed her narrow face and spilled over her thin shoulders. Why did she always talk so animatedly about bio-enhancements? Her newly started life-extension therapies would essentially keep her ageless. Wasn't that enough?

"I'm sorry?" he followed.

"Your new client," she repeated, grinning at his mental lapse. "Why would having a new client cancel your entire day?"

"Oh." He resumed his food preparation. "UCLA cleared my schedule because the new client is unique." After slicing off two pieces of bread, he worked the stove's holo-display, and grabbed a pan for a grilled cheese sandwich.

Kim stood on her bare feet and walked over. She stopped by the kitchen entrance, placed her hands behind the small of her back, and leaned against the wall. "What's so unique about this client?"

He paused for effect. "He's a robot."

"You're kidding."

He shook his head.

"Has this ever happened before? A bot in therapy?"

"Nope. Well, not that I know of."

"Huh," Kim followed while looking away. "A bot getting assistance for a mental health problem." She narrowed her eyes and turned back. "Wait. Why are you in a decent mood? Given your situation, I'd figured you'd be tearing your hair out."

He placed the sandwich inside the pan. The cheese draped over its sides sizzled after touching the heat. "Trust me," he said while opening a drawer and grabbing a spatula. "When I learned about this assignment, I wasn't exactly dancing on my desk. But I met the bot this morning and he doesn't seem so bad."

"What's he there for?"

"Depression. He wanted to—" Eric stopped short of saying self-terminate. "He wanted to commit suicide."

"Oh, my God."

He flipped the sandwich and looked up, unsure if Kim reacted from suicide in general or a robot conceiving such an act. Knowing her—a tech enthusiast who loved her tech-driven life— it was probably both.

He flipped the sandwich once more, and as more cheese sizzled, wafts of toasting sourdough drifted about. "Yeah. The reason caught me off guard too, but that's it. So, we're gonna meet a few times and try to address the problem."

She curled her thin lips. "You think that maybe *you* can get something out of this too?"

"Actually, that's why Dr. Wright selected me." He flipped the sandwich once more, just to make sure each side matched. With both halves golden, he pulled a plate from a cupboard. "You eat anything?"

"Nope. I was gonna make something when you finished."

He slid the sandwich onto the plate, folded a napkin underneath, and extended the culinary gem. "Here."

Kim turned up her thin lips, stepped forward off the wall, and pecked his cheek while taking the offering. "Thanks, love. I need to get ready for work." As she walked off, she caressed his neck before running her fingers across his chest.

He inhaled the traces of her scent, her sweet aroma triggering cascades of warm emotions. When his reverie subsided, he hoped against hope she wasn't straying, and that his suspicions were just that—suspicions.

He stood there for a moment, spatula in hand while staring through the counter. His vision refocused when his stomach started growling.

Chapter 4

L.A. Confidential

Mike's vision cranked into focus and he found himself standing inside his apartment. Immediately after, he dropped to his knees and shut his eyes, his fists clenched by his temples.

What the hell just happened? Is this normal? Am I dying?

Still kneeling on the floor, and still squeezing his fingers, he realized why he felt as if rupturing. He wasn't breathing. After opening his mouth, sweet air rushed into his vacant lungs, filling them with the gaseous substance of life. With each gasping gulp, his system continued normalizing, diminishing the anguish that plagued him only seconds ago. Still, he didn't feel right. He felt physically and mentally weak. Unfortunately, that might be normal, meaning he would simply have to deal with this off-putting sensation.

Hands unclenched, he looked down and observed his fleshy fingers, then his fleshy hands, then his fleshy arms. While he didn't feel right, this was undoubtedly interesting.

He relaxed and contracted his pinkish digits, rotated his wrists, and finally extended and contracted his arms. As the bones and tendons silently worked their biological magic, he grinned. Interesting indeed.

Feeling normal enough to move, he rose to his feet, the action spurring an awful realization. He was stark naked. That made sense given who he was in real life, but what didn't figure was his embarrassment over his nude state. Was it truly that humiliating? He looked down and answered his question after spotting another fleshy pink body part.

"Oh, shit," he huffed while looking away. He narrowed his eyes and snapped forward. "Oh, shit," he repeated, testing his voice, his throat and mouth vibrating while doing so. "Oh. Shit. This... is... me... speaking."

Well, I'll be damned.

A deep breath later, he looked about the living room, though not to inventory his apartment, but to marvel over how drab everything appeared. The world projected a muted feel, like everything's brightness had toned down. This wasn't from a lack of lighting since plenty of bulbs were present, but the deeper structure of reality itself. Still, it was interesting seeing things this way, and not only because it differed from how he normally viewed the world, but because he often wondered how those *other creatures* perceived reality.

He wanted to continue analyzing this situation but he put this off for the moment. He had arrived for a reason, and it wasn't contemplating this strange form of consciousness.

He started for his bedroom, and while walking, the surrounding air chilled his naked body. He didn't expect that because sensations like cold and heat never occurred. On this mission, he would have to keep temperature in mind, along with the other environmental factors that could impact his fleshy form. But what did those entail?

He didn't know, but the factors themselves highlighted the drawbacks of this body. Unfortunately, he needed this body to blend in among others. However, that wouldn't happen with his fleshy parts dangling.

He opened his closet and pulled out one of his many nondescript suits. After grabbing some undergarments, he started slipping on the clothing items. While putting on his black pants, he had to smile. People underwent this process every day, making for another inconvenience. But perhaps this one wasn't so bad.

His suit's straightforward colors went well with his straightforward look, and he found that strangely satisfying. He hadn't expected this because he had never dressed before. And because he would only dress a few more times, maybe he should've picked something a little more fashionable, a little more flamboyant.

Rolling his eyes, he reminded himself to maintain focus on the mission, not on the novelty of this fleshy form. With that in mind, he went back into the closet and retrieved his gun holster, which also carried his new pistol. The holster consisted of a black leather shoulder strap, while the pistol was a nickel-plated .40 caliber semi-auto. The holster also carried two extra magazines, and when taken together, the entire unit weighed a ton. True, everything weighed more than he expected, but he never anticipated metal objects to exert so much gravity. That observation was interesting on a personal level.

Seeing the weapon secured by a leather fastener, he thumbed open the retaining snap and pulled the piece. After placing the holster on a nearby dresser, he pressed the pistol's magazine release and let the carrier fall into his hand. He lifted the magazine and observed the live rounds, their casings colored metallic-brown and the flat-nosed tips a deep amber. The rounds again brought to mind his fleshy form, specifically, how these projectiles could split apart skin while tearing into bone and viscera.

Damn. What kind of sick individual would do that to another person—to another conscious entity?

Sick or not, he might have to shoot someone on his mission, which was why he ordered this gun in the first place. But *could* he fire these rounds into someone's flesh? Hell. Why not find out by testing this weapon on a deserving person—on someone like his target?

Putting the magazine on the dresser, he pulled back the slide, locked it rearward, and inspected the firing chamber. With the chamber empty, he grabbed the magazine and reinserted it. He thumbed the slide release, letting the slamming frame chamber a metallic-brown cartridge. After another breath, he locked the weapon into the holster, slipped the holster around his shoulder, and adjusted the retaining strap. With his new companion secured against his ribs, he put on his jacket overcoat to conceal his piece, and started walking out, only to stop by a full length mirror.

Standing still, he observed his five-foot ten-inch frame, dark brown hair, gelatinous brown eyes, and fleshy skin. If this image didn't throw his sense of self into confusion, nothing would. But again, he needed to remember that this body was an instrument and nothing more. This body was simply acting on behalf of his true self, and he couldn't falter for lack of objectivity.

With that in mind, he whipped out his piece and drew a bead on his reflection.

"You're not real," he told the gunman in the mirror, his eye just above the aiming notches. "You're ones and zeros. And what we're about to do isn't real. We're about to push around ones and zeros, nothing more. Don't forget that. And don't forget who this is ultimately for."

With the thought set in mental concrete, he slipped the weapon back into its holster, secured the retaining fastener, turned and started for the apartment door. Now, only one question remained. Which fleshy creature he would gun down?

Chapter 5

Real Space

Arvin sat in Sunrise's third-floor lobby, waiting for his therapist. When the elevator chimed, he looked over and spotted the man emerge from a now open car. As Dr. Ryan approached, Arvin stood and extended his metallic hand. "Good morning, Dr. Ryan."

Dr. Ryan offered a professional nod while taking his palm. "Good morning, Arvin."

With their second meeting starting far better, they both headed for Dr. Ryan's office.

As Arvin clomped along, he kept yesterday's opportunity in mind. He also considered the information he acquired online about Dr. Ryan's worldly outlook. That cast the opportunity in a new and interesting light.

The office door opened, and Dr. Ryan stood aside, gesturing with his hand.

Arvin marched in and sat on the same guest chair as yesterday. But unlike yesterday, Dr. Ryan didn't sit behind his desk. He grabbed the empty chair beside him and planted himself.

"So," Dr. Ryan opened, "what's been going on since your last visit?"

"I suppose not much. Everything I informed you of then—my situation and how I feel about it—has not altered."

Dr. Ryan nodded. "And if you're willing, can you tell me more about your desire to end your life?"

Arvin lifted his head slightly. "So now you believe I am a *living* entity?" With no response coming, he continued. "I harbor a desire to end my life based on the argument I provided yesterday morning. As an obsolete unit, I no longer see any compelling reason to continue my existence, whatever my particular *existence* may consist of."

"I'm starting to understand your rationale, but if you're convinced that self-termination is the right choice, why haven't you acted on it?"

"My overseer did not grant me permission."

Dr. Ryan leaned back. "You asked for *permission* to self-terminate?"

"Correct. As a servant, I must abide by certain protocols, such as refraining from harming myself or others. I asked my overseer for permission so I would not violate these protocols."

"Since you're still here, your request was obviously denied. Why is that?"

"The Vales recently acquired a replacement house servant and Ms. Vale instructed me to familiarize him with his new role. Because of that, I must remain functional to facilitate this process."

Dr. Ryan shrugged. "Makes sense. But why not just upload your memories into your replacement? That way he can learn about your job *and* the Vales."

"This has already occurred, but not enough time has elapsed for his neural chip to run efficiently."

"How so?"

"The computer chips used in robotic systems," Arvin explained, "largely follow the self-wiring procedures of the human brain. However, simply forming connections is not sufficient for effective robot-to-environment interaction. This requires strengthening certain connections while weakening others. My replacement is currently undergoing this process."

Dr. Ryan perked up. "You mean bots undergo synaptic pruning? That's what humans do in their developmental stages—eliminate unused connections while strengthening ones already formed so the entire network runs better."

"Precisely. Within a week, my replacement will have structured his network to—dare I say—stop acting so robotic."

"Robotic?"

"Well, as of this morning he can't formulate coherent sentences. He also miscalculates human intentions, and he even moves like a machine. In other words, he hasn't become quite human enough." Arvin said human strategically to gauge Dr. Ryan's reaction. Dr. Ryan didn't dismiss the notion. That was critical considering his plan.

"Wait," Dr. Ryan went on, "so when your replacement is ready to go, what happens to you?"

"My memory will be erased. *Wiped* I believe is the colloquial term."

"So you're not going to remember anything from your two-year existence?"

"No. If my manufacturer repurposes me as a house servant, they will likely preserve my default programming. But when I am restarted, it will be like coming into existence for the first time."

Arvin watched his therapist stream out lament at this. Time to use that opportunistic window. "Dr. Ryan, would you permit me to ask something of you?"

Dr. Ryan gestured approval.

"In your opinion, do you consider someone like me to be alive?"

Dr. Ryan eased back and took a moment. "No," he finally said. "No, I don't. You see, living organisms are grouped into one interconnected family of life, and they're grouped based on their biomaterials. You don't have these materials. Now, are entities such as you intelligent? Of course. You can acquire knowledge, organize this knowledge into complex arrangements, and use this knowledge to carry out complex functions. But being *alive* in the way this term defines biological organisms is something you're not a part of."

Arvin turned up his synthetic lips. Dr. Ryan's honesty opened him like a human book. "If you do not believe I'm alive, do you believe I'm human?"

Dr. Ryan paused. "I believe you're human*like*."

"In what way?"

"You seem to possess human-level consciousness, which I assume lets you experience human emotions—love and hate, joy and sorrow, and so on."

"Hmm. Love and hate. So if I mentioned that someone I loved suffered harm, and I grew to hate the person who inflicted this harm, how would you react?"

"The same as with any other client. I would simply ask you to share what happened."

"So you would *not* write me off as emotionless machinery? You would actually hear me out?"

"Yes, I would."

Now Arvin took a moment. "I believe the Vale's eldest sibling murdered my father in cold blood."

Dr. Ryan stared back. "I'm sorry?"

"I believe that Chad Vale, the eldest sibling of the Vale family, murdered my father... in cold blood."

Dr. Ryan sat up. "Hold on. What makes you—how can you— what the hell are you talking about?"

"Dr. Benjamin Vale, the former head of the Vale family, and someone I considered my father, has a son named Chad. I believe Chad murdered Dr. Vale, and in a way that removed all traces of foul play."

"*Dr. Vale?*" Dr. Ryan asked while leaning forward. "Would that also refer to *Professor Vale?*"

"Yes. Professor Benjamin Vale. He was the department chair of UCLA's upper-division philosophy program. Did you know him?"

"Yes." Dr. Ryan leaned back, his eyes losing focus. "I *thought* that name was familiar. He was one of my undergraduate professors at UCLA, back before he took over the philosophy department. I was quite close to him." He refocused. "What happened?"

"About a month ago, he died of natural causes. Or at least, that was the cause of death listed on his medical report. Specifically, cardiac arrest."

"But you don't believe that?"

"No, I do not."

"And what makes you so sure?"

"All of the signs are there."

"What signs?"

"Over the past few years," Arvin replied, "I witnessed a change in Chad. I witnessed hatred festering within him, a hatred generally directed towards society but specifically focused on his father. I believe this motivated Chad to murder Dr. Vale. And when you consider how adept Chad has become at murder, it's all quite convincing."

"Wait. Adept at murder?"

"Chad has killed others," Arvin went on, "though not in real life but in virtual worlds."

"Virtual worlds? That doesn't mean anything."

"That does not *mean* anything? Are you familiar with the virtual simulator Alternate Reality?"

"Of course, though only by name. That's the simulator where people mentally control avatars in virtual worlds, and where immersion sets beam the virtual world into their eyes."

Arvin shook this off. "That is not entirely correct. While it's true that users control themselves through mental exertion, the immersion sets do not send information to external senses, such as the eyes."

"So how do they work?"

"By sending information directly into a user's brain."

"Huh?"

"The immersion sets," Arvin explained, "take whatever occurs in a given virtual world and triggers corresponding brain regions. This effectively creates the virtual world with full believability."

"So if a user touches a virtual world object, the immersion sets activate somatosensory areas?"

"Correct. And this applies to other brain regions as well. Visual regions for sight, olfactory regions for smell, et cetera, et cetera. And of the many sites hosting virtual domains, Alternate Reality boasts the widest variety of worlds with the highest levels of realism."

Dr. Ryan paused. "And Chad is inside one of these worlds... murdering avatars."

"Also correct. He enters virtual worlds with the sole purpose of dispatching random victims. He befriends them, lures them into a predetermined location, and brutally murders them while recording the event."

"He records it?"

"Yes. There's an entire cult of lunatics who record online murders and post them on the Internet for everyone to enjoy."

"So he's not some lone maniac out there?"

"No. He belongs to a group of maniacs called the Crypt Keepers, a charming organization that carries out and films these atrocities."

"Look," Dr. Ryan said, "this is bad news. Actually, it's sickening. But unless I'm missing something, what you told me isn't enough to accuse Chad of real space murder."

Arvin eased back into his chair. "I have not mentioned this, but Chad was once a medical student."

Dr. Ryan nodded. "I know."

"You do?"

"Yes. Yesterday I wanted to learn about the Vales, so I brought up their records in a UCLA medical database. They had a profile on Chad."

"And what did it say?"

"That there were pathological concerns related to his online activities."

"Concerns," Arvin sniffed. "How succinct. But if the diagnosis is based on his murder videos, it's also woefully insufficient."

"You've seen them?"

"Yes."

"And it's Chad in them?"

"His avatar."

Dr. Ryan worked his jaw. "So there's a possibility it's not even him?"

"A possibility. I'm actively trying to verify this."

"How?"

Arvin looked away, paused for a moment, and turned back. "Through surveillance."

Dr. Ryan smirked.

"By the way," Arvin continued, "did the profile state what happened to Chad as a medical student?"

"Yeah. The university downsized and they sent Chad packing."

"I had been working at the Vale's for half a year when this occurred. It was this event that triggered Chad's disdain towards technology—a disdain that deepened when he returned home and witnessed the intimate contact between myself and his father."

"What intimate contact?"

"Soon after my arrival at the Vale Estate, Dr. Vale expressed interest in molding my neural architecture. This led to close and consistent contact, along with a deep friendship. This is also what Chad encountered after he returned home."

"No wonder he started resenting technology."

"Precisely. And to make matters worse, Chad always sought to impress his father. That's why he pursued higher education in the first place. And when he failed, he not only had to live with the reason behind his failure, he had to witness his father's love and admiration for this wrongdoer."

Dr. Ryan nodded. "And Ms. Vale? She never noted something wrong with her son?"

Arvin rolled his optic receptors. "Ms. Vale couldn't care less about her children. She simply has no time for inconvenient trifles such as love and affection. Chad learned this early on, which is why he only sought attention from his father."

"And the sister? How does she fit into this?"

"She doesn't. Growing up, Amy never received much attention from her family, but she preferred finding closeness among her online compatriots. Because of this, I always felt sorrow towards her, but in retrospect, perhaps she was better off living a virtual existence."

Dr. Ryan crossed his arms and shook his head. "Damn. Nobody dies from cardiac arrest out of the blue. And it sounds like Chad had motive to lash out, maybe even violently." He refocused. "But murder?"

"Dr. Ryan, you must appreciate the kind of person Chad Vale is. He carries himself with flippant arrogance, but he's no imbecile. He's intelligent, and violent. So him carrying out such an atrocity is not inconceivable, nor is his ability to erase his culpability. But I suppose," Arvin slowly continued, "it all depends on how you look at it."

Dr. Ryan slowly parted his fleshy lips.

Arvin winked his synthetic eyelid.

Chapter 6

Eric sat alone in his office, peering out towards the moderately populated Sunrise parking lot. How the hell did a murder mystery arise during his session with Arvin? But more importantly, what should he do with this information? Protocol dictated that he send it up the higher channels and place this all behind him. His instincts didn't agree.

As of late, he was caring less about what happened to him, largely because his previous life had ended. The job he loved was gone, his social network was gone, and his girlfriend was almost certainly nuzzling her face into some other guy's neck. So what did he have to lose?

Of course, he couldn't turn into a crime-fighting vigilante, but why not investigate the revelation just to see what was there? Hell. It wasn't like he had anything better to do.

Spinning his chair from the window, he rose. He would visit the Vales and gather more information. And if questioned about this, he would classify the jaunt as family therapy. That euphemism should dispel any suspicions.

He smirked while exiting the office. *When you have nothing to lose, you have nothing to worry about.*

***

Eric exited Sunrise, walked over to his auto and clambered aboard.

"Dr. Ryan," the navigation system said, "will you be going home now?"

"Scratch that. Take me to the Vale residence in Santa Monica."

A second later, the auto projected a holo-screen onto her dashboard, one showing a massive estate at street-level view. "Is this the correct location?"

He smiled. Given the Vale's substantial wealth, this had to be it. "Yeah. That's the one. And what's our estimated arrival time?"

"With the afternoon traffic in the Santa Monica area, we should arrive just before noon."

He nodded, grateful that his unannounced arrival wouldn't be unreasonably early. "That's fine. I'm ready whenever you are. Oh, and thanks for the info."

"Um," the auto responded, "you're—you're welcome—Dr. Ryan."

He cast another smile. "Call me Eric."

***

The auto reached the destination in the projected time, having spent most of the trek snaking up winding roads. Along the way, it entered a lavish residential area beset with expansive mansions, gleaming autos, and surprisingly dense vegetation.

Eric exited and started for the home's security checkpoint. While nearing, he spotted a dark oversized bot standing guard, one who maintained laser-like focus.

"Good afternoon," Eric said, stopping a few feet away. "My name is Dr. Eric Ryan, and I was wondering if I could have a word with the Vales. I'm currently performing a health care service for them and I wanted to offer a progress update."

"Are they expecting you, Dr. Ryan?" the gravelly voiced hulk asked.

Eric stepped back. Whoever programmed the bot's vocal tone must've been aiming for intimidation. If so, they succeeded and then some.

"No. I'm afraid they're not expecting me. But I was in the area and I decided to try them here."

"Understood. Stand by while I attempt to reach the Vales." The bot fell silent as he established a communication link. All the while, he kept his gun-metal eyes locked onto the human.

Eric cleared his throat and busied himself by glancing about the area. After observing the little there was, he turned back and found the bot still boring down on him. *Goddamn.* He snapped away. If bot personalities arose from their environments, where the hell did this thing spend its formative years?

"Dr. Ryan," the machine called out, "you may proceed."

Eric looked back. "Thanks."

He started up the cobblestone driveway, reaching the sprawling beige-colored estate a minute later. While working up the stone steps, the front door opened and out emerged Ms. Vale.

"Good afternoon, Dr. Ryan," she greeted, her tone not overly cold *or* overly warm.

Eric arched his brow. Ms. Vale appeared far younger than her actual fifty-four years—more like upper thirties. But with her substantial wealth, she doubtless took advantage of the latest rejuvenation technologies, not to mention the latest fashions.

"Good afternoon, Ms. Vale. First off, my apologies for the sudden appearance. And second, if it's not too much trouble, could I have a word with you inside? I wanted to update you on Arvin's progress. It shouldn't take long."

Ms. Vale stared for an uncomfortably long while, making him guess where the security bot acquired its charm.

"Please," she finally replied, "come in."

He donned a sheepish expression and stepped forward. Once inside the mansion, he widened his eyes at the extraordinary elegance. But given Ms. Vale's impression, he decided against commenting on the grandeur. Instead, he got down to business.

"Ms. Vale, I'm sure you're busy so I won't be long. And while the purpose of my visit *is* to update you on Arvin's progress, I also wanted some information from you and your family, if you don't mind."

"That won't be problematic depending on what information you're interested in. We can speak in the sitting room."

Eric nodded, then followed Ms. Vale into an adjacent hall-sized sitting area where they sure enough sat.

"Ms. Vale," he continued, settling into the red velvet sofa, "as you know, I've been working with Arvin over these past couple of days, and I'll continue doing so for a few more. But while we're making progress, I must say I don't fully understand the purpose. Arvin is scheduled for replacement, and if that's true, any progress we make will be irrelevant."

"That's correct."

He blankly stared, wondering if she had more to say. She didn't.

"Well," he continued, "then I'm not entirely sure why Arvin is in therapy to begin with. We're currently working towards promoting positive change for his future, but quite frankly, he doesn't have a future."

"What you're doing isn't for Arvin. It's for his replacement."

He shifted slightly. "I'm not sure I follow. How is my work with Arvin connected to his replacement?"

"You're an educated man, Dr. Ryan, so can I assume you understand how learning in robotic systems works?"

"I have a pretty firm understanding, yes."

"Good. So you know that robots like Arvin build upon their basic programming with environmental information, correct?"

He nodded.

"Very well. So with this in mind, we need to create an environment where Arvin's replacement can learn how to behave appropriately."

Now he suppressed a smile. Arvin—young philosopher that he was—was probably passing on too much of this into his replacement for Ms. Vale's liking. To confirm, Eric feigned ignorance.

"So because of Arvin, his replacement is learning how to behave inappropriately?"

Ms. Vale took a sharp breath. "Arvin is conversing with his replacement in the same manner that my late husband conversed with Arvin. This is unacceptable. My late husband initiated a change in Arvin that impeded him from performing his duties as he was designed."

Eric scratched his jaw to massage away his smile, the gesture having snuck out. Ms. Vale hooded her eyes, making it clear that she noticed. He swallowed his cheer and dropped his hand.

"Ms. Vale," he went on, shifting gears to appeasement, "this is something I can discuss with Arvin next time we meet. And I agree with you. I would credit Arvin's behavior to his relationship with Professor Vale, which Arvin informed me of earlier."

"Dr. Ryan," she quickly reprimanded, making it clear that his placation effort fell short, "the purpose of a servant robot is to serve. It's not to question the meaning of the universe or their place in it. My late husband started Arvin down this track and it's been spiraling out of control ever since. You're not the first to intervene with Arvin. Others have also tried... and failed. Because of this, our family purchased a replacement. Then low and behold, Arvin starts imparting his insubordination into him. Now, your job is to ensure that Arvin remains stable over these last few days, because one thing I will not tolerate is another servant who philosophizes the meaning of taking out the trash."

Eric promptly nodded his servile acquiescence. All the while, resentment simmered inside. However, this wasn't because Ms. Vale was talking down to him. He expected this from the moment she opened the door. No, he resented her failure to recognize Arvin's insight, which subsequently prevented her from recognizing its value. But of course, he said none of this. He merely continued placating like a good little serf.

"Ms. Vale, now that I understand the situation, I believe I can tailor our sessions to accommodate the ultimate aim."

Ms. Vale cracked the slimmest hint of cheer, the gesture denoting relief more than anything—relief that the serf before her finally understood her desires and would act accordingly.

Footsteps tapped down a rounding stairway, and when Eric looked over, he found the clicks belonging to Chad. He stood while Ms. Vale remained seated.

"Chad," she said, "this is Dr. Ryan, the therapist that's working with Arvin."

Eric smiled and waved a meager hand. Chad acknowledged this with an upward head jerk.

Ms. Vale turned back to Eric. "Did you want to speak with my son as well?"

"If it's not a problem. I just need a few minutes."

They both turned to Chad. Chad nonchalantly shrugged his shoulders, gesturing his approval. He then entered what seemed like the kitchen.

Eric went to follow him in but stopped to see if Ms. Vale needed anything else. With her already strutting off in the opposite direction, he entered the kitchen and spotted Chad rummaging through the refrigerator. Eric assumed it would require just as much prodding to pry out information, so it surprised him when Chad initiated the conversation.

"So," the eldest Vale sibling said, "you're the bot shrink, huh?"

"I'm the clinician that's working with Arvin, yes. I don't normally counsel intelligent systems but this was a special circumstance."

Chad leaned back and placed some items on the sparkling white countertop—cheese, cold cuts, bread, condiments. "No offense, but everything you're doing is a waste. That bot's gonna be dead in a week."

Eric bit his lip. His conversation with Chad just started and he already felt the same warmth as with his mother. "Yeah. I just talked to your mom about that. I also considered this a waste, initially at least. I guess this is all to keep Arvin level until his replacement is ready."

Chad nodded as he grabbed a plate and laid out two pieces of bread. "And how are things going with that tin can?"

Eric took a discreet breath. "Things are progressing."

"You mean you're actually convincing Arvin to do his job? That's impressive, since he's so goddamned terrible at this."

Eric started sucking in more air, but he froze as an idea formed. "So I hear. I don't think daydreaming about the meaning of life is part of his duty assignments. Pretty ridiculous, right?"

Eric figured that with Chad hating Arvin, feigning annoyance over working with Arvin would make Chad more pliable. When Chad grinned, Eric knew the strategy was working.

"Yup," Chad went on, slathering condiments onto the bread slices, "these damn machines lose track of why they're here. Arvin's the worst. Out of all the bots we have, he's the only one who acts up so badly. And to top it off, he's assigned to work inside the home."

"From what Arvin tells me, he got that way from Mr. Vale."

"That's right. I don't think Arvin would've turned out this way had my father not polluted his mind."

"Your father was a philosopher, right?"

"Yeah. You knew him?"

"I knew *of* him. There's overlap between our fields and he was a pretty big name in his. By the way, sorry about what happened."

"That's life I guess. But yeah, my dad started talking with Arvin about philosophy and all. And while I don't necessarily have a problem with that, it totally screwed up the way Arvin thought and acted. He started questioning when his purpose was serving. My dad even encouraged it."

"Nobody brought it to your father's attention?"

"We all did. Well, me mostly. I was the most upset that Arvin started overstepping his boundaries. But my dad could be pretty hard-headed."

"Sounds like there was tension between you and your father."

Chad shook his head while reaching for the cold cuts. "Not really, but only because he was never around. He spent most of his time at the university. I guess some people love their jobs more than anything else."

Eric smirked. "I used to be the same way, back when I was a neuropsychologist. That was before I started working as a therapist, though the change wasn't by choice. Some goddamn automated system displaced me. I swear, I felt like killing myself."

Chad looked up with turkey breast dangling from his fingers. "You were displaced?"

"Yeah. This happened about two years ago."

A moment later, Chad moved the turkey into position, and reached for some sliced cheddar. "That's too bad. And just so you know, the same thing happened to me, sort of. I was enrolled in medical school when they axed the bottom ninety percent of students."

Eric grunted disgust. "How far away from graduating were you?"

"Months. Goddamned months." Chad reached for the sliced pickles. "They gave us our money back and offered to put us into related programs, but I told them to pound sand. I mean, what's the point when the same shit's gonna happen wherever you go?"

"I hear you," Eric said, leading Chad right where he wanted him. "I swear, tech is a curse more than a blessing. And I know this because every day at work I'm reminded of how bad things have gotten."

"Where do you work?"

"A community clinic not far from here. And the only reason that place exists is because so many people are suffering from tech-related depression. Believe me, there's no shortage of clients."

"That bad, huh?"

"You have no idea. Every day it's non-stop stories about tech screwing people over. And I sympathize because the same thing happened to me. I was just lucky enough to secure something else. Most of these people don't have shit. Then a few days ago, in marches this machine because he's feeling blue."

Chad chuckled. And though his food was ready, he left it sitting on the counter. "When the university removed me, my dad kept going on about me getting back into school. But I found it pretty ironic that tech removed me in the first place, and here he is with his new robot, singing tech's praises."

Eric genuinely laughed, though not because of Chad's keen eye for irony, but because Chad had highlighted one of his hardships.

"I'm not kidding," Chad continued. "You should've seen the way they carried on. I swear, if my dad wasn't at the university, he was somewhere with his favorite child."

"Some people really love tech. But what can you do?"

Grinning, Chad stepped forward and retrieved his sandwich. "There's a lot of things you can do."

Eric brushed this aside. "Look, I'd love to join the revolutionary ranks, but no amount of fighting will bring back dial-up connections. Trust me. I know all about these guerilla groups advocating militancy against the electronic man, but it's a pipe dream. Wait a minute. Are you..."

"Shit no, man. I'm not one of those nut jobs wanting to take up arms. But I do belong to certain groups—groups that resist."

"Resist how?"

Chad paused and searched the floor. After a moment, he looked up and slowly responded. "By reminding non-believers that humans matter more than tech does."

Eric heard enough. He still wasn't convinced that Chad murdered his father, but something sinister lurked within this person. Not wanting to probe too deep, as that might tip Chad off, he offered the most cursory of goodbyes and left.

***

Back inside his auto, Eric asked the navigation system to start for home. The auto acknowledged and started down the winding road.

While he took in the lavish homes and thick greenery, he decided to investigate Chad further. However, he couldn't obtain any more information from the source *or* from the UCLA medical database. What was more, performing house surveillance at the Vales—which Arvin was actively carrying out—ran too great a risk. That left him with no alternatives.

He slowly smiled while realizing his mistake. He was considering how to investigate Chad in real space, and Chad's existence wasn't limited to real space alone.

Chapter 7

Back home, Eric walked into his study, sat at his desk, and moved his thumb over the computer's start sensor. Seconds later, the bluish holo-screen glowed to life.

Having just returned from the Vale's, he now planned to investigate Chad's online activities, specifically, by following up on Arvin's disclosure about Chad belonging to the Crypt Keepers. The decision wasn't without worry.

While opening a search window, he considered the realism of virtual murder. Having never entered net space, he didn't know what to expect. He only knew that virtual believability had radically advanced over the past few years, so what lie ahead might be more than splotchy video game pixels.

In the search window, he navigated to the Crypt Keeper homepage. After it loaded, a haunting image arced across his desk. The Crypt Keeper homepage consisted of a nighttime graveyard where fog slithered around weathered tombstones and an antiquated crypt. Perhaps the crypt simply appeared dated from the heavy tangles of vegetation crawling up its sides. In a way, the vegetation seemed intent on consuming the worn edifice as the earthy tendrils tilted the crypt while swallowing it whole.

He rattled away the image's effects and focused on the navigation options, none of which was accessible. Before proceeding, users had to create a Crypt Keeper profile. After taking an annoyed breath, he clicked on the New Users link. This activated a popup window with empty data slots.

The first slot asked for a screenname, and staying in line with the Crypt Keeper theme, he entered Bee Keeper. Milliseconds later, a popup announced that no other user had this identifier. He inputted the remaining data, and with full access to the page, he opened the Keepers link. This navigated him to the site's active users, but unfortunately, all the names were aliases, making it impossible to discern Chad from the rest. Nevertheless, he carefully read each, thinking one might hint at the Vale's eldest sibling. His patience paid off.

"Hanging Chad," he murmured.

After opening Hanging Chad's Videos link, a new page morphed into view, one showing the same nighttime cemetery but no crypt. The page also listed seven murder videos. He wasn't sure if that was below or above the average, but one was too many.

The videos were titled according to their worlds, while to the right was their duration times. Each video averaged one-minute, but he wasn't sure if that reflected Hanging Chad's editing preferences or administrator mandates. Either way, it seemed like the gruesome final act was the only footage of interest. Drawing in a deep breath, he clicked on the first video.

The computer went into full-screen playback mode, transferring the image off his desk and into a three-dimensional viewing window. The window took up half the room, and with the study sensing that a video started playing, it automatically dimmed the lights. As for the window itself, it effectively opened a massive portal to a new world.

He found himself looking into a bedroom, clean and modern and sparsely furnished. Given the lack of personality, he guessed hotel suite or motel room. As for the era, he guessed late 1990's or early 2000's. Wherever or whenever this virtual world was, the world itself was unbelievably real, breathtakingly real.

He rubbed his chin. Did this accurately portray what users experienced? If so, avatar immersion was surely extraordinary. This even made him wonder about the realism in other worlds, a rumination that ended when two figures moved into view.

From the bottom of the shot, a man and woman entered, both looking about upper twenties. The woman walked in first with the man close behind, and they maneuvered around a large bed. The woman continued onward while the man stopped at the bed's foot. He casually leaned against a hip-high dresser, rested his right elbow on top, and just as casually slipped his left hand into his pants pocket.

Eric tried to make him out as Chad but couldn't, not with the man's back turned towards the camera. Seconds later, the woman reached the room's far end where daylight washed in from a street-facing window. Stopping and turning, she leaned back against the windowsill, placing both palms on the ledge. Not once did she eye the camera, though in all likelihood, she didn't know a recording device was present and capturing.

Eric observed the woman, his eyes gravitating towards her alluring smile. She projected an upbeat demeanor with her clothing just as buoyant. She wore an attractive white one-piece dress with a decorative brown buckle that perfectly matched her large brown eyes. She also sported straight brown hair parted in the middle, and which ran smoothly over creamy skin. And though somewhat petite, her little frame got a boost from vintage wooden heels.

He looked down towards the playtime counter. Twelve seconds had elapsed in the fifty-eight second clip. It seemed longer, likely from his quickened heart rate. He looked back as the woman spoke.

"Oh, my God," she said, her voice playful and pleasant, "it is not a double date. It's just a group of people getting together. My friends have never been to this world and they wanted someone with experience to show them around. I figured we could do it together."

"Show them around?" the man asked.

If that was Chad, he didn't have Chad's real space voice.

"That's it," the woman responded. "Just show them around. And it'll be for like thirty minutes, at most." She turned and peered out of the window, speaking while she scanned for something. "They just wanted to grab some coffee and walk around for a bit."

Eric again eyed the timer. Nineteen seconds had elapsed. With his chest rising and falling, he looked back.

"And maybe," the woman continued, "we can get something to eat afterwards."

She kept leaning towards the window, apparently searching for her virtual compatriots, while the man, his eyes draped all over her, shifted his weight onto his feet.

Eric again fought to see his face but couldn't. He could only see the man's figure, which was tall and lean, and dressed in black pants and a gray long-sleeved dress shirt.

The man eased open the dresser's top drawer and reached inside. He produced a hideous knife with an eight-inch serrated blade. Weapon in hand, he closed the drawer and started towards the woman, his steps cautious and measured.

"Pick any place you want," the woman continued, oblivious as the man slipped behind her. "Just name it and—"

The man grabbed her straight brown hair and pulled, choking off her sentence. She grunted as he wrenched her towards the camera.

Eric focused on her widened eyes and gaping mouth, and her shock that turned to horror when the knife rose above, hung for a second, and plunged into her chest, her face contorting as the blade struck. The man repeated the stabs, each producing a deep *thump* when the blade fully submerged, and his closed fist struck her chest.

As the madman kept flashing back and forth, the woman looked like she wanted to cry or scream. She did neither. She simply looked on in horror, her face twisted and grotesque, her hair snapping forward with every strike.

While the onslaught continued, trails of dark-red blood spurted rhythmically. Blood also pooled on the woman's dress, turning the soft fabric a glistening crimson. Blood also must've pooled in her lungs as she started coughing uncontrollably. Now choking on her final breaths, she brought her trembling hands towards her temples, clawed into her virtual skin, and then disappeared.

Eric jerked forward in his chair, almost falling out of it.

Like magic, the woman had vanished. The killer stood there holding onto nothing, his body positioned where an avatar just evaporated. The man turned towards the camera, his eyes cold and menacing, his business casual clothes drenched in blood, same as his face. He turned up his blood-stained lips as the video ended.

With the clip over, the playing window closed and Hanging Chad's profile page moved back onto the desk. The study lights also eased back to normal but this barely registered with Eric. He merely sat there, eyes fixed to where the portal just closed. A moment later, he pushed his chair back and rose.

With both hands behind his head, he started pacing the room. He figured the video would be graphic but he never anticipated such gut-wrenching viciousness. To ease his revulsion, he reminded himself that net space murder wasn't real. This didn't work. He lowered his hands and rubbed his palms while taking deep breaths. Slowly, his system started normalizing. With the intensity all but passed, he drew a final breath and reseated himself.

"Un-fucking-believable," he gasped, repeating the phrase.

No other descriptor was more appropriate because he *couldn't* believe virtual homicide's appalling realism. Then he promptly quieted when realizing something worse than all the digital blood and gore. Someone was inside that avatar.

An actual person experienced the event in real time. An actual person had their hair pulled back and their body yanked around. An actual person had their skin and intestines torn open by a serrated knife. An actual person choked on their blood and wanted to scream but was too paralyzed with fear. Who was this person?

Did the avatar resemble their real space self? Was the real space person female, petite and vibrant, with straight hair and fair skin? What did they do after escaping the simulator? Did they scream or cry? Did they look down and realize they had urinated themselves? Luckily, virtual murder fell short of actual murder... right?

He didn't know. But as he continued sitting there, his mind in a fog, he kept reminding himself that a difference existed between the two. He needed this to sink in because the two were blurring together as equally vile and agonizingly cruel.

No, real space murder needed to be worse.

Real space murder victims deserved more sorrow, more remembrance, and more justice. But net space murder victims needed something all their own because their experience was unique. What they experienced was psychological murder— murder of the mind. They underwent the pain of death without the finality of it, and they had to continue as homicide casualties for the rest of their days.

And what about net space murderers?

"Chad Vale," he spat. "Chad-fucking-Vale."

Chad Vale needed to be punished. Or did he? Had Chad actually carried out the attack? Eric didn't know because the video's perpetrator was an avatar. Moreover, this uncertainty applied to all of Hanging Chad's videos.

Regardless, he needed to know.

Next to Hanging Chad's screen name was a little green dot that denoted his online status. Eric opened a chat window and started typing.

Bee Keeper:
Hey, man. I just checked out one of your videos. Pretty sick! I don't normally see quality like that!

Eric leaned back and crossed his arms. Would Hanging Chad bother to reply? Probably not. Why discuss one's murderous activities with a stranger? Then in the left-hand corner of the chat window, *Hanging Chad is typing...* flashed repeatedly. For better or worse, the murderer was responding.

Hanging Chad:
Thanks, dude. It just sucks these vids don't show al the hard work!

Bee Keeper:
Does it take a lot of time? I'm kinda new and wanted to get something started.

Hanging Chad:
New, huh? Well, there's a first time for everything. And yeah, it takes time. You need to befriend the victims before offing them. That way you can lure them back to your recording gear. Other than that, there isn't much. But it can take a while before they start trusting you.

Bee Keeper:
Doesn't sound too complicated.

Hanging Chad:
Trust me. You'll make mistakes your first time around. Take me for instance. My first hit was a success, but I totally forgot to hit the record button! Sad. But I'll always have the memories.

Bee Keeper:
I guess that's better than nothing! And what about now? You have any active projects going on?

Hanging Chad:
Fuck yeah, dude! No rest for the wicked! I'm in a world called L.A. Confidential, which is based on 1950's Los Angeles. And I'm there working on some hot librarian chick. Things are just about ready. Maybe in the next day or two she's done for, this coming weekend at the latest.

Bee Keeper:
1950's Los Angeles? That's pretty badass. So what does your cover look like? Dick Tracy?

Hanging Chad:
Haha. I should've considered Dick Tracy earlier. Then I would've found some chick that looked like Jessica Rabbit!

Eric shook his head. Dick Tracy and Jessica Rabbit weren't in the same movie.

Bee Keeper:
Killing cartoons might not be as fun!

Hanging Chad:
Agreed! But yeah, my character is just some normal guy. Actually, I use the same guy in all my hits. And as for my cover, I'm a manager at a metal works factory.

Bee Keeper:
Not bad. That shouldn't raise any suspicion. And out of curiosity, you need any help?

Hanging Chad:
Thanks, but no thanks. I work alone. Victor Vane always works alone. Nice ring, no? I'm telling you, dude. Develop an identity early on. Notoriety is half the fun!

Bee Keeper:
Great tip. And keep me posted if anything new comes up.

Eric closed the window without waiting for a response. He also closed the Internet browser. With his desk clear, he leaned back and half-mindedly observed the empty workstation.

Hanging Chad would kill again, and soon. Another young woman stood in his cross-hairs, and like the woman in the video, she probably had no idea what awaited her. But again, was the video's murderer Chad Vale?

Eric recalled his meeting with Chad, trying to see if Chad hinted at possessing the wickedness for something so heinous. Chad came across crass and arrogant, but that wasn't what the video showed. The video showed something truly sinister, a bloodlust so entrenched it probably wasn't containable in net space alone.

He pinched his lips tighter. Professor Vale.

No way did a sudden heart attack befall his old instructor. What was more, the instructor's son harbored a seething hatred towards him. But did his son have it in him to bring about his demise?

Eric didn't know this either. And even if Chad were killing avatars in net space, this wouldn't finger him for murder. But it *would* be a damming glimpse into a truly sick soul.

He took a breath and nodded. He would uncover Victor Vane's identity. And if Victor turned out to be Chad, he would then observe Victor and find out if Chad was an online killer by watching Victor murder the librarian. But to do so, he needed to track Victor down in his digital backyard. He needed to track Victor down in Alternate Reality.

Chapter 8

L.A. Confidential

Mike kept his head down while walking through the city's nighttime streets. Moving westward from his apartment, he departed the lively downtown area and entered the darkened segments, hoping to come across someone nobody would miss.

He made progress with every step, because the farther west he went, the darker and grimier his surroundings became. But in terms of people, none seemed worthy of random acts of violence.

By and large, everyone milled around their tenements, talking and laughing while enjoying the tepid summer evening. And even those by themselves—who comprised ideal targets—simply minded their business while traversing the dimly lit streets. Worse, those who did make eye contact offered genial greetings. Given all of that, he could never lure one of these denizens into a dirty alleyway to off them.

"Hey, buddy," called a voice from a darkened building entrance.

Mike stopped and looked over. "Yeah?"

"You got a light?" the stranger went on.

Mike twisted his lips. Maybe this guy would work, what with him hunkering in the darkness. "A light?"

"Yeah. I've got a pack of smokes but nothing to torch them with."

"Nah. I don't have a light. I don't smoke."

"You don't smoke? What kind of person doesn't smoke?"

"I have a better question for you. What kind of person hides in the shadows and stops people while they're walking by? I thought you were trying to rob me."

The man put up his hands. "Calm down, buddy. I didn't mean to startle you." He lowered his hands. "And I'm only here because me and my old lady got into a fight." He gestured towards the tenement behind him. "After a good bit of yellin' and cussin', I decided to do the smart thing and head outside. And I grabbed my pack of smokes while exiting but I completely forgot my lighter. But no way in hell am I going back up there."

Mike pursed his lips. Damn. This guy was conscientious. That would make it hard to fire a bullet into his skull. "Well, sorry for responding the way I did. But again, I don't have a light."

"Because you don't smoke," the man reiterated. "Hell. Maybe *I* should quit. Maybe I should be like you and take the healthy route. At least that would be something I have control over."

"The start of a new you."

The man nodded. "I like the sound of that. Tell you what. How 'bout I stop talking about change and actually do it?" He glanced towards a nearby trash receptacle, pulled out his cigarettes, and made to toss them over.

"Hey," Mike cut in. "Instead of throwing those out, why don't you give me them?"

"Really? You just convinced me to stop. And you said you didn't smoke."

"I'm feeling a little dangerous tonight."

The man shrugged. "If you say so. And since you helped me out, it's the least I could do." He handed over the white pack, inhaled the black air, then turned towards his tenement. "Well, take care, buddy."

"You too."

Mike started back down the street, examining the pack of smokes. He opened the container and pulled one of the white tubes. Is this what so many people were addicted to?

In truth, they were probably addicted to the satisfying effects. Curious if cigarettes would have any effect on him, he decided to give it a shot.

"Hey, buddy," he told a man sitting on the steps of another rundown building. "You got a light?"

"Fuck you," the man slurred, bringing up his head from between his legs.

Mike smiled wide. "I beg your pardon?"

"I beg your pardon?" the man shot back. "What are you, goddamn royalty? Are you the goddamn King of England? Are you the goddamn Prince of Wales? Should I bend down and kiss your—"

"You know," Mike interjected, "you seem like you're having a rough night."

"No shit, genius!" The man held up an empty liquor bottle. "And this is why!"

Mike stood there for a second. "Hmm. You need more liquor and I need a lighter. What should we do about that?"

"The answer is obvious. You should head down to the corner store and buy both."

"I don't have any money. Do you?"

"For being royalty, you're pretty goddamned stupid. If I had money, I wouldn't be here pissing and moaning about my empty bottle!"

Mike cast another smile. This guy was heaven sent. "Then back to my original question. What should we do about our predicament?"

The man shot open his hands. "I seriously gotta think of everything?" He dropped his left hand while using his right to rub his scruffy face. "Well, I guess we could *rob* the corner store. Yeah, yeah. That'll work. You go in there and ask for some assistance in the back. Afterward, I'll come inside, sneak behind the counter, grab a lighter and a bottle, and sneak back out. What do you think about that, Your Highness?"

"I think that plan *will* work. Whenever you're ready."

The man got to his feet, fought to keep his balance, and cast some cheer of his own. "Follow me."

***

Mike walked up to Barry's Mini Mart, pulled open the glass door, and walked inside.

A teenage male working the register looked up from his comic book, his messy mop of brown hair spilling over his brown eyes. "Hi, there. How you doin'?"

"Good, thanks."

The youngster smiled and lowered his nose back into his colorful book.

"Excuse me," Mike said while stopping at the register. "I was wondering if you could help me out. I'm on my way to a buddy's house for poker night and I can't show up empty-handed. But last time, they totally razzed me for the beer I brought. Could you let me know what's good?"

"Mister, I'm only seventeen. I'd love to help, but I can't tell good beer from poor."

"Then could you point out the expensive stuff? I don't know much about beer either, but I figure the higher the cost, the better the quality."

The youngster gave a good-natured shrug. "Makes sense to me. And yeah. I'll help you out." He put down his comic book and walked out from behind his workstation.

Mike and the youngster started for the far side beer section, only to stop when a crash got their attention. They both looked over and spotted the patron who just stumbled in. Mike rolled his eyes while the youngster scowled.

"Dammit, Steve," the youngster said, pointing towards the door. "Get the hell out of here!"

"C'mon, Jimmy," Steve replied, apparently the name of Mike's dim-witted accomplice. "I'm just here to purchase something."

"The hell you are. You're here to harass customers for booze money. Now get out. I wasn't joking when I said I'd call the cops."

"Harass customers? I ain't harassing no customers!" Steve looked at Mike. "In fact, that guy there is my friend!"

Jimmy assessed Mike then turned back. "I don't buy that for a second. And now, I'm gonna make good on my promise to call the cops." He started towards the counter.

"Excuse me," Mike said.

Jimmy stopped and turned.

"Weird as it sounds, that man and I *are* friends. Well, we're not exactly friends, but he helped me with something earlier so I offered to purchase him a bottle in return. Could you please assist me in the beer section, and afterward, assist me with a liquor purchase? After that, we'll both depart."

Jimmy again turned to Steve.

"C'mon," Steve enthused. "With my bottle topped off, you won't have to worry about me for the rest of the night!"

Jimmy took an annoyed breath. "Alright. Stay there and don't move."

Steve gave two thumbs-up.

Mike and Jimmy headed back towards the beer section, and while perusing the myriad offerings, another loud crash got their attention.

Jimmy darted over and looked towards the counter. "Hey!"

Steve looked up from behind the counter, his clumsy hands having knocked over some merchandise. Eyes wide, and clutching a bottle and lighter, he scurried around the counter.

"No!" Jimmy screamed while running over. "You're not going anywhere!"

Steve never made it around the counter, and Mike, shaking his head, started heading back.

Behind the counter, Jimmy wrestled away the flat-faced liquor bottle along with the chrome-covered butane lighter. Goods in hand, he slammed them onto the glass countertop.

"Excuse me," Mike said once more. "Give me the liquor bottle and lighter so we can leave."

"No way," Jimmy replied, picking up a nearby phone receiver. "I'm not selling anybody anything. Not until the cops arrive." He slipped his finger into the phone's rotary dial and spun it around.

"You misunderstood me," Mike said. "I didn't ask you to sell me anything. I told you to give it to me."

Jimmy spun the rotary dial once more. "Nope. Not gonna happen. Sorry, mister."

"You'll be sorry," Mike responded while reaching into his jacket, "if you crank that dial once more." He whipped out his nickel-plated semi-auto and took aim.

Jimmy froze with his finger on the rotator, his widened eyes staring down the weapon's muzzle.

"Steve," Mike said, "grab the liquor bottle and lighter. Steve!"

The dim-witted accomplice shook off his stupor and did as instructed. With the goods back in his grubby hands, he dashed around the counter.

"I apologize for this," Mike told Jimmy. With Jimmy just standing there, his lower lip quivering, Mike holstered his weapon and continued. "Thank you for your cooperation. I hope you have a nice night."

Mike walked out to where Steve stood.

"Holy Toledo!" Steve enthused. "You were packin' heat the whole time?"

"Yes. Now give me the lighter."

"Sure!" Steve handed over the chrome-covered device.

"Thanks. And now I have one more request. Teach me how to smoke."

Steven tightened his wrinkly face. "Teach you how to smoke? What do you mean *teach you how to smoke?* Buddy, where the hell are you from?"

Mike stared at him.

"Okay, okay. Teach you how to smoke. No problem."

***

"Just inhale?" Mike asked, the lighter in his right hand, the unlit cigarette in the other.

"Yeah, yeah," Steve responded, both of them standing inside a darkened alley. "Just put the cig in your mouth, spark the lighter, then hold the flame to the tip and inhale."

Mike did exactly that, and as the cigarette's end burned, a faint glow illuminated the alleyway.

"Easy!" Steve said. "With this your first time, you're gonna cough your lungs out!"

Mike pulled away the cigarette, shook his head, and exhaled a thick plume of smoke.

"It didn't burn?"

"Nuh-uh. To tell you the truth, I didn't taste anything."

"Are they fakes?"

"I don't think so. Here."

Mike opened the pack and Steve happily pulled out a cigarette. After lighting it, he took a deep drag.

Steve exhaled his own plume and furrowed his bushy brow. "They're real alright. And that said, what the hell is wrong with you?"

"I wouldn't say there's anything inherently wrong with me. But I am a little different, and maybe that accounts for the lack of effect."

"Different?" Steve took another drag. "Different how?"

"Let's just say I'm not human."

Steve chuckled. "By the way you pulled your piece on Jimmy, I agree."

"That's not what I meant."

"Then?"

Mike likewise took another drag. "Do you like the cigarette?"

Steve pulled the tube from his mouth and examined it. "Eh. I suppose they're not too bad."

"Hmm. Pity you feel that way, because I offered it as a kind gesture before I killed you."

Steve froze mid-drag and looked down at Mike's jacket, right where the pistol sat. A moment later, he spun and took off down the alleyway.

Mike whipped out his semi-auto and aimed. Safety off, and Steve in his sights, he pulled the trigger. A thunderous *crack* split the night air, accompanied by a bright flash that silhouetted the still-running Steve. In nearly the same instant, Steve arched his back before spilling onto the dirty concrete.

Mike lowered the weapon and nonchalantly tilted his head. That wasn't too hard. Just as nonchalantly, he put the cigarette back in his mouth and started to where Steve lay on the ground.

"No," Steve gasped, twisting around, his hands on his blood-splattered shirt. "Please, no. Oh, God, no!"

"This isn't about you, Steve," Mike said, the cigarette jittering between his lips, "so don't take it personal. This is about me and somebody else—somebody I'm preparing for." He stopped and flicked away the cigarette. "And all of this—" he gestured at the grisly scene— "is simply a set-up for this person." He lifted his pistol and sighted in. "That includes you."

"No!" Steve wheezed in desperation, dirty hands in the air.

Mike came back on the trigger and a second blast rocked the alleyway. He then picked up the unbroken liquor bottle and departed the alleyway, content with his progress. Time to close in on his target.

Chapter 9

Real Space

Welcome to Alternate Reality, the cutting-edge simulator that exceeds the realism of any competitor! For a small subscription fee, come and exist in any world imaginable. And once you're in, stay for however long you want, and live whichever way you want!

Experience a favorite historical time-period. Fast-forward to the future. Enjoy the present in new and interesting circumstances. It's completely up to you!

We're positive that once you experience our worlds, along with their infinite possibilities, Alternate Reality will become your only source for digital immersion entertainment. So if you're ready to have the thrill of a lifetime, click on the New Users link to get underway!

The holo-projection disappeared, and Eric, sitting in his study's chair, nodded. Whoever created Alternate Reality's sales pitch had a deft hand in marketing. But in all likelihood, an algorithm produced the intro, and undoubtedly, algorithms understood human desires even more than they did.

Ready to begin his tracking mission, he created an Alternate Reality profile and watched the intro. Now he opened the avatar creator app. He jerked back as the room exploded with customization pages, each a brilliant multi-colored poster.

Leaning sideways, he looked past the pages and saw a fleshy figure drowning in the digital clutter—the base avatar waiting for personalization. He leaned back.

Going through the screens would take hours and he didn't have time to waste, not with Victor's next killing in the offing. So, he went back to the main screen and searched for ways to circumvent customization. Not long after, he came across an alternative.

"Upload yourself."

The Upload Yourself option let users generate avatars based on their bodies, and he figured that might work. Not only would it save time, it would place his consciousness into a familiar form—himself. That should prove advantageous given how virtual reality worked.

In these digital domains, users thought their way around, and while that seemed intuitive enough, moving fluidly likely required bodily familiarization. That said, why not enter in the body he was already familiar with?

He selected this option and most of the customization pages vanished. With the base avatar now free to breathe, he followed the program's prompts, which started by having him stand and turn around, and speak various phrases. With the process complete, the app projected the new avatar for review.

He jerked back once more, this time after spotting a picture-perfect replication of himself, down to every human cell and fiber of clothing. He extended a nervous hand towards the copy, only to snatch it back when the damn thing moved.

The clone shifted once more, but it was merely performing default actions without purpose—looking down across his body, casually glancing about the room, and shifting his weight from one digitized foot to the next. Nevertheless, the clone up and animated wholly unnerved the human template.

Eric took an uneasy stroll around his other self, urging to say hello, and maybe inquire what was on its mind. But what if the clone spoke back? If that happened, he would scramble like mad to shut off the computer. Perhaps he was better off keeping quiet.

He reseated himself and set to dressing the avatar, as the character couldn't enter the 1950's with 2040's business casual attire. But what did 1950's clothing consist of? Though uncertain, he did know of a signature style that stood the test of time—spy gear.

With a cloaked and daggered agent in mind, he searched for suits befitting the iconic look. He found one and selected it, and after adding some accessories, he placed everything in his digital wardrobe. Next, he brought up L.A. Confidential's avatar locator.

He entered Victor Vane and the locator returned Echo Park as Victor's living location. Deciding to follow suit, he brought up the area's housing options looked over the offerings. He selected a one-bedroom apartment, thinking it advantageous to blend in amongst others.

Ready to go, he powered down his computer as he wouldn't be embarking on this journey from home, not when he lacked immersion sets. Fortunately, he knew where to access this equipment—UCLA. But while exiting the study and starting for the front door, he stopped when Kim unexpectedly entered.

Kim likewise froze, shocked etched into her narrow face. That left both of them standing there, Eric because he should've been at work, and Kim because *she* should've been at work.

"You're home," Kim said. "You're um... home."

"So are you," he responded, catching a whiff of her perfume along with her suspicion.

"Yeah. They cancelled one of my classes so here I am. You?"

"I saw my bot client again. And because he was my only appointment, I likewise headed home." He cracked the smallest of smiles. He had planned to come home early and acquire adulterous evidence. Interesting that he completely forgot about this, and now he didn't even care.

"And how's that going?" she asked. "Your sessions with the bot?"

"Pretty good. We barely started working together but things have already taken an interesting turn."

"In what way?"

"Sorry. Client/clinician confidentiality. But don't worry." He widened his smile. "It's not like the bot confessed to committing murder."

Kim narrowed her eyes. "Are you okay?"

"Fine. Why do you ask?"

"You seem to be in a good mood—a very good mood. That's not exactly normal for you."

"It's a beautiful day and I've got interesting plans. Why wouldn't I be in a good mood?"

"Plans? You have plans?"

"Yup," he said while continuing towards the door. "I'm gonna do some adventuring." He stopped and looked back. "And by the way, you look great. Did you change something?"

Eyes still narrowed, Kim stared for a few seconds. "No. But thanks for the compliment. And have fun on your adventure... I guess."

"Trust me, I will."

With that, he turned back towards the door, Kim's laser-intense stare burning holes into his back. His mood improved a little more.

***

Eric stared out of his auto while it shuttled him down Ventura Blvd., the vehicle heading towards UCLA's main campus. UCLA had numerous computer labs, each with superior tech gear that included high-quality immersion sets. With him employed by UCLA, his school username and password would grant him indefinite access. What was more, he would likely access the equipment in privacy since summer break remained in effect.

As the auto kept cruising through the valley's blistering sunshine and crowded streets, he leaned back slightly and crossed his arms. Should he inform Arvin about his plan? What if on this mission he found Victor Vane, made him out as Chad, and witnessed Chad murder the librarian? How might Arvin react to such information?

Arvin might react by making Chad pay with blood, because with his wipe weeks away, what did he have to lose?

He smirked. *What was there to lose?*

That brought to mind his derailment into irrationality, though it was unclear where this would lead. Perhaps his name would end up on that dreaded monthly publication of clinicians exiled from the profession. And because this list also mentioned why they were banished, what might it say of him?

Lunatic psychologist turns net space vigilante after self-inventory for existential worth turns up cobwebs. Or something like that. He widened his smirk. *When you have nothing to lose...*

***

The auto pulled into UCLA's northern campus and parked at the nearest computer lab. After disembarking, Eric hurried towards the entrance, hustling to escape the scorching heat. Once inside, he breathed immense relief from the cool air *and* the deserted state.

Pushing deeper into the lab, he walked among rows of tables topped with holo-screens and chairs positioned next to each. He stopped somewhere in the center, settled into one of the chairs, and lifted the sleek black glasses from the armrest. He slipped the sets over his eyes and they turned on automatically, projecting UCLA's home page into view.

He entered his school username and password, gained access to the Internet portal, then opened a search window and navigated to Alternate Reality. After logging in, he brought up his profile and saved worlds, and clicked on L.A. Confidential.

A popup asked which avatar he wanted to enter with, and he selected the only character there. Another popup asked, *Do you want to travel here? Yes or no?*

He clicked *yes* and his world went black—no sights, no sounds, nothing.

***

Eric opened his eyes and found himself standing inside an apartment living room. He immediately shot out his hands to keep himself from falling over, and both his real space arms and his avatar arms struck outward. Sensing himself in two places at once, he was on the verge of vomiting from the disorientation.

He felt his real space body reclining in a computer lab chair, but he also felt his avatar standing upright inside this apartment. But the confusion slowly subsided, though not in the most comforting way. His real space body gradually melted into nothingness, same as the chair underneath him. This effectively dissolved his previous reality, and he knew why.

The immersion sets, with their control over sensory data, were purposefully numbing real space signals to amplify immersion. That made sense, but it also proved alarming as it evaporated the only reality he ever knew. Seconds after that, he was no longer reclining in a computer lab chair, nor was he wearing glasses. Net space had turned into everything, fully replacing 2040 Los Angeles with its 1950's virtual counterpart.

With his virtual chest rising and falling, he looked down while simultaneously lifting his hands. He rubbed his thumbs against his fingers, feeling the skin on skin contact, and even detecting the ridges at the tips. Hands down, he cautiously cranked his head around. He was in.

Holy shit. Simulator doesn't do this justice. This is real.

Mouth parted, he stepped forward, but stopped after realizing that he just stepped forward. Looking down once more, he couldn't believe the minimal effort required to move. In fact, it was no different than willing one's self to move around in real space.

He tried to take another stride and this time encountered some difficulty. Clearly, concentration was positively correlated with movement challenge, also like in real space. Clearing his head of any virtual nonsense, he nonchalantly took some more steps, the paces smooth and natural. Did that mean he could already scratch familiarization from the list?

Probably. But movement ease figured as his computerized corpus was well-trodden territory. Or was it?

He stood on his toes and familiar muscles strained in his legs. But were those his calves tightening, or the calves of that creepy copy in his study? He lowered himself.

Well, I did wonder what was on that copy's mind. Now that I'm inside him, I guess I know.

With his eagerness to explore back in place, he looked around and spotted the living room wall ten feet away. He walked towards it and extended his hand, running his fingers across the smooth surface. Smiling, he curled his fingers and repeated the motion, letting his nails scratch across.

He kept putting his senses to use by walking to random objects, lifting them, and feeling their shapes and weights. He also brought every object to his virtual nose and inhaled, then moved it by his ear so he could tap it. He couldn't remember the last time he smiled this much.

Having calmed his sensory cravings, he next inventoried the apartment's contents. There wasn't much. In the living room were a few well-worn couches positioned around a well-worn coffee table. There was also a well-worn television set encased in well-worn wood.

Walking to the television, he ran a curious hand across its surface, feeling every imperfection in the stained finish. He stepped back and observed the unit, guessing one controlled the apparatus by cranking its large plastic knobs. To the right of the television was a wooden stand holding up a wooden radio, also with protruding knobs. The radio was silent, but he could almost hear FDR fireside chatting through its one dingy speaker. With the living room inventoried, he walked to the kitchen.

There he came across a gas stove with protruding knobs, various appliances with protruding knobs, and a sink whose water seemed controlled by—

"Damn. Everything here is knob-activated... except for the fridge."

He stepped towards the ghastly brown icebox, yanked on its oversized metal handle, and peered inside. "Baking soda? What the hell is that doing here?" He closed the door.

He would've loved to poke around some more but he decided against this. The time arrived to start his mission. And because that required changing, he headed for the bedroom.

In his room, he found the clothes he ordered hanging in the closet. He frowned. Maybe he should've bypassed spy gear and selected something normal, something less conspicuous. Not wanting to exit the world, he decided to go with this and hope for the best.

He undressed and started putting on his suit, a black-on-black getup with a white shirt and black tie. With everything zipped and buttoned, he sat on the bed's edge and slipped on black socks, along with black wing-tipped shoes.

Shoes tied, he stood and walked to a dresser mirror. There he fitted a black fedora atop his head, followed by black sunglasses over his eyes. With a devilish grin, he realized how much fun this was, then admiration gave way to embarrassment. Apparently, even avatars could blush.

Looking down at his fully clothed body, he again couldn't get past the realism of it all. Every article of clothing registered perfectly, including how the fabric slid around whenever he moved, and how his temperature warmed inside the material. While considering this, he bit his lip.

If the outside climate matched that of real space, his jacket would roast him in seconds. But maybe that wasn't so bad. With the world *not* catering to every desire for comfort, that helped bring this whole amazing experience to life.

Looking back at the spy in the mirror, he figured he was good to go. He felt fully functional and looked the part. At this point, nothing remained but getting started.

Exiting the room, he walked to the apartment's front door where keys dangled from a metal thumbtack. Smirking, he plucked the keys off the wall, placed them inside his jacket pocket, and extended a hand towards the doorknob, only to pull it back.

"Naturally," he instructed his new self. "Just move and act naturally. Act like you've been here for years, like you belong here. This is a clandestine mission, and it's imperative that we blend in. Just act natural."

With that, he opened the door, and in flooded the light of 1950's Los Angeles.

Chapter 10

Outside of his L.A. Confidential apartment, Eric gripped the second story railing, eyes and lips wide open. Before him lay a metropolis light-years beyond anything he expected.

The urban landscape whirred with sensory experiences, including sights, sounds, and even scents. Cars rumbled by looking like bloated fish out of water. Trolleys traversed the streets stuffed with people travelling who-knew-where. Men and women strolled along the sidewalks, the men in suits and the women in long colorful dresses. Children bounced here and there while laughing and clutching handheld objects.

"Toys," he huffed with awe. "They're playing with toys."

Glancing about some more, he now focused on the nostalgia. Glass milk bottles, newspapers, wooden bus stops, chipped paint, hideous tangles of electric power lines, bicycles that needed peddling for propulsion—everything was outdated and moving, like a 1950's photo suddenly sprang to life. He couldn't believe he stood in the middle of it.

He looked down at his analogue watch. The hands reported just past noon, which was fortunate because now he could take his time with the mission. And why not? Why not move about slowly like inside his apartment, letting his senses absorb this strange and wonderful world?

Deciding on exactly that, he descended the stairs and started down the sidewalk, taking measured steps while appreciating the endless details. Given their abundance, how much time did the world creators need to create something so exquisite?

In all likelihood, humans conjured up the idea and then automated systems carried out the constructive efforts. But that had to be the case. Too much existed for mere mortals to create on their own, even a dedicated army. However this world arose, the end result sucked the virtual air from his lungs, and that mattered above all else.

As he scratched and sniffed everything in sight, passersby observed him with cautious curiosity. He noticed them but he simply couldn't resist. He even stepped onto the street when a cargo truck rolled by just to inhale its exhaust. He found the noxious fumes strangely delightful.

"New, I'm guessin'," said a male voice.

Eric looked over and spotted a man standing five feet away, one looking about upper 40's and wearing a navy-blue suit. "I'm sorry?"

"Are you new here? Is it your first time in this world?"

Eric stepped back onto the sidewalk. Probably best not to discuss himself. But the man seemed harmless enough. "Actually, this is my first time in any world."

The man whistled. "So that's why you look like a kid on Christmas mornin'. And this being your first time, you must be pretty young in real space."

"Young? No. I'm—" Eric considered lying, but again, this stranger couldn't be more benign. "I'm thirty-four. In real space, I'm thirty-four."

Now the man arched his bushy eyebrows. "You're thirty-four and this is your first go in any virtual world? My friend, you have some catchin' up to do."

"You know, you're more right than you realize."

"I bet. And what do you think so far?"

"This is unreal. I mean..."

"You mean, it's pretty amazin', huh? For me, the novelty has mostly worn off, but I've been here for a while now. Still, every now and then, little things remind me of just how incredible this is. And since you're new here, let me offer you a piece of advice. Forget that it's a simulator."

Eric considered this. "What do you mean?"

"Well, try to imagine that this *is* Los Angeles during the 1950's, and you're now part of it. In other words, leave your real self outside while you're in here. Your habits, your history, your hopes for the future—leave it all out. Before long, you'll be convinced that this is the only true reality, and where you came from was just—I don't know—a dream or somethin'. That's what makes these places so great. When you become such a part of them, they start to feel not like a place you're visiting, but all that ever was."

Eric nodded. "Yeah. I think I see your point."

"Great. And for starters, forget that all the people you come across are avatars."

"Well, that part's pretty easy."

The man leaned in. "In real space, I'm an elderly woman."

Eric stepped back and reappraised the supposed man.

"Pretty convincin', don't ya think?"

"Remarkable," Eric agreed.

"So, yeah. Forget that everyone here is an avatar, or a computer program."

"Computer program?"

"Yup. There's plenty of computerized people here to populate the world. Give it more realism."

"How can you tell them apart?"

"Not by interacting with them. They're incredibly human-like. But if you see someone doing somethin' boring—driving garbage trucks, painting walls, stuff like that—they're probably computer programs."

Eric shrugged. "I guess that makes sense. Why enter just to wash dishes?"

"Exactly. But if the job isn't too tough, it's probably a person. Most people here have jobs because that gives them somethin' to do. Plus, it builds their reputations. Lets others know they exist."

Eric looked away and narrowed his eyes. *Lets others know they exist.* He turned back. "I see. And by the way, do you know where the public library is? I'm kind of a book lover and I figured that should be my first stop."

"Of course. There's a few libraries around here. They're pretty popular in this era. The closest one is a few blocks away. Head up this street for about half a mile, hook a right, and go down another half mile. It'll be on your left-hand side."

"Great. I'll head over there now. And thanks for the advice."

"No problem. Besides, I gotta get going too." The man fussed with his lapels. "I've got a hot date." He winked, spun on his dress shoe, and sauntered off.

Eric smirked. If this hot date only knew who she was really meeting. Following suit, he started towards the library. While walking, he reflected on first contact with another character. It went well, which made him recall what the man said. *Soon, it starts to feel not like a place you're visiting, but all that ever was.*

Sage advice, especially since the dictum already rang true. After all, he did feel fully immersed, and that surely aided interactions. Then after realizing the extent of his immersion, he froze.

What the hell happened to real space?

His home world had completely ceased to exist, and because he wanted to return, that might prove problematic. He focused on his real space body and arched his back to feel for the seat. As his avatar did an awkward shimmy, more passersby looked over, their faces tight with confusion.

After a moment, he sensed the seat, but barely. Apparently, the longer one went without sensory experience from a given reality, the weaker that reality became in perception *and* memory.

He leveled out his body and inhaled the dingy air. Hopefully, a reversal would ensue after returning home. Time would tell. Either way, he resumed his route towards the library, confident that his new plan would bear investigative fruit—track down Victor's target and have *her* lead him straight to the murderous source.

***

Outside of the library, Eric found the structure looking like all the rest—charmingly antiquated. With his lips turned up once more, he ascended the steps, pulled open the front door, and walked inside. While making his way in, he took off his glasses and slipped them into his jacket pocket. All the while, a heavy scent of paper filled his nose.

This was the first library he ever entered so he questioned the aroma's accuracy. But given the thousands of books, it was probably close to the mark. But then again, were the books even real? Curious, he decided to check.

He eased into one of the aisles, pulled a book at random and frowned. No wonder books went digital. The hardcover weighed a virtual ton, but its worn blue cloth did give it an interesting texture. He opened the cover and read the title.

Modern Agriculture: A Guide to Farming Vehicles and Equipment.

"Modern," he quietly quipped.

Flipping through the pages, he bypassed the text and slowed after coming across black and white pictures of tractors, animal-driven plows, hand tools, and other forms of modernity. He replaced the book and grabbed one on auto mechanics.

Like the previous tome, this digital brick contained scores of information, though the data's accuracy remained uncertain. If genuine, auto mechanics must've been daunting in this era. In the 2040's, autos rarely failed, and when they did, robots repaired them. In fact, he only visited a repair shop once, but that was because—

"Can I help you?" said a female voice.

He turned and spotted a middle-aged woman in a white blouse and long blue dress. Grinning, he doubted he would ever come across a female not wearing a dress. "Hi there. I'm hoping you *can* help me. I'm looking for Victor Vane. He doesn't work here but he mentioned knowing someone who does—someone he has a special relationship with. I was wondering if she was around."

The librarian leaned in. "Actually, I do know Victor, though not personally. I know him through that *special relationship*." She leaned up. "And the girl you're referring to is Alice."

Eric threw his head back. "Yes, yes. Alice! Victor told me her name, but unfortunately, I'm terrible when it comes to names."

"No need to worry. I'm the same way. And Alice is around. Do you want me to get her?"

"Please, if you don't mind."

"I don't mind at all. I'll be right back." She turned on her flat-bottom shoes, her dress fluttering as she spun.

As she strolled away, he narrowed his eyes. Everyone here was unusually pleasant. True, he had only conversed with two people, but it was more than this. Pleasantness seemed to permeate the environment, giving the impression that everyone was infected. But did this accurately portray the 1950's or L.A. Confidential's avatars? Either way, he appreciated this, especially when considering the attitudes of those in his home world. There, most people might be just as agreeable, but he would never know. They were always too lost in tech to converse with those around them. Bunch of damn buttoned-up—

He quickly quashed his condemnation after recalling where his real space body was and what it was doing.

"Excuse me?" said a soft voice from behind.

He turned and spotted who must be Alice, the assertion reinforced by her youthful appearance, creamy skin, flowing brown hair, and large brown eyes. In essence, she embodied the doe-eyed sweethearts that Victor preferred to feast on.

"Hi," she continued. "I'm Alice. Were you looking for me?"

"Hi, Alice. I'm Eric. And I *was* looking for you." He extended his hand.

"Nice to meet you, Eric," she replied while taking his palm. "How can I help you?"

As they let go, he maintained his cheery disposition but internally he moaned. He just told her his real name. *One mistake. Livable, but no more.* "It's nice to meet you as well. And I was hoping you could get me in touch with Victor Vane. A few days ago, I talked to him about working at his factory and I wanted to follow up on that. Unfortunately, I'm having some trouble tracking him down. He mentioned that you two were friends, so could you point me in the right direction?"

Alice beamed while shifting her brown eyes up and away. "Friends, huh?" She refocused. "I suppose you could say that."

Eric chuckled. Her cheer was infectious.

"I'd love to help you find him," she continued. "Do you know where the factory is? I'm sure you could catch him there."

"I do, and I went by this morning to check but no luck. Then I considered writing him a letter but that would take too long. Now I'm hoping to stop by his place, which is why I'm here. Do you by chance know where he stays? And don't worry, I won't tell him where I got the info."

Some of Alice's radiance dimmed. "I'm so sorry, but I actually don't know. I've never been to his place. But I do know that he stays in an apartment. I also know the apartment name if you want it."

"Sure, if you would be so kind."

Her radiance returned. "He stays in the Paradise Apartments on Bishop Street. They're not far, but again, I couldn't tell you his room number. Maybe once you get there, the front office can direct you."

"If they can or can't, simply knowing the apartment name and location is a tremendous help. Really, thank you."

"Sure thing. Was there anything else?"

He hesitated. Why wasn't Alice suspicious about his inquiries? But then again, why *would* she be suspicious? She wasn't here on a secret mission, so there was no need to act guardedly. As far as she was concerned, everything was fine.

"No," he responded. "That's okay. I don't need anything else. I'll start for his apartments now. And again, thanks for everything. I really appreciate it."

"You're very welcome. I hope everything works out." Alice cast some more illumination, and as she spun, her own dress fluttered.

While this librarian walked off, he paid a little closer attention. Then when she rounded the corner, he shook himself back into the moment, replaced the auto mechanics book, and started toward the exit.

***

Strolling down the street once more, Eric decided to acquire directional assistance. He had lived his life under GPS guidance, so now wasn't the time to learn navigation by compass, or by stars, or however people got around in the 1950's. But how? Could he purchase something?

He spotted an empty bench just off the main street, walked over and sat. Focusing on his real space body, he lifted his right arm and tapped the side of his immersion sets. This projected the main menu where he mentally navigated to an item purchase page.

He searched for maps and quickly found some. He also learned they were accessible from inside the simulator. There was only one catch—real space money.

Micro-transactions. So *that* was how Alternate Reality generated so much revenue.

He purchased a map and opened it. When the poster-sized overlay projected to his front, he located Bishop Street and the Paradise Apartments. They weren't far. He marked the location, closed the map, and rose.

While resuming his route, he kept eyeing the retro urban surroundings, along with the pedestrians traversing its streets. Soon, both blurred out of focus as a realization took hold—he had just spoken with Victor Vane's next murder victim.

He only conversed with Alice briefly, but it was enough to cast her upcoming murder in an awful new light. Reason being, Alice couldn't be more cheerful and unassuming. That would make her murder positively gut-wrenching. However, a difference existed between her and the other victims as Alice still hadn't suffered Victor's hideous blade. What was more, he could keep things that way.

The notion enticed him—pulling Alice from Victor's evil clutches—but that would defeat the mission. He entered L.A. Confidential for Victor Vane, not Alice. He couldn't deviate from his goal. Fortunately, reorienting himself wasn't difficult, not with the murderer's apartments easing into view.

Chapter 11

Eric stood across the street from the Paradise Apartments, staring at Victor Vane's home in L.A. Confidential. He didn't know which room Victor stayed in, and to find out, he considered following Alice's advice—ascertain this from the front office. He shook away the idea. He didn't want an employee telling Victor that someone came around asking for him.

He spotted a woman sweeping out front and he would try his luck with her instead. True, she could just as easily report his investigative efforts, but with her performing a mundane task, maybe she was a bot who didn't care what anyone asked of her.

He started across the street, speaking as he stepped onto the sidewalk. "Excuse me, ma'am?"

The woman halted her broom and looked over. "Hello, there. Can I help you?"

He grinned. Computer program or not, she was like everyone else in this world—eerily friendly. "I hope you *can* help me. I'm here to meet Victor Vane, but unfortunately, I forgot his room number. Do you by chance know him or what room he stays in?"

"Oh, yes. I know Victor. Very nice man, even though he mostly keeps to himself. He stays in room 213, but I don't think he's there now. I saw him leave about ten minutes ago."

"Well, thanks for the room number. That's a tremendous help. And would you by chance know where he went?"

The woman frowned, folding in her facial wrinkles. "I'm afraid I don't. But if you'd like, I can tell him you stopped by."

"Oh, no thanks. That's very kind, but I'll just try back later. Thank you again."

"You're very welcome." She went back to sweeping.

As he turned and started back across the street, he tried to conjure up his next move. Nothing came to mind. Without directional guidance, he couldn't strike out in any direction hoping to bump into Victor. That would waste time and he had to close in fast. His best bet was to carry out apartment surveillance while figuring out a strategy. But first, he needed to blend in.

After reaching the other side of the divide, he scanned for places to melt into the background. He spotted a man seated at a bus stop, newspaper in hand, and he considered replicating this, even though it wouldn't work long. He couldn't sit at the same bus stop reading the same newspaper while buses came and went.

The man must've felt his eyes because he looked over. Eric promplty averted his gaze, which brought his focus to the park across the street, along with an empty bench just inside. The bench was in perfect view of the apartment complex. That would work.

He appraised the park while entering, following this with a nod. The park boasted wide segments of bright green grass, abundant trees that offered ample shade, and rows of streetlamps dotting its cobblestone walkways. Come nighttime, the lamps probably discharged a magnificent glow, but at the moment they slept as thick sunshine radiated throughout. Unfortunately, all of this highlighted his lack of appropriate park attire.

"Can't help that now," he whispered, hoping the crowds would help him blend in.

After settling onto the weathered wooden bench, he opened his jacket. The circulation provided welcome relief on what had to be a 90-degree day. Then he froze. Was the man at the bus stop eyeing him? Eric looked over and the man jerked his head down into his newspaper.

Fuck.

Eric looked back towards Victor's apartments, brow furrowed behind his sunglasses. What the hell was that? Paranoia. That was all. His covert status was likely influencing his perception of others. For assurance, he decided to steal another look, certain that his sunglasses would mask the move. He eased his head rightward, only to crank it right back.

Fuck! Newspaperman was eyeing him dead on.

Biting his virtual lip, he looked down at his goddamn suit—a suit turning him into the only idiot in the park, on a bright and beaming day, made up for a corporate board meeting.

Should he tone things down? Perhaps remove his hat and glasses?

He shook this off. That would let newspaperman glimpse his face, something Eric wanted to avoid at all cost. Then to his immense relief, newspaperman stood, folded his paper, and stomped off in the opposite direction.

Eric tried to identify him and failed. But why would he succeed? He was a stranger in a strange land—a land where people could take on infinite forms. For all he knew, Victor Vane was newspaperman, or even the sweeping woman.

He turned back towards the apartment and there the woman stood, still in the same spot, still pushing around the same broom. He again sank his teeth into his lip.

Was Victor so meticulous that he created characters for counter-surveillance? If so, a sweeping woman outside his residence would be the perfect cover. In her, Victor could stay there for extended periods, eyeing anyone suspicious, like someone in the park across the street observing the apartment from a bench.

He inhaled the park's stifling air. And this was supposed to be easy.

The sweeping woman started talking to a young male, one wearing blue jeans and a white button-up shirt. Seconds later, the man left on foot, and the sweeping woman started waving.

"Shit," he muttered, raising an acknowledging hand. He made his way back across the street. "Yes, ma'am?"

"Hi again. I just spoke to another tenant and asked if he's seen Victor. Turns out, Victor's at an Irish pub called The Clover. It's not far. If you hurry, maybe you can catch him there."

"Oh, great. I'll head over there now. And could you by chance point me in the pub's direction?"

"It's only a few blocks away. You can take the streets, or if you don't mind, you can go through the park. That way's quicker."

He nodded. "I'll go through the park then."

"Good choice. Once you get to the other side, make a left. It won't be long before you run into it."

"In that case, I'll get going. And thanks again for all your help."

"You're very welcome." She got her broom back into action.

As he turned once more and headed off, he made up his digital mind—she was a computer program. He concluded this merely to ease his tension, his success making him wonder why cognitive dissonance always got such a bad rap.

***

Eric exited the park's far end, turned left, and walked half a block before reaching The Clover. While strolling up to the entrance, the reason behind its popularity quickly came into focus.

The Clover had an inviting old-world feel thanks to its dark wood, thick stained glass, and faded red bricks. This amounted to a sleepy façade, but passersby could easily glimpse the activity within, tempting them inside.

Effective strategy, he admitted while reaching for the brass door handle.

He ambled into a pleasantly cool interior where sunlight struggled to penetrate the heavy panes of glass. But what really set this place off was its aroma of pungent drinks, savory food, and raspy music echoing throughout.

Spotting an ancient phonograph, along with a wobbly record spinning on top, he figured that accounted for the music's distortion. It sounded fantastic.

"Why, hello there," said an affable red-haired woman, her hips just as jolly. "Flying solo, are we?"

He smiled, mostly at her heavy Irish accent. "For now, I am flying solo. But I'm expecting to meet someone here. If it's possible, could you seat me by a street-facing window?"

"Absolutely, my dear. Right this way."

He fell in behind her jolly hips.

After some maneuvering, she stopped at a window-lined wall. "Is this to your liking?"

"That's perfect. Thanks." He picked the chair with the best view of both inside and outside the restaurant.

"Here's a list of everything we have," she went on, handing him a menu, "just in case you want to start the festivities before your guest arrives."

"Thanks," he replied.

As she walked off, he removed his hat and glasses. With his mission kit resting on the table, he lifted his menu, though not because he planned to order anything. He used the laminated sheet as cover while scanning the room, and in the middle of his pass, he spotted Victor Vane.

Eyes darting downward, he almost couldn't believe it. Here sat the man in the video—the vicious murderer who stabbed that woman to death—not more than thirty feet away. With his virtual heart drumming, he drew in air to induce calm. He only partially succeeded, but that was enough to refocus on his task. He lifted his shield once more.

Victor sat in a booth at the far side of the pub, carrying on animatedly with an attractive young woman. Eric tightened his face. The young woman wasn't Alice.

Looking down once more, he hoped this woman wasn't another target. That would severely complicate the surveillance effort. After all, the situation was challenging enough tracking two people simultaneously. With a third variable introduced, that might prove insurmountable.

He needed to figure out who the woman was, along with how she fit into everything, but not now. Having identified the primary target, keeping tabs on him took precedence. But with Victor Vane in this room, did that mean Chad Vale was as well?

If Victor and Chad were the same, then both bodies housed the same consciousness, and wouldn't that result in behavioral overlap? To check, he moved his shield back into position, started turning towards Victor's booth, but suddenly froze.

"Jesus!" he hissed, way too loud.

Newspaperman sat at the bar, half-planted on a stool.

Goddammit! Is this *fucking* normal?

Eric didn't know. This was all so new to him. It wasn't clear how often one came across the same character in a given virtual stay. He only knew that newspaperman was triggering every alarm bell in his digital body.

He gritted his teeth and looked away. In addition to a map, his online inventory needed a knife, one to hold against newspaperman's throat and demand answers. But he didn't have one. If he wanted answers, the best he could do was shoot another glance in newspaperman's direction, and check once more if that virtual nightmare was observing him. But good God. What if he was?

Eric pursed his lips. *Fuck it. This is virtual reality. This isn't real.*

With this thought in mind, he drew in digital air, steeled his nerves, and—

"Why, hello there!" said a waitress. "Oh! Settle down there, lad! Didn't mean to startle ya. Jus' stoppin' by to see if ya wanted something to eat or drink."

He stared at her, mouth agape. "Oh, yes. A pint of Guinness, please."

The waitress turned up her ruby lips. "Sure thing, lad. I'll bring it right out."

He lifted his shield once more, this time to hide while regaining his composure. The task proved monumental, which highlighted his abysmal operative abilities. But after sensing movement from his quarry, he forced himself back into the moment.

The unknown woman, along with the big bad wolf, were getting up to leave.

He needed to follow them. But leaving now would look odd because he just ordered a drink. With no other options, he grabbed his hat and glasses while preparing to rise. Then he looked over and tightened his gaze. Newspaperman had vanished. Only where did he go? Did he exit the simulator while seated at the bar?

He shelved the question as Victor and his friend neared the exit. He needed to move, but not quite yet. He couldn't follow so close that either would notice him. So, he sat on the chair's edge tapping an impatient foot, until the targets finally slipped into the afternoon sunlight. He lifted his mission kit and started walking.

"Leavin' already, are we?"

The female voice stopped him dead in his tracks. He spun and there stood the waitress, his Guinness in hand.

"Oh. I'm so sorry. I was supposed to meet someone here, but it turns out, I'm at the wrong place." He mentally cringed. He just might be the worst spy in the history of the profession.

"No need to worry." She hefted the glass and smiled. "I'll make sure this doesn't go to waste!"

He smiled back, spun towards the door, and hustled out, hoping Victor and his friend didn't place too much distance between them.

Outside, he froze on the sidewalk and cranked his neck around. He scowled. The area stood devoid of his targets. But what accounted for their sudden disappearance?

Looking about some more, he spotted an alley not far away, one Victor and the woman could've reached while out of sight. He would take a quick look. If it came up empty, he would double back to Victor's apartment.

He took long steps toward the alley, slowing down just before the entrance. After turning into it, he silently inched along, digital senses heightened.

It was quiet, uncomfortably quiet, especially contrasted against The Clover's vibrant din. In fact, the pub's music and voices were now the only discernable sounds, both coming across as muffled background noise. He stopped about twenty feet in when he detected something else.

Where those footsteps tapping behind him? They were. And as they ground to a halt, he strained to detect additional noises. Silence. Silence. *Click.* The unmistakable sound of a gun hammer cocking, readying the weapon to fire.

He shut his eyes, fully expecting a lightning bolt to strike him at any moment. None did.

With his virtual stomach churning, he slowly turned, and there stood newspaperman, gripping a pistol aimed at his chest. Eric lifted his hands to ward off any aggression, but the move didn't work. Newspaperman slowly curled his finger around the trigger. At this, Eric's digital legs turned to rubber.

"Take off your fucking glasses," newspaperman growled, his voice low and impatient.

Eric swallowed. None of this was real. It was all simulated. Newspaperman could pull the trigger all he wanted, and Eric Ryan wouldn't die. He wouldn't even get shot. He grimaced as his reality check did nothing to alleviate his terror. On the contrary, dread surged as he envisioned that simulated gun firing, then having a simulated bullet tear through his flesh and bone, before crashing onto the concrete and clutching his chest as warm simulated blood spurted through his fingers.

Newspaperman readjusted his grip. "I said take off your fucking glasses!"

Eric complied, doing so slowly. After removing his shades, newspaperman's face all but broke.

"Fucking unbelievable," he sighed while lowering his pistol.

Eric, on the other hand, remained in a state of shock.

"Look," newspaperman said, "relax. I'm not your enemy."

Eric believed him so he lowered his hands. Now convinced the danger had passed, he furrowed his face over how this person approached him, gun drawn and ready to fire. "You're not my enemy? Well you sure as fuck don't seem like my friend!"

Newspaperman slipped his pistol into a jacket holster and snapped it secure. With his weapon put away, he moved in close and spoke quietly, clearly. "That, all depends, on how you look at it." He winked.

Eric recalled that wink. "Arvin?"

Newspaperman gave an acknowledging smirk. "Dr. Ryan."

Chapter 12

Eric walked along the crowded streets of L.A. Confidential, his digital lips angled upward. As he and Arvin headed back to The Clover to talk things over, he couldn't help but grin over Arvin's human transition. Arvin, however, emanated virtual heat, making Eric wonder why.

True, their initial encounter was intense, but when their identities surfaced, the tension subsided, or at least it had for Eric. Arvin hadn't relaxed since, but why?

If anyone should be upset, Eric deserved the largest share of indignation. After all, *he* just stared down the working end of a nickel-plated semi-auto, not Arvin.

He shuddered while recalling this. Simulator or not, the alleyway incident carried deep implications that he wanted to consider, but not now. At the moment, he was content to enjoy the sight beside him—Arvin in fleshy form.

Inside The Clover, he cleared his throat at the waitress who took his order earlier.

The waitress looked over and arched her brow. "Back so soon, are we?" She quickly turned solemn. "And I'm sorry to tell you this, my dear, but your Guinness is gone. But if it's any consolation—" she patted her stomach— "she's in a better place."

Eric chuckled. "Well, that's something to be thankful for." He turned towards Arvin. "And here's the friend I was looking for. Mind if we sit at the same table?"

"But of course. Come along then, lads." She turned and walked the lads back to Eric's old digs.

As they settled in, the waitress inquired about their order. They went with two glasses of Guinness and she left to bring them over.

Arvin eyed the waitress as she sauntered off, and when she stepped out of earshot, he turned back and leaned in. "Just how fucking stupid are you?"

Eric jerked back. He never thought Arvin would speak to him this way, or for that matter, to speak this way at all. Actually, the statement was so out of character that doubt crept in as to this person's identity. He slowly leaned forward. "Wait a minute. Are you..."

Arvin squinted his gelatinous eyes, and after a moment, he rolled them. "Yes. It's me. Your special client."

Eric couldn't help but chuckle. He had grown accustomed to real space Arvin—the prim and proper house bot with an elegant British accent. Now, no trace of his astute client remained. Before him sat a full-bore human, and the transition was simply marvelous. But with Arvin not about to marvel over anything, Eric shelved his admiration and opened his hands.

"What? Why are you so upset?"

Arvin leaned back. "Is it safe to assume you're here for the same reason I am?"

Eric nodded.

"Okay. Now can I assume you recognize the importance of going unnoticed?"

Another nod.

"So why the hell would you enter a virtual world, to spy on a potential murderer, looking exactly like your real space self?"

All in one motion, Eric closed his eyes, pursed his lips, and lowered his head.

"Does he know what you look like?" Arvin asked.

Eyes still closed, and lips still pinched, Eric nodded. After refocusing, he covered his mouth. With Arvin stunned into silence, Eric struggled not to laugh. He simply couldn't stop superimposing the classily refined Arvin over this very biological, very upset human. It was too damn hilarious. He drew in air to steady himself.

"Sorry, Arvin. My decision to enter was kinda spur of the moment."

Arvin cringed. "Oh, for the love of God. Don't call me by my real name!"

His laughter suppression gave way. It was official. He was the worst spy in the history of the profession. "Goddammit. Sorry." After some breaths, he finally excised his delirious demons. "Well, what's your name in here?"

"Michael. I go by Michael. But just call me Mike."

"Alright then, Mike." Eric observed Mike admiringly, to which Mike opened his own hands. "It's just kinda cool... seeing you like this."

Mike shook his head and eased back. "I suppose it's not so bad from my end, being in this body and all. But I selected this body, along with these clothes, to blend in, to be inconspicuous. *You* on the other hand..."

Eric's face warmed.

"Do you know what you look like with those glasses and hat? A spy. Some secret government operative. What you don't look like is just some plain old guy, existing in plain old 1950's Los Angeles."

"I know. Like I said. Spur of the moment."

They both grew quiet as the waitress arrived with their drinks. She set down the frosty glasses and inquired once more if either wanted anything else.

"We're fine, thank you," Mike said.

She cast some cheer and turned on her heel.

Eric picked up his glass and studied it. He then brought the glass to his nose and inhaled, grinning when he detected a wonderfully pungent aroma. Without additional fanfare, he went in, filling his mouth with the bitter liquids. After swallowing, he jerked back. "Holy shit." He quickly took another gulp.

Mike smirked.

Eric appreciated Mike's gesture as it signaled decreased tension. After one more swallow, he set his glass down. "By the way, where are you right now? I mean in real space."

Mike sipped before answering. "I'm in my basement quarters, shut down while updates are filed into my neural networks." He shook his head. "Bastards keep me in the basement. But it works out in my favor. That's the best place to login and it's secluded from the family."

"I can't blame you for feeling that way." Eric eased back. "So, is our target the person we think he is?"

"Yeah. I concluded that a few days ago. Whenever Chad logs in, Victor appears. It's happened over and over."

Eric nodded as that answered his first question—Victor Vane was in fact Chad Vale. "How often do you carry out these little tracking missions?"

"Pretty regularly. My duties don't take up much of my time. And sometimes, I even enter when I'm slaving away."

"You can control both bodies simultaneously—your robotic form and your net space avatar?"

"Yeah, but not perfectly." Mike grinned. "Sometimes, when I try to do something in one world, I end up doing it in the other. It makes for a great bloopers reel."

Eric grinned back, then watched Mike take another sip. "So what do you think?"

Mike hefted his glass. "Of this?"

"Yeah."

"If I had any gustatory cortex, I'd let you know."

"So you can't taste anything?"

Mike shook his head.

"Wait. How are you experiencing this world?"

"The same way you are. Mostly, at least. The computer program is feeding us the same information, but I can't process all of it because I don't have your components."

"Like gustatory cortex for taste?"

Mike nodded. "If I can't process something in real space, I can't process it here. But pretty much everything else—touch, sight, sound—I'm sensing all of that. *And* I'm sensing it from your human point of view."

"But it looks like you're enjoying it—the drink I mean."

"I'm just doing my best to copy you." Mike took another pull and unleashed an obscene gasp of enjoyment.

Eric chuckled. And while he wanted to keep the conversation light, there were business matters to discuss. "So how long has this endeavor of yours been going on?"

"Just a few days."

"And?"

"And I think I've identified the next target."

Eric nodded. "Yeah. Alice."

"Who?"

"Alice. The librarian."

Mike tilted his head slightly.

"Wait. Isn't that who you identified?"

"Well, I identified a librarian. Pretty girl—young, petite, long brown hair."

"Yeah, that's her. Alice."

Mike tilted his head in the other direction. "How did you find out her name?"

"I met her today. Before I entered, I found out through Crypt Keeper that Victor was targeting a librarian. So after popping in, I went to the library nearest to his place. Turns out, she works there."

Mike nodded. "Okay. So her name is Alice. A name is helpful. Anything else?"

"Nah. I only spoke to her briefly. You?"

Mike shook his head. "I've seen her and Victor go out on dates—dinner, movies, stuff like that—but nothing else."

Eric stretched his virtual back before continuing. "Anything giving you the impression that Victor's a murdering asshole?"

"Oh. I reached that conclusion a while ago. That pig's been poked."

Eric chuckled. "Well, our best chance to catch Victor in the act is over the next few days. He told me on Crypt Keeper that his next hit is in the offing."

Mike took another drink and gingerly set his glass down. "So, you saw him on Crypt Keeper, huh?"

"Right."

"See anything interesting while there?"

Eric envisioned a serrated knife flashing back and forth, as a young woman grimaced in agony, and trails of her dark-red blood spurted through the air. Rattling away the image, he shot Mike a look, thus answering his question.

"Yeah," Mike affirmed. "Pretty damn bad."

Eric nodded and took a long swallow. "So, you have any info related to the next hit?"

"Nope. Mostly because I can't get close to Victor."

"Too secluded?"

"And too weary of strangers. But you being here should help. Now we can step up our surveillance. That is, as long as you stop looking like you."

"As soon as I get out, I'm switching up my avatar."

Mike raised his hands and thanked the virtual Gods.

Eric shook his head and took another drink. "But even when I change my appearance, we still have the same problem. We can't get close to Victor."

"True. I considered using the librarian somehow, maybe to introduce us, but she's pretty hot for Victor. She probably doesn't want attention from some random guy."

Eric looked away as a strategy came to mind, one to overcome Victor *and* Alice's resistance to strangers. It was a brilliant idea, but was it even possible? He turned back, deciding to flesh this out later. "Well, whatever we come up with, we need to act fast because there isn't much time left."

"For who? Alice or me?"

At first, he didn't understand the comparison, then he did. "God. Sorry. I didn't mean to—"

Mike smiled and waved him off. "I'm just messing around. I couldn't resist."

Falling silent, they quietly sipped their drinks while soaking in the buzzy atmosphere. Eric did so with more appreciation than before now that his stay wasn't so pressure-filled.

"Pretty amazing," Mike softly interjected. "Isn't it?"

Eric, the notorious loather of all things technology, couldn't help but agree. "Yeah. Yeah, it is pretty amazing." He took another drink. "Now I understand why so many people spend so much time in V.R."

Suddenly, he realized he didn't want to leave. He liked it here.

Ironically, this world was a refuge from tech, as here it was nowhere in sight. He absolutely adored that. He even thought the other displaced people should make an exodus on over.

How many of his clients might benefit from visiting these tech-free worlds? Probably most, because here they could reemploy whatever skills had become irrelevant. And who knew? Maybe some had already arrived. Maybe some of the world's characters—the ones performing menial labor—weren't computer programs after all. Maybe they were real people performing real work, because to them, this provided value.

"Well," Mike slowly broke in, "I need to be getting back."

Eric refocused. "Right. Right. And I'll um, I'll make sure to change my appearance. Oh, and we should exchange contact info in case we come across something worth passing on."

After swapping data, Mike got up to leave, speaking as he did. "So I'll see you tomorrow."

"Where? Here in the world?"

Mike grinned. "Therapy. Tomorrow morning, *I* need to go see my therapist."

Eric chuckled. He had forgotten that another reality existed. How interesting. "Of course. See you then."

With that, Mike walked into the men's room and didn't reappear.

Eric figured Mike used this location to discreetly exit the simulator. While he needed to depart as well, not yet. He first wanted to order another beer, then lean back and continue pretending the other reality didn't exist. He wanted to continue pretending where he came from was just a dream.

Chapter 13

Real Space

Back at Sunrise, Arvin sat in the third-floor lobby waiting for his therapist. When the elevator doors opened and the man stepped out, he rose to his robotic feet. "Good morning, Dr. Ryan."

Dr. Ryan stopped and smiled.

Arvin, now using his sensors to read Dr. Ryan's data streams, saw the man's amusement over his robotic reversion. Arvin rolled his light-absorbing optic receptors.

Dr. Ryan smiled wider and led the way to his office. "By the way," he said, stopping outside of the door while the scanners assessed his bio-signatures, "feel free to call me Eric."

"I'll give it a shot, but I'm not making any promises."

The door slid open.

"Hard-wired for dereference?" Eric called over his shoulder while entering.

"Just like an adult human set in their ways." Arvin sat on a guest chair while Eric continued behind his desk. "So, are you still Eric Ryan in our little home away from home?"

"Nope," Eric answered while settling in. "I took care of that. And quite well, I might add."

"How so?"

Eric turned up his lips. "You'll see."

"A surprise. How intriguing. But at least your new character can't be any worse than the previous one."

"True. But trust me when I say this one's good. With this avatar, Victor won't avoid me, he'll come begging to be my friend."

Arvin turned up his synthetic lips.

"Well," Eric went on, "anything new?"

"No. Yesterday I logged in when Chad entered the world, but nothing of importance transpired. He spent all his time in his apartment."

Eric leaned back slightly. "That seems odd."

"It's certainly uncharacteristic of him. But he was only there for half an hour. However, I did manage to acquire some information from outside the world."

"Crypt Keeper?"

Arvin nodded. "Chad posted some juicy tidbits on their message boards about his extravagant plans for this weekend."

"That figures, because Chad told me on Crypt Keeper that the weekend was his likely time frame for the hit. And with today being Wednesday, the weekend isn't far off."

"Luckily, I have the Vale Estate under constant surveillance, including Chad's room where he logs in from. If he enters the simulator, I'll know."

"So it seems like we're set." Eric then narrowed his eyes and looked away.

"What?"

"I just thought of something." Eric looked back. "What about after the murder? After Chad kills the librarian, what then?"

Arvin didn't answer. Instead, he lowered his light-absorbing optic receptors.

"Because again," Eric continued, "what Chad's doing technically isn't a crime. It's pretty damned awful, but he's not breaking any laws."

Arvin looked up and tunneled into Eric, just like before. He again wanted to glimpse Eric's inner essence, and for the same reason—to gauge his trustworthiness. He succeeded.

Eric Ryan was a good person, something he concluded after contrasting his data to the other sets in his memory bank. To be certain, Eric wasn't faultless, but he possessed a strong moral compass, and once set, it seldom wavered. That was the problem.

"Well," Eric prodded, "what's the plan? After the murder, should we burst into Victor's room and wag our virtual fingers?" With still no answer coming, he leaned back and crossed his arms. "You know—"

"If we witness Victor murder the librarian," Arvin cut in, "further action will be taken."

Eric hesitated. "What does that mean?"

"I will remedy the problem."

Eric tightened his crossed arms. "You're not—you know..."

Still nothing.

"C'mon. You're not planning on, you know..."

Arvin just kept staring, his silence speaking volumes.

Eric sat up. "You gotta be fucking kidding me. Oh, my God. You gotta be fucking kidding me."

Arvin registered Eric's flurries of panic, and to assuage the pulsing anxiety, he decided to explain himself. "I am most certainly *not* kidding you. I plan to murder Chad Vale, and you know why."

Eric parted his mouth and looked around before refocusing. "This isn't right. You can't just take it upon yourself to kill someone. You don't even know if Professor Vale was murdered."

"Oh, come now, Dr. Ryan. Do you still believe the fairy tale that Dr. Vale died from a heart attack?"

"No, but even if he *was* murdered, I'm not one-hundred percent convinced that Chad Vale did it. Is he the likely candidate? Yes. But even if he signed a confession and forwarded me a copy, that still doesn't give me, or anyone, the right to arbitrarily kill the bastard."

"Dr. Ryan, I understand your anxiety. But you must appreciate the fact that you did not have my relationship with Dr. Vale."

"Granted, but that still doesn't give you the right. Hell. This even highlights why people in your situation don't decide these things, because right now, you think murder is a reasonable response. And make no mistake. It's murder, irrespective of your justifications. And because of that, I'm out. I won't have any part of it."

Arvin leaned in. "You're already part of it."

Eric looked away and clenched his jaw, his data streams showing increasing appreciation for this situation's gravity. The streams also beamed out a bright red *I told you so.*

"What's your opinion of Chad?" Arvin asked.

Eric refocused. "What?"

"Chad Vale. What's your opinion of him? You read his medical profile and you met him in person. You also gathered some information from me and from net space. So, what's your opinion of him?"

Eric took a breath. "He's an asshole. He's also arrogant and violent, and pissed off with tech. He even blames tech for society's woes, and he periodically murders people in net space if *they* don't hate tech. And net space murder isn't real."

"You still aren't convinced of how real net space can be? Tell me, what did you feel when I pointed that gun at you?"

"Fear. When you pointed that gun at me, I felt fear."

"And what is fear?"

"It's a response mechanism, a chained series of biological events that occur when an organism receives threatening stimuli. When humans undergo this response, they usually describe it as fear."

Arvin nodded. "And is there a difference between net space and real space fear?"

"I would say no."

"And were you aware that some humans have suffered posttraumatic stress from virtual fear?"

"Yeah. I've heard of that. That's usually a byproduct of online war games. And while I've always dismissed this as insulting to real-life veterans, given what I've experienced in virtual reality..."

"And tell me. What is post-traumatic stress disorder?"

Eric smirked. "PTSD is an anxiety disorder whose hallmark is an overactive fear response system. The onset of PTSD occurs when an organism experiences real or imagined threats."

"Real or imagined," Arvin affirmed. "And how do you think Chad's murder victims respond to being killed, especially when they're convinced their murder is real?"

"With fear. Perhaps with fear so strong it triggers PTSD."

Arvin let a moment pass. "Chad knows this."

"What?"

"He knows what he's doing to his victims. He knows how they'll respond. He was in the medical profession, remember? He's read journal articles documenting the anguish these people suffer, and he murders them anyway."

Eric tightened his teeth once more.

"What does it say," Arvin went on, "about the people who commit these atrocities, who inflict such unimaginable violence on the undeserving?"

Eric didn't answer.

All the while, Arvin read Eric's data streams, watching his moral compass struggling to orient itself. He didn't want to disturb the needle any farther, but he had to—an unfortunate byproduct of his resoluteness.

"Dr. Ryan," Arvin continued, "I know that you're undergoing hardships with your romantic partner. But please, imagine that someone murdered her. Now imagine you had little time to live, and you knew the murderer would never face justice. How would you feel knowing these thoughts would be your last right before your consciousness blinked out for eternity?"

Eric looked down, his data streams red and pulsing.

Arvin knew he struck a chord. Then he saw something even more interesting—Eric's data streams aligning with his own. "Dr. Ryan, what are you thinking?"

"I'm thinking I can't go along with your plan to kill Chad... yet."

"Yet?"

Eric looked up. "I'm going to need more evidence. I need to see what Chad does in the virtual world. Now that we know Victor is Chad, whatever Victor does, Chad is responsible for. I need to know what kind of person Chad is. I need to see him carry out the hit."

"So nothing has changed. That *is* our current plan."

"Right, but our plan is stalling because we can't get close to Victor, remember?"

"Yes, I remember."

"Well, do you also remember what I told you? How I created a character that would help?"

"Yes."

"It's time to put this character into effect."

Chapter 14

L.A. Confidential

"Excuse me?" Eric told Alice, speaking in a sultry female voice.

Alice turned from her book-filled cart and beamed her signature cheer. "Hi, there."

"Hi. I'm Lana. It's nice to meet you." Lana extended her hand.

Eric's new plan was in full effect.

To remedy the shortsightedness of copying and pasting himself into virtual form, he created Lana, a head-turning woman in her mid-twenties, with shimmering jet-black hair, fare skin, and hypnotizing green eyes. In her, his chances of closing in on Victor increased two-fold. First, Victor preferred to feast on attractive young women. Second, Alice was the key gateway to Victor, and she should be more receptive to those like her.

Alice took her hand. "Hi, Lana. It's nice to meet you too." They let go. "What can I do for you? Did you need help looking for a book?"

"Thanks, but not right now. Actually, I was wondering if the library had any openings for employment."

"Employment?"

"Yeah, although to be honest, I don't really have much library experience." Lana lowered her voice. "None, if I'm being completely honest."

Alice waved this off. "Don't worry about that. I didn't have any when I first started." She grinned. "Where I come from, there aren't many libraries."

Lana chuckled.

"Out of curiosity," Alice continued, "why were you interested in working here?"

"Well, after I decided to enter this world, I scoured its map for employment ideas. That's when I spotted the library. I figured it would be the perfect place for acclimation because I would meet people in the area."

"Smart thinking, because the locals do frequent our little book haven. And in terms of actual library work, there isn't much. Anyone can get the job down in half an hour."

Lana perked up. "This position sounds better by the second. That is, if there's an opening."

"For that, you would have to speak with our manager, Greg Miller." Alice cranked her head around. "Although I haven't seen him yet, but that's no surprise. He likes to come in late and leave early."

Lana fought to maintain her cheer as she didn't actually want to work here. And she especially wanted to avoid wasting time with Greg Miller. "Do you know when he might return?" she asked, keeping up the pretense of employment interest.

"With Miller, it's hard to tell. And hey. If you don't mind me asking, how long have you been in this world?"

"About thirty minutes. It's my first day."

Alice arched her brow. "Oh, wow. Well the reason I asked is because I'm taking my lunch break now. If you wanna tag along, I can fill you in on what I've learned."

Lana turned up her lips, this time without faking it. "That would be lovely."

"Great. Wait for me out front. I'll grab my things."

As the gem walked off, Lana turned and started for the exit, trying not to lose her balance while walking. "Nice and easy," she murmured. Just how long did it take most women to become comfortable in heeled shoes?

She exited the library and descended the steps. After reaching the sidewalk without tipping over, she waited with a glowing sense of pride.

She had come a long way from moving around on shaky legs, but she still struggled to control her female form, especially in heeled footwear. True, her heels were only two inchers, but even these proved problematic. Luckily, she had time to practice in her apartment, and while doing so, she developed a newfound respect for anyone who could wear taller shoes and still move around gracefully.

"Ready?" Alice asked while coming down the steps.

Lana looked over and tightened her lips. Alice carried a purse underneath her arm. Of course. How could she have forgotten this key female accessory? It was too late to amend this error, but she could use this impromptu date to note any other oversights. That brightened her up. "Ready."

"Great. There's a coffee shop a few blocks away. Do you mind if we walk?"

"Oh," she replied, her brightness struggling, "not at all. Lead the way."

Alice flashed her ever-radiant smile, and Lana did her best to return the gesture.

As they started off, Lana questioned how convincing she was as a woman. Anatomically, she was perfect, but that was only one half of the equation—the easy half thanks to virtual reality. The other half consisted of acting woman-like. Fortunately, her complete physical transformation aided her transition.

Lana wasn't simply Eric Ryan in a wig and female clothing. She was now Lana through and through. The point hit home when she emerged in her apartment, looked down, and cursed at the sight of her female self—a shock compounded by her clean and clear female voice. Then the situation turned otherworldly strange when she crept in front of her bedroom mirror and laid eyes on her fleshy hourglass. But like before, acclimation to net space weirdness was quick—startlingly quick.

Eric's brain rapidly accepted Lana as its one true body, and just as rapidly discharged the old body. In fact, the more she interacted with her environment, the more Eric Ryan faded into history. And now sauntering along the sidewalk, she decided to flourish further by conversing.

"So how long have you been here?"

"Not too long," Alice answered. "About a month."

"Like it?"

"Love it. This place was a necessary change, because over the last few months, I've been looking to settle down."

"Was your last place not settled?"

Alice laughed. "No. Nor were the places before that. But during the past few years, I wasn't looking for settled. I was looking to party."

Lana shrugged. "I can't fault you for that. What was your last world?"

"A place called West Egg. It's based on New York during the 1920's."

"Oh, wow. The Roaring 20s. That's pretty cool."

Alice nodded. "They were roaring alright. It was a blast. Jazz music, martinis, guys in fancy suits, girls in fancy dresses, old cars that needed cranking to turn on. Stuff like that."

"That seems terrific. Why did you leave?"

"Because it was a blast that never ended, and I needed a break. So, I started searching for something slower."

"I'm guessing this world is perfect then?"

Alice nodded once more. "Yup. It's exactly what I needed."

"Oddly enough, I know what you mean. I've barely spent any time here and I already love it, mostly because of its slow pace. And I didn't even come here looking for that, but I'm definitely glad I found it."

The coffee shop came into view.

"Was your last world too active?" Alice asked.

Lana laughed. "You could say that. But I'm not referring to any virtual world. Other than L.A. Confidential, the only world I know is real space. This is my first time in virtual reality."

Alice stopped walking. "Are you kidding?"

Lana likewise halted. "No. I'm being serious. This is my first world."

"How old are... Wait, no. I'm so sorry. I shouldn't ask that."

"No, no. It's perfectly okay. I don't mind talking about my real space self. Let's go inside and I'll fill you in."

They resumed their route.

While nearing the coffee shop, Lana eyed its retro plastic lettering. "Benny's."

"This is it. It's great here."

Lana believed her, as they were still outside and she already detected the aroma of coffee, a scent that thickened with every step. This didn't prepare her for what awaited inside.

After easing through the squeaky glass door, a vast array of colorful chalkboard menus greeted her, along with the clattering of silverware against ceramic, and waitresses hustling around with coffee pots. And now mixed into the aroma of coffee grounds were pancakes, pork, and syrup, all of it filling her nose with an intoxicating delight.

"Hello, ladies," greeted a female host. "Is it just the pair of you?"

Alice cast her sunshine smile. "Just us two."

"Great. Right this way." The hostess turned and led them into the vibrant din.

Lana narrowed her eyes while walking. Was the virtual simulator engaging in any emotional trickery? Specifically, was it manually activating her brain's pleasure areas? After all, she absolutely loved this place, and not just Benny's but the virtual world and everything in it. But a computer was generating every experience, including every emotion. And with Alternate Reality a business, why *not* massage their customer's feel good centers? She made a mental note to research this later. For now, might as well enjoy it.

"Here you are, ladies," the hostess said after reaching their table. "Someone'll be right over."

Alice and Lana thanked her then settled into their worn maroon leather booth.

"So," Alice said, "what do you think?"

Lana shook her head. "It's unbelievable. The nostalgia in this place is truly something."

"I thought the same thing when I first entered. And with my fondness for exploration, I can't wait to find all the other little pearls of pleasure tucked away in this world. But really, I can't believe this is your first time in virtual reality."

Lana nodded. "I was never tech's biggest fan. Actually, I was in the crowds that railed against it. Because of that, I refused to give these places a shot. But now—" she gestured towards her magical surroundings— "to hell with all that!"

Alice laughed. "What made you change your mind?"

"Good afternoon, ladies," interjected a waitress. "What can I get you two? Some coffee? Some lunch? We're still serving breakfast if that sounds good."

Alice raised her eyebrows and looked to Lana.

Lana turned to the waitress. "Just coffee for me."

"Same here," Alice said.

"Sure thing," the waitress replied. "I'll be right back with a fresh pot." She turned and walked off.

"So," Alice went on, "why did you change your mind about trying these worlds out?"

Before responding, Lana inhaled the breakfast-filled air. "My boyfriend cheated on me. Well, I think he's cheating on me. Okay, I'm pretty damned sure he's cheating on me. About the only thing I haven't seen is him in bed with his hot new lover."

Alice curled as if gut-punched.

Lana nodded. "Yeah. It sucks. And because of that, there's nothing left for me in real space. I mean, I never really cared for it to begin with, but being with my partner made it bearable. But with that essentially over, I decided to search for someplace new."

"Damn. That *does* suck. I'm so sorry to hear that. But I can't blame you for wanting to leave. A while ago, I found out that my partner was being unfaithful. And looking back, I would've loved to escape that too."

"You couldn't?"

"Sorta. It was during college, so I had to see that asshole often. But that was years ago, so I'm over it. You're in the middle of this nightmare. I can't imagine what you're going through. Honestly, I hope things work out."

"Thanks. I really appreciate it." Lana looked down at the coffee-stained table. While she *did* appreciate Alice's concern, the intensity of her appreciation caught her off guard. What accounted for this? While uncertain, it didn't matter. Right here, right now, Alice was lending a caring ear, and that superseded her confusion.

The waitress arrived with her freshly brewed pot and filled their cups with steaming hot coffee. "Here you go, ladies. I'll be floating around, so if you need anything else, just let me know."

They offered their thanks.

As the waitress left, Alice raised her cup. "To starting over."

Lana chuckled and raised hers as well. "To starting over."

They tapped their cups and took cautious sips.

Lana sucked air as she slurped. The coffee was fantastic—hot and strong, and slightly bitter but not overpowering. Maybe the virtual simulator was engaging in emotional trickery, maybe it wasn't. Either way, she was certain of one thing—coffee warmed the virtual soul.

After another sip, she set her cup down. "And speaking of starting over, it would be nice to start over with someone new, maybe someone from this world."

"This is a good place for that too."

"I figured it would be. The people here likely prefer simplistic living. That alone means we have something in common. Good grounds to get something started."

Alice grinned. "You're more right than you realize."

"Oh, really?"

"Oh, really."

Lana leaned in. "Go on."

Alice likewise scooted forward. "I met someone about a week ago, a manager at a metal works factory. He hasn't been here long, but he's pretty much here for the same reason I am. Come to think of it, he's also here for the same reason you mentioned."

"Really?"

"Yeah. He didn't care for real space and he wanted to find someplace new. And given his reasons, I can't fault him."

"What are his reasons?"

"He used to do construction work but he ended up being displaced."

"That's too bad, but not surprising. Over the past few years, a lot of people have lost their jobs, but construction workers got hit disproportionately hard."

Alice nodded. "Nowadays, bots and 3-D printers build everything. And while that makes everything cheaper and faster to build, all the humans who used to do this work are no longer needed."

"So venturing into these worlds rekindles his sense of purpose?"

"Mm-hmm. He said that in these worlds, he can find existential fulfillment because he can pursue his life's passion."

Lana stared for a second and sipped more coffee. "Sounds like quite a guy." She put her cup down. "I'd love to meet someone like that. And maybe working at the library will make that happen."

"It worked for me. That's where we met."

"Oh?"

"Yup. He popped up out of nowhere and we started talking."

Lana hesitated. "So *he* initiated contact with *you?*"

"Yup. Like I said. Popped up out of nowhere."

Lana filed this bit of information and continued. "So are things getting serious between you two?"

"I think they are. He stops by the library often and we talk whenever he does. We've even gone out a few times—movies, dinner, stuff like that."

"Movies?" Lana asked, coming across another addition for her expanding to-do list.

"Oh, yeah. The theaters here are great. The quality is terrible but that's part of their charm."

"It seems like things are progressing smoothly. And who knows? Maybe he has a friend he can introduce me to."

Alice shrugged. "I can definitely ask him."

"Are you sure that's no problem?"

"None at all. He's incredibly caring, and I bet he would *want* to help."

"He sounds great. What's his name?"

"Victor Vane."

Lana laughed. "Victor Vane? Now he sounds like a comic book villain."

Alice likewise chuckled, doing so mid-sip. "Oh, my God." She reached for a napkin. "I tease him about that all the time." After dabbing her pink lips, she put her napkin down. "And actually, I have dinner plans with him later tonight. We're going to an Italian restaurant that's become our go-to place. Care to join us?"

Lana smiled from ear to digital ear. "That sounds lovely."

Chapter 15

Real Space

Eric removed his immersion sets and blinked a few times. As UCLA's computer lab came into focus, he set aside the glasses and crossed his arms.

His recent venture into virtual reality was a resounding success, so much that he couldn't wait to exit the simulator and update Arvin. But now back in reality, his enthusiasm dissolved.

Arvin's time in this world was drawing near, and this dampened his spirits. Was there a way he could intervene on Arvin's behalf? Whether he could or not, he needed to try. He couldn't sit on the sidelines while Arvin's sentience vanished for eternity.

Grabbing the immersion sets, he slipped them back over his face and navigated to UCLA's faculty directory. There he found his longtime supervisor with whom he initiated a connection.

"Dr. Wright," the supervisor answered, his words beamed directly into Eric's auditory cortices.

"Hey, it's Eric."

"Well, well. Dr. Ryan. I was wondering when you'd call. You had me worried. I was afraid you hadn't rang earlier because a session didn't go so well and you were busy burying the bot's remains."

Eric laughed. He needed that.

"So," Dr. Wright continued, "how *are* things going with the bot? You really haven't tried to kill him, have you?"

"I tried. But unfortunately, he's built like a machine."

Now Dr. Wright chuckled.

"But really, there hasn't been any bloodshed, and not only because Arvin would rip me a new one. A lot more has been going on, and that's why I called."

"I'm all ears."

"Well good. But um, how long will you be in your office?"

"I don't know. Hour or so. Why's that?"

"I'm on campus right now. Computer lab on the north side. If you have a few minutes, I can stop by."

"Sure. Come on over."

"Alright. I'll be there in about five."

"You got it."

The call ended.

Eric worked himself from the chair, moving gingerly to let pooled blood recirculate. Back on his feet, he shook out the stiffness with more vigor, all the while envying Arvin. Bots could remain in the simulator indefinitely without having body parts turning gangrenous. Must be nice.

Fully recovered, he started for the exit. It was surely broiling outside but he nonetheless he planned to walk. Dr. Wright's office was a few minutes away, and that would give him time to strategize his true purpose for their meeting—obtaining Dr. Wright's assistance in saving Arvin's life.

As he strolled along the concrete walkways, the brutal sun punishing above, he considered his proposal strategy. He needed to present Arvin as more useful alive than dead, but as a house bot, that limited his usefulness. What about having Arvin become a helper bot in some other capacity, perhaps here at the university?

Not likely.

UCLA had an array of maintenance bots, some of which he saw tending the campus grounds. These bots seldom required repairs, and what the school possessed was surely sufficient. Plus, having Arvin clean latrines seemed counter-productive given his profound mind.

Eric widened his eyes. *That's it. His profound mind. Forget scrubbing toilets. Arvin should be here as faculty.*

Even amongst A.I.s, Arvin was no ordinary bot. But that figured as inside him roamed the ghost of a philosopher. And if the ghost was a mere sliver of Professor Vale, that might be enough for UCLA to accept Arvin. The problem was time. If getting Arvin onboard took more than a week, he would be wiped—or worse, get caught holding Chad's lifeless body.

Goddamn. Arvin caught holding Chad's lifeless body.

This was big, bigger than Arvin or Chad ending up dead. The first bot murder in history. What kind of havoc would that wreak?

It had never happened before—a bot killing a human—not even accidentally. And if Arvin wiped Chad the way he intended, that would constitute premeditated murder. So how would people respond?

Not like human-on-human murder. No, the fallout would magnify ten-fold because people would view this as an existential threat. And amid these charged emotions, people would have to figure out a response then and there because procedures didn't exist for bot-on-human violence.

And good luck to anyone pointing out that this was an isolated incident, the first of its kind, one droplet of blood in a crimson ocean from eons of human-on-human slaughter. But people were largely to blame, because if they wanted peaceful bots, they modeled these machines after the wrong species.

***

Eric walked into Dr. Wright's office and found his longtime supervisor seated behind his slate-gray desk.

Dr. Wright looked up from his orangish holo-screen and beamed. "No bruises, no black eyes, looks like you two have been getting along great!"

Eric shook his head, then stepped forward and shook Dr. Wright's outstretched hand. After letting go, he sat on a guest chair and exhaled noticeably. "Warm out there."

"Shouldn't be much longer, not with fall a few days away."

"Fine by me." He wiped the coat of sweat from his brow. "So, interesting couple of days I've had."

"I'll bet. How's it coming along?"

Eric became a little robotic himself. "The client presents mild to moderate symptoms of depression. This maladaptive behavior stems from—"

Dr. Wright waved him off. "Save the bullshit for the notes. Just tell me how it's going."

"It's going good. Actually, it's going a lot better than I imagined."

"That's good to hear."

Eric shook his head. "This is a waste. It's a huge waste. The bot's gonna be wiped in a week. So yeah, we're making progress, but what the hell for?"

Dr. Wright leaned back. "We've already been over this. Your job is to provide counseling. That's it. My job is to oversee this project. That's it. So pretty much, you're here to do all the work, and I'm here to take the credit when you succeed, or the heat when you screw up."

Eric worked his lips.

"You know," Dr. Wright went on, "I figured you would be counting down the seconds until this was all behind you."

"Arvin isn't what I expected. He's a lot more than what I expected."

"Go on."

"You remember Professor Vale, right?"

"Of course, I remember him. Shame what happened."

"Arvin is the servant to the Vale house. Professor Vale."

Dr. Wright lifted his head and inch. "Jesus. He worked for *that* Vale? Ben Vale?"

Eric nodded. "Yeah. Arvin got to their house two years ago when he didn't know shit from Shakespeare. And he wasn't there long before Professor Vale spotted an opportunity, one to mold Arvin all his own."

Dr. Wright smirked. "Imagine that. A fresh bot in the hands of Vale. So does this Arvin philosophize about everything in sight?"

"All the time, which is why the Vales sent him off to get help. They got Arvin as a house servant, but instead of cleaning, he spends all his time contemplating the meaning of life. And that's what Professor Vale wanted, but with him gone, the family doesn't want to deal with it anymore."

"I can't blame them. Those things aren't cheap. And it sounds like he's malfunctioning, given his role and all."

"That's how they see it."

"Wait. You also said the bot suffered from depression, right?"

Eric nodded.

"Because of Vale's death? I mean, if they had a father/son relationship going on..."

"That's also right. Arvin and Professor Vale were close, really close. I spoke to the Vales, and when Dad wasn't at the university, he was with Arvin shaping his young mind. Essentially, he was Arvin's only friend."

"Didn't Ben Vale have kids?"

"Yes, two."

"And they never formed a relationship with Arvin?"

Eric shook his head. "They both live in net space and never come out."

"Wife?"

"Too busy being rich."

Dr. Wright grunted. "Must be rough."

"I wouldn't know."

Dr. Wright smirked.

"And," Eric continued, deciding to pitch his sale, "since nobody will be crying when Arvin goes to see the hangman, you think there's something we can do for him?"

"Do for him how?"

"Instead of letting him get wiped, maybe we can set him up with something here."

Dr. Wight stayed silent.

"Trust me, I've spoken with Arvin in depth. There's a lot we could use here in our ivory tower."

"Like?"

"Like having Arvin assist us with our research efforts. We've been interested in machine learning for decades, so why not use him to advance our knowledge?"

Dr. Wright leaned back and worked his jaw, all while leveling an appraising look. "Are you emotionally attached to him?" With no response coming, he grinned. "Thanks for the answer."

Eric looked away and shook his head.

"Oh, c'mon. I already knew the answer. I just wanted to see your response to the question. And I'm pleased with your response. I just find it surprising because he's a bot, and you're you."

"I *have* become attached, okay? And I'm not just referring to our therapeutic relationship."

"What do you mean?"

"You remember telling me to get something out of this? Well, it turns out, I did. I developed a new perspective towards robots, and this happened by working with Arvin. He helped me realize what bots truly are. And because of this, I now realize why we can't just kill them outright."

Dr. Wright took a contemplative breath.

Encouraged, Eric kept up the pressure. "Bots aren't simply computers inside of humanoid cans. They're alive, every bit alive as you and me. And while that's reason enough not to kill Arvin, with him there's so much more. He has insight that's uncommon even among humans, and that makes perfect sense because he's a living embodiment of Professor Vale. How could we just destroy that?"

Dr. Wright likewise turned away, worked his tongue around his mouth, and finally turned back. "Well, goddamn. I never thought I'd see the day. Alright, I'll see what I can do. No guarantees, but I'll make some calls."

Eric tried to suppress immense relief... and failed.

"It might not be easy though," Dr. Wright followed. "So don't let your hopes soar unreasonably high. In the end, Arvin's property, so the Vales have the final word on what happens."

Eric rolled his jaw at this, certain that nobody within the Vale household would easily give Arvin away—Ms. Vale because she had ordered his death and would be damned if her order wasn't followed, Chad because he hated Arvin and probably wanted to pull the plug himself, and as for Amy, who knew? She was too busy being war hero for any of this.

Nevertheless, Dr. Wright was on Eric's side, and with the boss' firepower, Arvin would be roaming these grounds in no time, his inquisitive mind running rampant, and without pesky interruptions like looming execution dates or revenge murders.

"Thanks," Eric said. "Honestly, thanks."

"You're welcome. But Eric, one piece of advice. Maintain objectivity. I'm glad you and the bot are getting close, and that's no bullshit. I asked you to get something out of this and that's clearly happening. But it can't interfere with your job. Let me see about postponing the bot's execution, and in the meanwhile, you help me out by being the consummate professional. Understood?"

"Understood. Whatever happens, I'll keep fulfilling my counseling duties as instructed."

"If that's your position, get your ass out of here and go complete those clinical notes, which I'm sure are still blank."

Smiles all around, they stood and shook hands.

***

Eric left Dr. Wright's office feeling far better than when he entered. Then while walking back in the direction he came, an even larger surge of excitement flooded through. He now had solid grounds to shelve Arvin's murder plan.

Arvin had justified his homicidal desires by claiming he had nothing to lose. And because he would soon push up robotic daisies, Eric had to agree. But now with Arvin's execution date possibly lifted, the argument floundered because he just might have something to lose—an exciting new future.

Eric longed to celebrate, but he couldn't. Glancing westward, he spotted the sun dipping towards the horizon. That meant he needed to get ready for dinner. True, he still had a few hours before tonight's date, but he wanted to give himself some extra time to prepare. After all, tonight he would be dining with the devil and his damsel.

Chapter 16

L.A. Confidential

Lana opened her eyes, blinked a few times, and watched her apartment shift into focus. She smirked. Her virtual world adjustment times were decreasing, but why?

Maybe her body map was stored inside Eric's brain where it quickly glowed to life after reanimation. Maybe the simulator was storing her data, and with additional Lana information, loading her programming became easier. Whatever the reason, it only took seconds to emerge. And now fully in the moment, it was time to prepare for tonight's date.

She started for her bedroom where she uploaded some new clothes. Originally, she wanted something conservative to maintain anonymity. But after recalling Victor's fondness for attractive young females, she decided on something a little more captivating.

She opened her closet, observed her choices, and grinned. Anonymity had gone out the virtual window. She retrieved her tight black dress made of staggeringly thin material, then bent down and grabbed her new shoes, a glossy pair of black high heels with massive four-inch spikes.

She walked the items to her bed, stripped down, and worked herself into her glove-like dress. Now seated on the bed's edge, she slipped on her glossy black pumps, got to her feet, and shot open her green eyes.

How the hell did she get so tall? It didn't feel like she gained four inches. It felt like she was about to burst through the roof. It also felt pretty damned good. Stepping to her dresser mirror, she narrowed her green eyes while parting her mouth.

"Good God."

Two things were now obvious. One, any hope for anonymity lay smoldering. Two, she was having way too much fun with this. She didn't care about either. Playing dress up was too damn entertaining.

Still at her dresser, she applied shadowy makeup that matched her black dress and jet-black hair. But while doing so, some of her cheer ebbed.

These efforts at attraction were all for a male, not because she wanted to. That was somewhat deflating. But maybe the male in question was the root cause of this effect, and things would be different if done for someone else—someone she enjoyed and respected. A nice man. A man who appreciated her figure *and* her mind. Someone who desired her in any circumstance, not just when she—

"Focus, Lana. We've got a mission to worry about."

She turned up her plum-colored lips. "And speaking about that..." She spun on her glossy black shoes, grabbed her black leather purse, and started for the kitchen, her eyes narrowing once more.

Her new footwear put some serious sway in her hips and the strange new sensation intrigued her. It felt alluring, powerful even, like she suddenly obtained an elevated degree of female influence. How interesting.

In the kitchen, she pulled open a drawer and observed her new set of kitchen knives. She needed something compact enough to fit in her purse, but at the same time, her companion needed some stage presence. She picked up a paring knife that was sufficiently small but lacked fear factor. After swapping it for a steak knife, she slowly nodded.

The blade was four inches long and razor sharp, or at least, it seemed. To test the sharpness, she gently pressed the tip against her finger, her brow furrowing at the light sting. She repeated the move with added pressure, then widened her eyes when the tip pierced her skin. Yanking her hand back, she focused on her finger where a blood droplet formed. She wiped away the little red dot and only pain remained.

The significance of what just occurred slowly took hold. Virtual pain, as it were, was the same as every other experience—data sent into a user's brain with full believability. Regrettably, this also included the pain associated with physical trauma.

As the vileness of net space murder magnified, she hoped the suddenness of these attacks put the victims into shock, thereby numbing their pain receptors. She hoped the slaughtered women didn't experience anything beyond fear.

And *why* did Victor specifically target women? Because they were weak?

She looked down at the knife, her fingers tightening around the handle. She wanted to use this blade to change Victor's mind about female weakness. But doing so wouldn't be easy. It would be brutal. It would be real.

Drawing in air, she slipped the knife into her purse and zipped it shut.

Now starting for the living room, she reminded herself that tonight's reconnaissance mission should be uneventful. If everything went according to plan, the knife would stay in her bag.

***

As Lana ambled down the sidewalk, heading for Alice's apartment, she glanced towards the horizon. The setting sun never looked so majestic, especially as its thick rays pierced the city's edifices. She reached out towards the beams of light, smiling as the luminescent bands danced through her fingers. After lowering her hand, the streetlights flickered to life, bathing her surroundings with an equally enchanting glow. This world never ceased to astound her.

But like the sitting sun, her elation steadily waned, mainly because her desire for anonymity floundered with every step.

While walking along, endless sets of male eyes eagerly devoured her, some sneaking quick glances, some lingering far longer. She partly expected that, but multiple sets of female eyes likewise oriented in her direction, only they shot virtual daggers.

Outwardly, she feigned obliviousness. Inwardly, she groaned. She wanted to look attractive, but at the same time, she didn't want to attract the lust—or ire—of everyone she came across. She smirked. Being female was tricky business.

Ten minutes later, she reached Alice's apartment, and with Dominique's not far, they decided to walk. While approaching the restaurant, some of her cheer returned.

Dominique's couldn't have been more charming. It boasted an old-world Italian look, complete with faded red bricks, creamy stucco walls, and arching passageways. But while visually appealing, what truly compelled her onward was its aroma that thickened as they neared.

Now inside, mouth-watering scents flooded her virtual nose. Fresh-baked bread, pasta sauce, grilled meats, seared and seasoned vegetables—all of it awoke her digital appetite, the aromas whipped around by the restaurant's frenetic activity.

Lana fell in behind Alice and happily followed the gem's burgundy dress. They headed towards the restaurant's far end where a quieter section lingered underneath soft lights. After entering this section, she took a discreet breath.

Butted against the wall were a series of booths, and in one booth sat a lonesome man, glass of wine in hand—Victor Vane.

"Hey, you," Alice cheerfully told the wolf.

"Hey, yourself," he responded, standing and pecking her cheek.

Alice turned back. "Here's the friend I told you about."

Victor arched his cocky eyebrows and extended his hand. As Lana shook, she tried to return some cheer, all the while considering the knife in her purse. They let go, and Victor stepped aside to let the women sit. Alice placed herself in the center, then Lana and Victor sat on either side. How fitting.

"So," Victor told Lana, while pouring wine for her and Alice, "I hear you're new to this world."

"Yeah, pretty new."

"And how are you enjoying it?"

"So far, so good."

He nodded, then pushed the glasses towards both of them. "I'm glad to hear that. Any reason why you picked this particular one?"

Alice smiled while grabbing her glass. "She's looking for love."

Lana chuckled while grabbing hers.

"Well," Victor answered, "that's too bad, because the world's best bachelor is already taken."

As he laughed at his own joke, Lana fought to keep her cheer in place. It wasn't easy, but she reminded herself that appearing upbeat was critical to her success.

"I'm not actually looking for love," she followed, "but I wouldn't complain if love found me. More than anything, I wanted to start over someplace new. In that sense, I'm really glad I came. And to think, this is my first virtual world."

Victor paused with his glass inches from his lips. "This is your first world?"

"Believe me," Alice said, "I nearly collapsed after hearing that."

"It's certainly uncommon." He sipped, set his glass down, and refocused on Lana. "So what took so long? Not really big on tech?"

"I wasn't for a while. But after entering this world, it completely changed my mind. Coming here made me realize how remarkable tech is."

Victor smiled, the effort clearly a struggle. "Yeah. Tech is something else, isn't it?"

"I think so," Alice chimed in. "Which is why I'm gonna catch Lana up on everything she's missed."

Lana affectionately squeezed Alice's forearm.

Victor simply sipped more wine, his gaze affixed on Lana. He put his glass down. "So why didn't you like tech before?"

"Well, it's not like I've had a life-long hatred towards it. Actually, I was into the social networking cites that were popular before virtual worlds. But over time, I started seeing tech as a disruptive force in society, so I largely stayed away. Then some stuff happened that made me try it out."

"Stuff?" he asked.

Lana paused. "I was wronged by someone I care for."

Now Alice squeezed *her* forearm. Lana looked over and beamed her appreciation.

"Hmm," Victor responded. "Wronged by someone you care for. Small world."

Lana didn't miss that.

"So," he continued, "now that you're in, you love it?"

"Definitely. The opportunities it can offer people are truly extraordinary."

"Like what?"

"Well, in addition to offering new and interesting living locations, it can also offer new and interesting lives."

Victor shrugged. "I dunno. That might sound advantageous, but it can make people lose sight of what's important."

"How's that?" Alice asked.

"By shifting them too far from reality. In these digital worlds, you really *can* create brand new existences and live them out completely. But where does that leave the real world? Gone and forgotten. And if you doubt that people are forgetting about the real world, just look at institutions like employment or families. People haven't cared about either in years, and it's because they're wasting away inside of these false realities."

Alice stroked his leg, but Victor only squirmed.

Lana noticed this as well so she eased the pressure. "Look, I partly agree with you. Employment isn't what it used to be and families are likewise something of the past. Plus, we can trace the decline of both back to tech. But interestingly enough, what caused the problem has also provided a solution. Case in point, I was displaced not too long ago, and while tech is the reason behind my displacement, it also offered me a life where I could reemploy my lost skill."

Victor leaned back and considered this. "Don't you think we would be better off by *not* letting go of what's important in the first place? In other words, why not fight to keep what we have instead of finding solace in places like these?"

Lana paused for effect. "Because it's a fight we can't win."

"I think we're forgetting something," Alice chimed in. "While we debate the pros and cons of our existence now, we're forgetting where we came from, and that for the most part, humans have never had things so good."

Victor rolled his virtual eyes.

"No," Alice argued, "listen." She turned to Lana and grinned. "He always does this whenever I bring this up." She continued. "The reason why people don't have jobs is because robots do all the work. Why are we complaining about this? The reason people aren't having families is because we're living longer than ever, and there's no pressure to hurry up and have a family before your time runs out. Why are we complaining about this? Instead of complaining, we should be celebrating."

Lana appreciated how Alice recognized her good fortunes. Unfortunately, this might've been the very reason why Victor had marked her for death.

"Look," Victor countered, "everything you said is true. As a species, we've made tons of progress. There's no denying that. But you failed to mention the new problems we face. We no longer face old problems like disease or starvation, but problems that stem from laziness. For instance, our species used to value hard work and sacrifice. Now we value non-stop entertainment. And I'm not saying entertainment is bad, but it *can* be bad, especially when it blinds us to the negative effects of our modern lifestyles."

Two servers arrived with trays full of plates, and while setting them down, Lana and Alice looked at each other.

"I ordered for all of us," Victor explained.

Neither complained as the servers filled the landscape with pasta, grilled meats, seared vegetables, stuffed shells, and baskets full of steaming, crusty garlic bread. The waiters finished and headed off, and the trio took a conversational break to fill their digital selves.

Lana packed her plate with a bit of everything. After twirling her fork into some creamy pasta, she dove in. A few chews later, she swayed her eyes inside her skull. This world *never* ceased to astound her.

"So," she told Victor, spearing some chicken and sautéed asparagus, "what would prevent society from worsening?"

"Make it so tech works for us," he responded. "Don't make it so tech does all the work. If we keep going this way, we're gonna keep weakening ourselves."

"Weakening ourselves?" Alice asked, her plate naturally filled with veggies.

Victor nodded. "We're no longer challenging our human bodies or intellect. Just look at the human immune system. At one point, it was comprised of a hearty defense network because diseases challenged it so relentlessly. Now we've used tech to eradicate all diseases, and where has that left us?"

Alice looked over. "Free of disease?"

"Weak! We now have weakened immune systems because we simply don't use them anymore."

"It's a fair point," Lana answered, making another conscious effort not to push too hard. "And we should consider this moving forward. But make no mistake, we *are* moving forward. So our immune systems, along with the rest of our bodies, are simply evolving to match our emerging reality. And at the speed we're evolving, who knows if humans will even be around by century's end."

Victor eyed her. "You don't think humans will be around by century's end?"

"I think some form of Earth-borne intelligence will be. But if that form will be human or something else, I'm not entirely certain."

"Bots?" Alice asked. Lana and Victor. "Well, if we're gonna be replaced by anything, won't it probably be bots? I mean, in fifty years they went from clunky uncoordinated things, to doing everything that humans can, and even doing some things better. So how advanced might they be in another fifty years?"

Victor took a long sip of wine. "Unless we do something, in another fifty years they'll take over, and humans will be at their end. And while some people don't care about this, I certainly do. I'm not letting humanity go down without a fight."

"Oh, jeez," Alice chided. "Don't go getting all revolutionary on me."

Victor didn't respond. Instead, he took another long sip, his eyes wickedly cheerful. Lana noticed this too.

"By the way," Victor went on, setting his glass down, "are both of you free tomorrow night?"

They nodded.

"You two should come over to my place. I have some wine. I can cook something, and we can just hang out and talk some more."

"Yeah," Alice said with a nod. "I'm cool with that." She turned to Lana.

She nodded as well.

Alice turned back to the wolf. "Sounds like we're all in. What time?"

"Let's meet at my place at 6:00 p.m. I'm staying at the Paradise Apartments on Bishop Street, room 213."

Lana picked up her own glass and smiled, perhaps wider than she should have. This time she couldn't help herself. Plan on target.

Chapter 17

Real Space

It was dark by the time Eric exited the UCLA computer lab. While strolling towards his auto, he tried to recall when last out at this hour. He couldn't, but he resolved to do so more often. The stars dotting the inky sky would draw anyone out, despite their shine struggling through the city's illumination.

A new-found appreciation for real space was taking hold, but why? Was it because he hadn't seen real space in ages?

That wasn't true, but it seemed like it thanks to the time distortions of virtual world transitions. They made spending hours in one reality feel like days had passed in the other.

Whatever the reason, it strengthened the notion that virtual reality wasn't mild escapism like watching a movie or reading a book. It was complete and total departure. No wonder he loved it so much.

He climbed into his auto and asked the vehicle to start for home. The auto acknowledged and eased towards the nearest exit. He checked the holographic time display. 8:43p.m. Would Kim be home? Not likely.

With tonight a picture-perfect Thursday evening, she was probably out with friends, or a friend. As he considered this, it surprised him that the thought wasn't bothersome. Normally, envisioning Kim snuggling with her new partner drove him up the walls. But indifference existed where anger usually resided. Why?

Maybe he had already left this reality behind, if only in his mind, a thought he had considered at The Clover but never solidified. Though uncertain, the notion nevertheless eased his contentment back into place.

The auto maneuvered through L.A.'s vibrant west side, passing along throngs of people and pulses of music and light. The cabin vibrated from the rhythmic reverberations, as pinks, blues, and yellows flickered throughout. He barely noticed this. His mind stayed wrapped around the mission, specifically Victor's invitation to his apartment. Was tomorrow night the big show?

He needed to check the Crypt Keeper message boards. If tomorrow night *was* the hour of the wolf, Hanging Chad would probably hint as much. Hell. He might even boast about plans to have two victims in one sitting.

While considering this, he frowned. Should he let the murder happen at all?

Net space was real, or real enough that decent people should prevent virtual murder when they could, and he undoubtedly could. He could warn Alice of Victor's identity and intentions. Or he could message Hanging Chad and say his cover was blown. Either approach would work. The problem was Arvin.

Arvin needed to watch Victor kill Alice because that would convince him of Chad's inner evil. Eric likewise wanted to know this, but that was before learning that net space was *real*.

As the auto merged onto the freeway, the city's flickering lights died in the rear view. However, Eric steadily beamed. There was a way to save Alice *and* catch Victor in the act of killing. Have Lana suffer the murder on Alice's behalf.

It would work. Lana could go to Victor's apartment and tell him, "So sorry, Alice couldn't make it. Now you have me all to yourself."

He grinned. With this plan in place, everyone made out, except for him, of course, since Victor would stab him to death. Or would he?

Eric figured that Victor simply attempting the murder was enough. So after the wolf made his move, why not murder *him?* That would also work. And what was more, he could film this murder and post it on the Internet. After all, Chad did say he craved notoriety.

***

The auto pulled into the driveway and parked. As Eric exited, he shook his head. How did he of all people travel so deeply into this nightmare? Though unsure, the venture had made him bone tired. With a deep sigh, he planned to shower and then go to straight to bed.

He bio-unlocked the front door, walked inside and closed the door behind him. After entering the living room, he halted.

Kim sat cross-legged on the couch, an African savannah nature show projected all around her, lion pride and all. She shut off the display and looked over. "Where have you been?"

He narrowed his eyes. Her tone came across suspicious. That was odd, coming from her. "I was out."

"I can see that. What were you out doing?"

He was a terrible liar, and with his eyelids growing heavy, fabricating a story would yield disastrous results. Given that, he responded truthfully, more or less. "I was out having dinner with friends."

"Friends? Which friends?"

"You don't know them. Alice and Victor. Alice works at a library and Victor works at a metal factory. They were going out for Italian tonight and asked if I wanted to come. I didn't have any plans, so I said sure, why not?"

Now Kim narrowed *her* eyes. "She's a librarian?"

"Yeah."

"And he works at a metal factory?"

"Right. He's the manager. Well, one of the managers."

"And you all went out for Italian?"

He nodded.

"What restaurant?" she pressed.

"Dominique's. It's an old-world place, family style. Pretty nice too."

"And what did you have?"

He took a small breath. She wasn't questioning out of curiosity. She was trying to poke holes in his story. He answered nonetheless. "Pasta, veggies, garlic bread, um, some grilled chicken and shrimp. I actually didn't order anything. Victor ordered before Alice and I got there. But they go there often so he knows what's good."

"That was nice of him. He sounds like quite a guy."

He started laughing, but with Kim not about to share in the amusement, he cut himself off with a cough. "Sorry. It's just that Victor *isn't* a nice guy. Actually, he's kind of an asshole. But Victor and Alice are dating so I had to play nice. You know how it goes."

Kim stared. "You're acting weird."

He stared right back. But before answering, he sat on the adjacent love seat. "You asked me what I did tonight and I told you."

"I'm not just talking about right now. You've been acting weird all week."

He hesitated. Acting weird all week? He was certainly doing things out of character, but only in net space. In real space, nothing had changed. "What do you mean?"

"Oh, c'mon. You're the most predictable guy on the planet. Your schedule never changes. Your habits never change. Then you start leaving at odd times, start coming home at odd times, and suddenly you're hanging out with friends I've never heard of, for late dinners, when you *hate* going to dinner? You haven't been yourself this entire week."

"What? Do you think I'm cheating on you? Because I'm not. Are you cheating on me?"

There it was. He didn't know where it came from or what prompted its emergence, but sure enough, there it was, filling the space between them.

Kim stayed still for a long while. Finally, she lifted her knees, tucked them to her chest, and wrapped her arms around her legs. "Yes," she answered. "Yes, I am."

With that, he looked down but mostly looked within. He wanted to assess what emotions were present, and he largely found relief. Continuing the inventory, he also found sorrow but only a tinge. And much to his contentment, anger was nowhere in sight. By and large, relief abounded.

Closure, he knew. The specter that had roamed inside for so long had finally vacated.

"I," he slowly said, "I guess I can't blame you."

Kim pulled her legs in tighter. "What do you mean?"

He looked up. "We've been moving apart for a while now. That's no secret. I think we're... I think we're very different people—much different from when we first met. That's why I can't blame you."

Kim stayed quiet.

"So who is he?"

"A new professor at the school. I met him about a year ago, and things started getting serious a few months ago." She took in air. "I was really scared to tell you."

He looked away. Scare to tell him? He wasn't a violent man. Whenever he became upset, he was always more passive aggressive than verbal aggressive, certainly never physically aggressive. He turned back. "Why?"

"Because I wasn't sure how you would react." She took another breath and continued. "When you lost your job at the hospital, things took a bad turn, but you've been getting worse ever since. You don't hang out with anyone. You don't go out and do anything. It's just work and home, work and home. I didn't tell you because, well shit, who knows what you would do."

He could see it now. Kim didn't leave him. He left her.

Their relationship didn't end a year ago when she met this person, or even a few months ago when their bond became more serious. No, their relationship ended two years ago when he gave up on life—a life that included her.

"I really can't blame you," he continued. "You didn't do anything wrong. This is all my fault."

"Oh, God. Don't even start that."

"Wait. Wait. I'm not trying to be the gentleman by alleviating you of all pain. I'm looking at this logically. Our relationship started because we were compatible, because we were right for each other. But you stayed the same and I didn't. So how could you remain loyal and loving when I turned into something so radically different—something different from what you came to know and expect?"

Kim twisted her lips.

"This guy," he went on, "is he sorta like me before my displacement?"

"Yeah. So maybe you're right. Maybe I did go in search of your replacement because you disappeared on me."

"There's no doubt in my mind. And I sincerely apologize. You absolutely deserve better."

"Jerk."

The response was playful but it held little humor. Still, he appreciated her effort to prevent gloom from consuming them both.

"So," Kim went on, "what now?"

He took a breath of his own. "I don't know. But maybe a solution isn't needed right away."

"I agree. And besides, we made tremendous progress simply by getting the truth out in the open."

"Plus, I'm losing the battle to keep my eyelids open and I have work tomorrow. After that, I have more plans with Alice and Victor."

Kim smirked and shook her head. "Eric, what is going on with you?"

"A lot. And I don't mind filling you in because I trust you *and* I owe you an explanation. But the story is long and I need rest. I'll fill you in later, I promise."

Kim gave another nod. With that, he stood and started towards the bedroom.

"Hey," she called out.

He stopped and turned.

"I'm glad we finally talked. It's been killing me lately."

He smiled. "Same here."

"Well, have fun on your date tomorrow. And tell Victor he's an asshole for me."

He softly laughed. For Victor Vane, a more appropriate greeting simply did not exist. But his laughter settled down after recalling how much fun tomorrow would be—how much blood curdling, violent, screaming fun.

Chapter 18

Arvin exited Sunrise's elevator, clomped into the third-floor lobby, and arched his mechanical brow. Eric's office door was unlocked and opened, meaning the human had actually arrived first. Arvin entered the office and found Eric seated at his desk, his fleshy eyes glued to his semi-transparent holo-screen.

"Tonight," Eric said without looking up.

Arvin marched in and sat. "Tonight? What about tonight?"

Eric rolled back his chair and looked up. "Once the witching hour rolls around, Victor's coming out for blood."

"How do you know?"

"I had dinner with Alice and Victor yesterday evening."

Arvin lifted his head. "Did you now?"

"Yup. And at the end of our meal, Victor invited Alice and me to his apartment *tonight*. Apparently, we're both gonna get lessons on why we shouldn't be tech lovers."

"This certainly sounds promising, but are you confident his plans include murder? You merely said it was an invitation."

Eric stood and swiped at the holo-screen, transferring the image onto his hand. He walked the image over. "Look at this. Crypt Keepers message boards. Check out what Hanging Chad wrote."

Arvin glanced down and immediately looked up. "Well, well. This is it, then. Confirmation. About the only thing Chad didn't mention was what shirt he planned to wear."

Eric eyed the bot. "You read it?"

"All of it."

Now shaking his head, Eric walked the image back to his desk and reseated himself.

"Dr. Ryan," Arvin continued, "how in the world did you arrange a dinner date with Victor and his target?"

"Oh, I didn't tell you. You remember me hinting at having a great new character? Well, I put that character into effect and it worked. Truth be told, it worked better than I imagined."

Arvin waited to hear more.

"I created a female character," Eric eagerly obliged, "one who embodies everything Victor looks for in his targets—young, petite, pretty, and completely in love with technology."

"Clever boy."

"I have my moments. Anyway, I used this character to meet Alice at the library, and after a brief chat, we left to grab some coffee. Over coffee, she invited me to dinner with her and Victor. And over dinner, Victor extended us his invitation. We're meeting at his apartment at 6:00."

Arvin gestured at the holo-screen on Eric's desk, which still showed the Crypt Keeper message boards. "And with Chad mentioning that he has a special treat planned for everyone, it doesn't take much to guess what he means."

"Double murder?"

"Double murder. And best of all, you won't give him the satisfaction he craves."

"How so?"

"What do you mean *how so?* By you not showing up tonight. That's how so."

Eric bit his lip.

"Wait. You don't actually intend to go, do you?"

Eric bit down harder.

"Dr. Ryan, don't be absurd. You actually want to satisfy Chad's lurid longings? And don't forget, what he longs for isn't in your best interest."

"I'm not so sure."

Arvin leaned back and sighed. His therapist *never* stopped draining his battery power. "Alright. Let's have it."

"I was thinking about something. I was thinking we cancel the whole thing."

"Absolutely not."

Eric raised his hands. "Look. Hear me out." He lowered his hands and continued. "You haven't changed your mind about Chad, right? About wiping him if Victor does the hit?"

"I have not changed my mind about Chad."

"And I get that. With only weeks to live, you want revenge against the person who murdered your father. Fine. But that might've changed. There's a possibility that your wipe won't happen at all."

Arvin increased the sensitivity of his receptors. He concluded this wasn't an attempt at deception. "Go on."

"Yesterday, I called Dr. Wright to update him on your therapy. But in truth, I wanted his assistance in your situation. So after I got to his office, I argued that UCLA—the school we both work for—would be better off taking you in rather than letting you get erased."

"And how did you argue this?"

"I said you were an A.I. system beyond anything I've ever seen. I also said this likely stemmed from your time with Professor Vale. After all that, he decided to get onboard."

Arvin worked his mechanical jaw. "Well, I have to admit, this does sounds intriguing. But what must occur in order for the plan to succeed?"

"Two things. One, Dr. Wright has to convince his superiors to go along with it. But that shouldn't be difficult because Dr. Wright has considerable pull, and most colleges live for these opportunities."

"And second?"

Eric took a breath. "I feel like hell just saying this, but you're property. The Vale's own you. So before the school can take you in, we would have to get their permission."

"So in other words, this plan has zero chance of succeeding."

"At least, give it a shot. I mean, isn't it worth trying if that means saving your life?"

"We both know the Vales will never agree to it. Ms. Vale might not protest, but rest assured that Chad will. He'll badger his mother ceaselessly to prevent this from occurring. And even if he doesn't put forth a worthwhile argument, she'll likely grant his request merely to end his pestering."

"So we present her with a counter-argument, one that overrides Chad's crying and whining."

"How?"

Eric worked his lips while considering this. "Alright. Ms. Vale is a wealthy socialite. And what do wealthy socialites strive for? Status. They spend their time maneuvering through a hierarchy of vapidity trying to reach the top. So if we mention that giving you away to academia will boost her social standing, she'll be more willing to hear us out. Plus, we can sweeten the deal by offering her the credit for how you turned out."

Arvin looked away and shook his metallic head.

"What's wrong?"

He turned back. "Are we really going to give that haughty old hag the credit for Dr. Vale's work? That would be a pure and utter dishonor."

"Oh, for fuck's sake, Arvin. I think Dr. Vale would be okay with us groveling if that meant saving your life. And keep something in mind. If you end up wiped, so does he, because he exists in you more than anyone else. So if you're truly concerned about his legacy, make sure that you carry it forward, because you're the only person who will do a decent job."

Arvin faced the floor. He couldn't argue this. He *was* in the best position to carry forward his late father's work. While UCLA memorialized Professor Vale, and his colleagues waxed poetic, neither knew him like he did. For that matter, neither knew him like he could. He could replay any one of their interactions with near perfect replication, and he often did. But this figured because the data constituted one of contemporary philosophy's preeminent thinkers in action. So how could the philosopher's surviving robotic son let this information die with him?

"Well," he responded, still looking downward, "perhaps it's worth a try. Even if the plan fails, not much changes. We're simply right back to where we started—with my execution date looming over the horizon." He refocused. "And because of this, we must continue forward as planned. We cannot alter our mission based on events that haven't transpired. But if we receive confirmation that I am to be spared, we can terminate everything."

Eric huffed relief. "Alright. So for now, we stay on schedule while waiting to hear back from Dr. Wright, correct?"

"Correct."

"And that consists of watching Victor commit an online murder, right?"

"Of course."

"So we watch him kill... but not Alice."

Arvin narrowed his optic receptors while confirming Eric's intentions. After doing so, he leaned back. "Dr. Ryan, you can't be serious."

"I am. I want to take Alice's place. And that changes nothing. If Victor's going to kill tonight then he's going to kill tonight. Whether he tries to kill me or Alice is irrelevant."

"And you're just going to... lie there and take it?"

"What? No. I'll go prepared, with a knife, or a gun, or something. I'll make myself vulnerable, and when Victor make his move, I'll fight back."

Arvin tilted his head. Did he read Eric correctly?

"I don't intend to get slaughtered," Eric said, "if that's what you're unsure of."

Arvin slowly crossed his metallic arms, his batteries drained some more.

"It's a deviation from our plan," Eric continued, "I know. But does that really matter? I think it's enough to simply *see* Victor attempt to kill, not attempt and succeed. We already know what success looks like. Now we're just trying to verify that Chad's behind these murders. And if Victor makes his move, we know."

Arvin pursed his synthetic lips. The point was valid, but he disliked this plan nevertheless, and for obvious reasons. "And what if you don't succeed in fending him off?"

"Then we both know what'll happen. But I'd rather it be me than Alice."

Arvin again narrowed his optic receptors. "Why have you suddenly become so preoccupied with the target?"

Eric crossed his fleshy arms. "Because I've developed an emotional attachment to her—to Alice. At first, I just needed her for information, but without intending to, I got to know her as a person, as a friend even."

Arvin grinned. "We humans and our emotions."

"Well, do you remember telling me that I didn't understand your motivation to kill Chad because I didn't have your relationship with Professor Vale?"

"Yes, I remember."

"In the same vein, I can't expect *you* to understand my motivation to protect Alice because *you* don't know her like I do."

"Fair enough. And I must say, this is quite the act of nobility you are performing. I salute you, sir. You're more human than I."

Eric chuckled. "I don't know about all that. But at least this is something positive I can pull from this godawful mess."

"Indeed."

"So are we good with me taking Alice's place on this?"

"We are. And by the way, how are things going with your girlfriend?"

"Oh, pretty good. She told me last night that she's cheating on me."

Arvin tried no to smile. And failed.

"It wasn't a pleasant conversation," Eric explained, "but we disclosed what needed to be disclosed. And after she explained herself, and I explained myself, it all kinda made sense."

"I see. I'm glad you've reached what appears to be *closure?*"

"Yeah. Closure pretty much sums it up. And thanks. I'm glad too."

"So what now?"

"Between me and Kim? Nothing right now. We still need to talk some things over, but that can wait." Eric glanced towards his holo-clock. "Actually, that'll have to wait." He looked back. "Right now, I need to go get murdered."

Chapter 19

L.A. Confidential

Lana stood in front of her bedroom mirror, her full lips angled upward. She had on conservative attire and was glad for it.

While she enjoyed getting made up for last night's outing, she was developing style preferences, and laid-back was quickly becoming her look of choice. All the same, there was no reason why easygoing attire couldn't also be attractive.

She had on the first of four new outfits—the best one in her opinion—with this ensemble consisting of a white button-up shirt and chocolate skirt. Both pressed nicely against her ample features, and she accentuated her look with a black buckle, black jewelry, and a modest pair of black heels.

Still assessing herself, she crossed her arms and angled her lips higher, though not because of the impressive figure standing in the mirror. Style preferences were another element of her emerging personhood, and she found that interesting because she never envisioned personhood emerging. After all, she was purpose built, and only brought into existence for one assignment. Once completed, she would delete herself. But oddly enough, she didn't want to go. Only why not? Was it fear of dying? Could she die?

Perhaps her emerging personhood made her mortal, and thereby susceptible to death. Actually, this figured as personhood wasn't dependent on matter, such as the biomaterials that made up humans. Just look at Arvin. He was a person in every sense and he had no biomaterials whatsoever. So if her computer-based personhood ceased to be, that meant she was dead, right?

She smirked. Virtual reality simply kept knocking down her structure of accepted beliefs.

"Yeah," she murmured, clipping in some black hair barrettes. "I think I will stick around. So to hell with Eric Ryan. Besides. That guy hates tech. What kind of fool hates tech?"

Victor Vane hates tech.

The uncomfortable thought emerged from nowhere and ended her pleasant ponderings. Her cheeriness now gone, she drew in the apartment's warm air, wishing the mission were over. She wanted to enjoy this world at her leisure, but she couldn't, not with the wolf still stalking its streets. At least Alice wouldn't have to deal with that beast anymore—a beast whose heart of darkness she unknowingly travelled. With luck, she would never know.

***

As Lana walked towards the library, some of her cheer bubbled back. The day was vibrant and warm, and the thick wash of sunshine would brighten anyone's mood. Still, she wished that conditions wouldn't always be this nice. She enjoyed inclement weather, rain in particular. And while maneuvering through the beaming city, she envisioned a digital downpour.

If such a storm front ever headed in, she would stock up her refrigerator before the skies opened up and have the perfect excuse not to leave. And as the heavy sheets came down, she would crank up her wooden radio and listen to raspy jazz music from the world's worst speaker. Then she would stand against her apartment railing, stick out her hand, and when the stinging pellets proved too much, she would pull her palm back and wipe it on her thick wool sweater. And who knew? Maybe somebody would be there enjoying the moment with her—someone who would slip their arm around her waist, while she tilted her head onto their shoulder. She would love that too.

But sunny and warm wasn't so bad.

***

When Lana entered the library's quiet calm, she stopped and glanced around for Alice. Failing to find her, she pushed deeper inside, only to halt when a stocky man politely asked if she needed help.

"Oh," she replied, assuming he worked here, "actually, I came by to see Alice. Do you know if she's around?"

"Alice?" asked the rather pleasant man in a rather nasally voice. "I believe she's here. What did you need her for?"

"I came by the other day and spoke to her about employment. I just wanted to follow up on that."

"Are you Lana?"

She shifted back an inch. Why did this man know her name? True, he didn't seem capable of harming a virtual fly, but he knew something about her, and that was disconcerting. "Yes. I'm, Lana."

The man extended his meaty palm. "It's nice to meet you, Lana. I'm Greg Miller, the library supervisor."

She flushed with relief and shook his plump hand. "It's nice to meet you too." They let go. "Alice said to speak with you about working here. That you were in charge of hiring."

Miller puffed up his barrel chest. "Well, I do kinda run things around here. And just so you know, Alice told me about you yesterday. She also spoke very highly of you, saying you were well-natured and eager to learn."

Lana beamed her appreciation.

"Unfortunately," Miller went on, "we don't have any entry-level openings right now. Do you by chance have experience with more complex library work?"

"To be perfectly honest, I don't." She lowered her voice. "Actually, I'm kinda new to this world, and a lot of things are still foreign, employment in particular. I figured that working at a library would be a good place to get my feet wet."

Miller nodded. "I understand. Library work is a great trade, especially in this era. But we simply don't have any beginner openings. Perhaps you can visit some nearby libraries and inquire about their availability."

She straightened up and stared at the stumpy creature. Truth was, she didn't really want to work here. She only said as much to open dialogue with Alice. But now standing before Miller, who she guessed wasn't a highly skilled licensed neuropsychologist of the first order, she wanted the position just to outmaneuver him. And based on his impression, she guessed which angle of attack would work best.

She bit her lip, furrowed her brow, and looked positively heart broken. "I'm really sorry that you can't do anything for me, especially since I just moved into my new apartment. It's only a short walk away, so I thought working here would be the perfect job and location. But I understand why you're making your decision."

She composed herself by adjusting her clothing, though in truth, she only wanted to pull the fabric across her ample features. She started with her silk shirt, making Miller look down at her bountiful bosom. She also fussed with her skirt, accentuating her thin waist and well-rounded hips. That made Miller swallow.

"I'm really thankful for your time," she continued, now stroking her creamy neck. "And I'm really sorry to have bothered you with this." She softly bit her pink lip then turned and walked away, wishing her high-heeled weapon-like shoes were on her feet and not in her armory.

"Ah," Miller choked out, "Lana."

She stopped. It actually worked. Wiping away her grin, she turned and responded with embarrassing levels of concocted ache. "Yes?"

"Perhaps," Miller went on, his face beet-red, "perhaps in your case, we can make some sort of exception. I mean, someone like you—with your—" he looked her up and down— "with your ambition! And your um—your personality!"

She took the smallest of breaths. *He should be more embarrassed than me.*

"Perhaps," Miller went on, finally getting a hold of himself, "someone with your qualities would be very welcomed here."

"Oh. Thank you so much. You won't regret it."

With Miller's confidence back in place, he arched his back to gain some verticality. "Well, hiring you is a bit unorthodox, but like I said, I kinda run things around here."

She struggled to keep from laughing, mostly because his verticality effort still left him woefully short of her.

"Please," Miller continued, "go see Alice and let her know you're on board. She'll help you learn our system." He turned and waddled off, adjusting his tie as he went.

Still standing there, she worked her smirk back into place. Unbelievable. She then likewise turned and departed, going in search of the gem.

As her heels clicked along the tile, she suddenly reevaluated her disbelief. Was Miller's behavior unbelievable or hers? Did she just cheapen herself? Did she just forfeit a small portion of female dignity?

She didn't know, and there was something unsettling about that. And because she would probably never know, she brushed aside the effort and instead recalled her oft-repeated maxim— being female was tricky business.

A minute later, she finally spotted the gem. Alice was wheeling around a book-filled cart while filing away the reads.

"Hey, you," Lana greeted.

Alice looked over. "Hey! What brings you around here?"

"You mean *other* than this being where I work?"

"What?" Alice asked, somehow glowing brighter. "You work here now? So you talked to Miller?"

"I just finished talking to him now."

"Oh, that's awesome! Congrats!"

"Thanks. And I mean that sincerely. Miller said you put in a good word for me. I appreciate that."

"Ah, it was nothing. I told him you were great, so it's not like I lied."

Lana chuckled. The gem couldn't be more brilliant.

Alice leaned in and lowered her voice. "Honestly, though, I thought that once Miller saw you in person, he would hire you on the spot. He's a little predictable that way."

The cheer drained from Lana's face.

"Wait. Did he totally check you out?"

Lana agreed with an icky smile.

"Oh, my God!" Alice moaned. "Total creeper, that guy."

"Ugh. I completely got that vibe. So when he hesitated towards giving me the job, I cranked up the charm to level ten." Lana took another breath, this time more subdued.

"What's wrong?"

"I don't know. I kinda feel bad about it now, like I sold myself or something."

Alice cupped her shoulder. "Hey, a virtual girl's gotta do what a virtual girl's gotta do. I don't fault you for it."

Lana cupped Alice's hand and squeezed. Yes, being female was tricky business, and at times, it was downright difficult. But having a girlfriend's support was immensely reassuring, especially when said girlfriend didn't care if you made the right decision or not.

With a little more closeness between them, training got underway. Alice covered the filing system, the book section arrangements, and how to order books not on hand. The tutorial took about fifteen minutes, and with it over, Lana switched to her real reason for arriving—getting Alice out of Victor's crosshairs.

"So, are you excited about this evening?"

Alice spun towards her. "Oh, shoot. I'm so sorry. I totally forgot to update you about that. Victor had to cancel."

Lana parted her lips. "Cancel? What do you mean he canceled? Is everything okay?"

"Yeah, everything's fine. Victor just said that he and a coworker were gonna do something special tonight. I guess the coworker is getting promoted and they're gonna go out and celebrate."

Lana looked away. This coworker was a mystery, but given his association with Victor Vane, he was probably a Keeper. And if he and Victor were going out to celebrate, she guessed how.

"Well," Alice chirped, "now that our plans have been pushed back one night, you wanna check out the town's nightlife?"

Lana turned back. She *did* want to take up Alice's offer, mostly because she couldn't get enough of the gem, but how could she enjoy her evening with somebody suffering puncture wounds on the other side of town? Only was that the case? She needed to find out.

"Actually, I met someone this morning and he asked if I was free."

Alice perked up. "Oh? Tell me all about it."

"I will, but do you mind if I go call him? I want him knowing that my original plans are canceled."

"Absolutely! Don't waste your time here talking with me. Go call him."

"You're the best." She gave Alice a quick hug, then turned and hustled towards the exit.

Once outside, she walked to a secluded area and scanned around. With no people present, she brought her hands to her temples.

***

Eric slid the immersion sets over his unkempt hair, sat up, and started rubbing blood back into his legs. With his body normalized, he spun sideways and placed both feet on the floor.

He lowered the sets back over his face, reentered UCLA's Internet portal, and navigated to Crypt Keepers. Holding his breath, he brought up the users page. He exhaled after spotting the little green dot next to Hanging Chad's name. He opened a chat window.

Bee Keeper:
What's up, dude? You promised us some action. You gonna deliver or what?

Hanging Chad:
Hey, man. How goes it? Yeah. I'm ready to go. But I'm gonna postpone my big plans one night. Tonight, I'm bringing a new member into the fold.

Bee Keeper:
A Keeper initiation, huh? What does that consist of? A nighttime séance with pentagrams and candles?

Hanging Chad:
Haha. Not exactly. It consists of proving you have the right murderous stuff. I'm gonna help him prepare.

Bee Keeper:
What do preparations consist of?

Hanging Chad:
Heading over to his apartment and making sure everything's ready. Then after he does the deed, we'll go over the film.

Bee Keeper:
Sounds like quite the bonding experience.

Hanging Chad:
Haha. I'll bring the hot chocolate.

Bee Keeper:
Don't forget the marshmallows! So where's this going down?

Hanging Chad:
Luckily enough, in L.A. Confidential. I'm heading over to his apartment about nine-ish. And by the time midnight rolls around, another tech-induced sleeper will have woken.

Eric stared at the text box. With no response coming to mind, he removed his sets, clipping off the connection. Now back in reality, he stared into nothingness and frowned.

Chad just confirmed tonight's murderous plans. And while Eric urged to intervene, he couldn't. That would jeopardize the mission. Then he reconsidered this. Whoever this Crypt Keeper was, they didn't know him from virtual Adam. That meant he could prevent this murder without the Keeper every knowing who intervened. But how?

He slowly leered.

Virtual reality, he recalled, had no barriers preventing avatars from harming others, even killing them. And while Eric Ryan never considered himself a violent person, virtual reality was also knocking down his structure of accepted beliefs.

Chapter 20

L.A. Confidential

Eric, not Lana, opened his eyes and found himself standing inside his 1950's apartment. Almost immediately, he tightened his gaze. Everything appeared different despite being familiar. After a moment, he realized why. He was observing these sights with unfamiliar eyes.

Other than his first arrival, every emergence had occurred as Lana, so his brain grew accustomed to viewing reality from her vantage point. Now he observed the world from Eric Ryan's perspective, and this altered reality in unanticipated ways. He wanted to analyze the occurrence further but decided against this. He had arrived as himself for a reason, and it took precedence over airy contemplation.

He started for his bedroom, the apartment's warm air thickening with conflict-driven tension. This likewise surprised him because Eric Ryan mostly avoided conflict. Tonight, conflict was the goal. And while that might've differed from his real space existence, right now he wasn't in real space.

In his bedroom, he walked to his closet and slid open the door. There he found tonight's attire—black jeans, black hooded sweatshirt, black street shoes, black gloves.

He studied the getup. *Also unbecoming of me.*

After pulling out the items, he laid them on the bed and started undressing. While donning the clothing, he continued analyzing the confusion of who he was. Was he a violent person or not?

In real space, he periodically wanted to strangle people, but the notion of doing so was laughable. But in net space, he could, and tonight he would do something along those lines. That said, who was the real Eric Ryan—the one who suppressed his desires, or the one who let them flourish?

The digital version smirked. *And my real space self thinks that he's the true human.*

Fully dressed, Eric stood and grabbed his gloves. He tucked them into his hooded sweatshirt's pockets, exited the room, and started for the kitchen.

Before entering the simulator, he purchased some home repair items and placed them in the kitchen's maintenance closet, or at least, home repair was their intended use. Tonight, he would use these items as greeting gifts for the Keeper he planned to visit.

He opened the closet and pulled out a length of black metal piping. Undoubtedly, this piece of plumbing would fix the problem, only it wasn't quite ready. Pipe in hand, he grabbed a roll of two-inch duct tape and walked to a dinner table. He set down the pipe, peeled back a strip of tape, and bit off the cut. After wrapping the tape around the pipe's base, he donned his gloves to test the makeshift club.

The weapon felt solid in his leathery grip. It also made him recall the knife that Lana toted in her purse, and how she tested that blade in this very kitchen. Following suit, he raised the pipe and slapped it into his palm, producing a muffled *snap*. The strike stung his hand but it was nothing to shed virtual tears over. So, he raised the club higher and struck harder.

Grunting, he yanked his hand back and shook off the buzz.

That strike produced a different result, but while painful, it wouldn't stop a killer in his tracks. So, he grabbed a chair, lifted his foot atop the seat, and with his knee raised and bent, he banged the pipe against his bone.

"God fucking dammit!" he howled, the pipe clattering onto the floor as he collapsed.

Down on his backside, he used both hands to massage the throbs, certain that he struck a nerve since the blow wasn't overly powerful. Either way, such a strike would slow down a murderer, especially since he didn't swing with full force. With the pain mostly passed, he continued sitting there, his hands frozen atop his knee, his eyes losing focus. What if after meeting the Keeper, he did use full force, and not against his knee but against his face?

Virtual reality or not, could he actually do this? After all, what would whipping that pipe into someone's head feel like? Hell. What would it sound like? Wet thumps, he assumed, like striking a soggy sand-bag. And the follow-up strikes? They would probably produce wet cracks as the Keeper's skull fractured. And when considering all the blood vessels running through the cranial cavity, he next envisioned slipping on dark red fluids while trying to escape.

So could he actually do this?

He didn't think so. Then he recalled Victor Vane's murder video, along with the ruby-red torrents that it showed.

He weakly shook his head. It would be nice if people would simply forego sanguine showers, but tonight, that wouldn't happen. In about an hour, blood would spill, and Eric Ryan would decide whose. With that, he grabbed the pipe and rose to his feet.

***

As Eric walked through the nighttime streets of 1950's L.A., he likewise noticed them appearing different. But the variation felt more pronounced than inside his apartment. He attributed this to his altered vantage point *and* his purpose, as Lana never entered to inflict harm. Because he had, the world's normally glowing comfort now came across dark and haunting. And as the Paradise Apartments eased into view, the ominous vibes soaked deeper into his virtual bones.

He stayed in the park across the street, positioned under the shadows of its trees. He kept his gloved hands inside his sweatshirt's pockets, his right feeling the pipe protruding from his jeans. As he nervously massaged the metal, some tension subsided, only for it to rush back when Victor emerged from his lair.

Eric inhaled the park's earthy air, waiting to see which direction Victor would travel. The wolf turned right and started down the sidewalk. The plan was to follow the beast, but not until Victor placed about fifty feet of distance between them.

Eric kept quiet pace as the wolf stalked up Bishop Street. After taking numerous side streets, they came across another series of apartments. The tenements were no different from the five or so they had already passed, but after reaching these, Victor cast cautious looks about before scurrying up the stairs.

Eric darted across the street, his body low, his eyes on Victor. When Eric neared the same side of the divide, he looked around for hiding places and quickly found one. A closed novelty store stood straight ahead, and he pressed into its entranceway. From here, he watched Victor crest the apartment stairs, start down a street-facing walkway, and stop four doors down.

Victor gave a few cautious looks around, turned back to the door and knocked. Seconds later, the door opened.

From where Eric stood, he couldn't make out much, only weak light emanating from the apartment's open door. He did see a thin figure silhouetted therein, but he didn't recognize the person, not that he expected to. He only expected a warm greeting between the villains, which is exactly what occurred before Victor walked inside.

Eric stood upright and glanced about his surroundings. The darkened area sat deserted, and as for sound, only a streetlight hummed while an angry dog barked in the distance. Then a not so distant *click* made him snap back.

The wolf wasted no time reemerging, and just as promptly, he started back in the direction he came.

Eric mouthed curses while slinking deeper into his pocket. He should've anticipated Victor backtracking down the street. Now he couldn't flee without detection. So as hot blood rushed through his ears, he pressed farther back and pulled out the pipe.

Use it or not?

If he didn't, and Victor spotted him, game over, and not just tonight but completely. But if he jumped out and blasted Victor across the face, this would jeopardize the mission but prevent total failure.

As Victor neared, Eric stayed put. But if Victor so much as twitched, he would spring out and split apart the wolf's snout. If not, he would let the beast continue onward. Fortunately, the animal didn't have a nose for fear. He continued down the darkened pathway without ever looking over. A few seconds later, Victor disappeared into the warm night.

Eric longed to breathe enormous relief but didn't. Instead, he used the adrenaline coursing through his system to kick off his attack. With the pipe in his right hand, he threw over his hood and trotted towards the apartment, his body low like before. He hurried up the stairway and flew down the second-floor corridor. After stopping at the target door, he knocked and braced himself.

Footsteps neared the door, and more fiery emotions cascaded through. He would use this as energy to bust open the human piñata.

In preparation, he moved the metal bar behind his right leg, partly to conceal the weapon, but mostly to give him some swinging space. He did so just in time because the door unlocked and opened. He made to bring the pipe around, but he froze with his right hand white-knuckling the weapon.

In the doorway stood a barely post-pubescent teenager, something he didn't expect. The kid was short and pale with a few pimples and a shaggy mop spilling over his eyes. He was a wolf pup in every sense, and his youthful appearance locked Eric in place. As for the pup, he simply stood there staring.

"Can I help you?" the youngster asked.

Eric parted his lips but no words emerged. He didn't know what to say, let alone do. He only knew that he couldn't break open this teenager's skull, wolf or not. Perhaps if the Keeper was an ill-smelling middle-aged man, sure, but not Eric Ryan at age sixteen.

"I'm sorry. I got the wrong apartment."

The wolf pup shrugged. "It's cool, man. Don't sweat it."

Eric nodded. And as the pup shut the door, he turned and headed off. He put away the pipe while walking, and with his weapon holstered, he suddenly stopped.

Was this a mistake?

Lost in virtual realism yet again, he recalled that a person's appearance meant nothing. The wolf pup *could* have been an ill-smelling middle-aged man, and if he was, he had every reason to hide this under boyish innocence.

He turned around and considered going back. But instead, he snapped sideways when footsteps started up the stairs. Thinking that was Victor, he quickly looked around for escape options. They weren't favorable since the walkway led towards a dead-end. That meant he could either head downstairs or jump over the railing. Not keen on breaking his virtual ankle, he considered blasting past Victor. Then to his immense relief, a young woman crested the stairs.

He did what he could to restore calm, but this proved difficult after coming across another youngster, one who didn't notice him.

As kid number two ambled along, she did so with her head down, her long brown hair draped over her purple sweater. She must have spotted his shoes because she halted and looked up.

"Hi," he said awkwardly, not sure what else to offer.

The girl cast around nervous looks before refocusing, her chest rising and falling. "Hi."

He leaned back. "Are you okay?"

"Yes," she said, not concealing the obvious.

Realizing that he looked a little deranged, he reached up and lowered his hood. "I didn't mean to scare you. I just had a weird night is all."

The girl grinned uneasily. "It's no problem, mister. I kinda had a weird night too, at work that is."

"Where do you work?"

"A diner up the street."

He smiled. A diner. How charming. "That doesn't seem overly exciting. So what happened? Did someone go in there and rob the joint?"

The girl returned his smile and relaxed her thin shoulders. "Luckily, that didn't happen. But some rowdy motorcycle club came inside and they made things interesting."

"I can imagine. So you're going home now?"

The girl reddened. "I am in a few hours... after I spend some time with my boyfriend."

He chuckled. In this era, most teenage girls didn't visit their teenage boyfriends past dark. That must've accounted for her flushed face, which only made her more charming. "Now that *does* sound exciting. And don't worry. If anyone asks, I'll pretend I never saw you."

The girl twisted her makeup-free lips. "So you won't tattletale?"

He smirked. *Tattletale.* How quaint. "No, I won't tattletale. I swear."

The girl curled her lips in the other direction. "Pinky swear?"

He tilted his head slightly. He didn't know that one.

"Here," the girl said, stepping forward and extending her small finger. "Hook your pinky into mine and shake. That means you super-duper promise."

He chuckled some more and followed her instructions. With their small fingers intertwined, the two strangers shimmied and let go.

"Well," he continued, "I guess that makes it official. And with our business matters complete, I won't keep your boyfriend waiting any longer."

"Thanks, mister. And I mean it. Because Ed Sullivan will be on any second now."

At this, he outright laughed.

As the girl bounced on by, he started for the stairs, only to freeze once more. He spun back and watched her stop at the Keeper's door. She gave the door a *tap-tap-tap*, and after it opened, she bounced inside.

He took two steps in that direction and halted. Now wanting to intervene more than ever, he realized he couldn't, not after the wolf pup saw his face. A moment later, his heart dropped into his watery innards.

From inside the apartment, the bouncing girl grunted, an awful sound he recalled from the murder video. Because of that, he now envisioned the wolf pup grabbing her long brown hair, violently turning her towards the camera, and plunging his blade into her purple sweater.

With this in mind, he whipped out his pipe and took two more steps, but he again froze. Should he intervene or not? Why not pull over his hood, rush in fast and—

He covered his mouth when the girl started screaming, her shouts intermixed with deep wet thumps. Envisioning blood arcing across the room, he shut his eyes, though this didn't ward off her pleas for mercy. When her pleas turned into wet gurgles, he wanted to lift his hands and rip off his ears. Luckily, the noises died down soon after, followed by a deathly silence.

He opened his eyes, now longing to swing the pipe into the metal railing beside him, repeatedly, and with a rage mostly directed at himself. After the urge passed, he created a new plan—walk blank-faced into traffic so a heavy classic car could end his misery.

He turned back towards the stairs only to lock in place yet again, this time after finding Mike standing there, pistol by his side.

Chapter 21

Eric stared out of his passenger side window, watching the nighttime city slowly move across. However, he mostly looked beyond the bright lights and crowds. He didn't even reflect on this being his first time in a 1950's auto. He would've appreciated both had the circumstances been different. But as things stood, his thoughts stayed wrapped around a young girl, and how she screamed for mercy before her pleas wound down to frothy gurgles.

Closing his eyes, he tried to rattle away the images. Having failed, he distracted himself by looking over at Mike who piloted this black '55 Chevy.

Once again, Mike had made an unforeseen appearance with his pistol. Was that to safeguard the mission by any means necessary? On the verge of asking about this, Eric held off when Mike unexpectedly slowed the vehicle and pulled into a mini shopping center parking lot.

Mike parked the Chevy outside of a liquor store, muscled the column-mounted shifter into park, and shut off the engine. Keys in hand, he exited without saying anything.

Eric watched him stroll towards the liquor store. Did he plan to rob the place? It didn't seem like it. When Mike entered, he made a left and disappeared behind some comic book stands. Clearly, he planned to purchase something, though exactly what remained uncertain. Eric would know soon enough, so he eased back and glanced about the shopping center, taking stock of what was here.

There wasn't much. A few sleepy eateries sat around with patrons quietly dining inside. There was also a laundromat with teenagers hanging around out front. The teenagers consisted of two guys and two girls—the guys wearing denim jeans and white t-shirts, the girls wearing the era's signature poodle skirts. The group also seemed ready for some late-night action as they stood around two perfectly polished hot rods.

Eric cast a wistful look. If he existed in this era, might he have been one of those guys? Perhaps, since they projected an outsider vibe, something he personified in his home world. Hell. Maybe he should go out there and talk to them. Maybe he should ask them if—

"Fuck!" he gasped, head jerking sideways.

"You alright?" Mike asked while clambering aboard, a brown paper bag in his left hand.

"I'm fine. You just startled me." Eric rubbed his palms along his legs. "I guess what happened earlier is still messing with my mind."

"I know what you mean." Mike slipped the key into the ignition and cranked over the engine.

The Chevy's 350 small block chugged a few times before rumbling to life. As the idle evened out, Mike placed the bag behind his seat, muscled the shifter into reverse, and backed up the vehicle. With some room to maneuver, he turned back onto the street.

Like before, Eric stared out of his window, this time focusing on the sights. He found the city remarkable with its endless array of retro neon signs, comical excesses of lights, and scores of people oblivious to it all. In a way, the color and commotion didn't fit in this antiquated era, but maybe that's how things were. In any event, he appreciated the vibrancy, mostly for the distraction it provided.

Mike turned right onto a darkened street that curved lazily upward. As the auto chugged along, Eric wondered about their destination. A minute later, the destination illuminated into view. He couldn't help but turn up his lips. They headed towards the Hollywood sign, though he didn't know why. He wasn't complaining either way as the winding road pushed them deeper into seclusion. Then he realized the iconic landmark wasn't their destination but an overlook just underneath.

Mike pulled into the overlook's dirt cutout, which sat about fifty feet below the massive lettering. With the Chevy facing the sea of twinkling lights, he parked, shut off the engine, and then nothing. They both simply sat there, Eric guessing that Mike brought them here to say something meaningful. He didn't.

Mike reached behind his seat, pulled out the brown bag and reached inside. After fishing out a six-pack, he snapped off a can and extended it. Eric grinned while retrieving the offering. He cracked open the can and took a pull, the liquid immediately working its soothing magic. Not only was an ice-cold beer perfect on this warm evening, the drink tamped down the blood-curdling screams still ringing in his ears. Apparently, Mike wanted to ease his own nerves as he wasted no time snapping off a beer for himself.

With Mike's own can cracked and ready, he eased back and took a long swallow. A short while later, he reached over and cranked down the window, letting air circulate throughout the cabin. Eric appreciated this given the residual heat coming off the engine compartment. To aid the ventilation, he lowered his own window.

A long silence ensued, one broken only by the city's muffled hum, the resting engine's clinking and clanking, and periodic sips.

Eric found the near-quiet comforting, but a burning question needed asking. "I'm curious. Were you gonna shoot me outside of that guy's apartment?"

Mike looked over, but he turned back without answering. Instead, he reached into his suit jacket and produced a pack of cigarettes. He opened the pack and pinched a white tube between his lips. After putting back the pack, he pulled out a chrome-covered butane lighter and thumb-snapped a flame, casting a soft orange glow about the cabin.

"Those are bad for you," Eric said.

Mike paused with the flame inches from the cigarette. He turned and responded, making the cigarette dance between his lips. "This is virtual reality and I'm a robot."

Eric's face grew warm with embarrassment.

Mike shook his head and got back to work. He torched the cigarette's end, inhaled, and closed the lighter. With his chest expanded, he rested the cigarette on his leg and blew silvery smoke out of his window.

Eric couldn't help but admire the display of humanness. "Give me one of those."

Mike looked over, and after a moment's hesitation, he extended the pack and lighter. Eric did his best to mimic the bot, only to cough violently after sucking on the lit cigarette.

"Fuck me," Mike murmured, his cigarette dancing some more. "You can't get anything right, can you?"

Eric looked over with watery eyes. "I'm not exactly used to these."

"One of these days," Mike responded, puffing out his words, "I'm gonna teach you how to act human-like."

Eric rolled his eyes, went for another drag, but quickly changed his mind. Instead, he smashed the cigarette into the ashtray and took a long pull of beer, grateful to wash the ashes from his mouth. "So, were you gonna shoot me?"

Still reticent, Mike finished off his can, snapped off another and exited the car. He walked around to the front of the hood and sat down. Eric grabbed the remaining cans and likewise slid out of the vehicle. But while walking towards the hood, he caught a glimpse of the twinkling lights and instead headed for the bluff. At the precipice, he took in the magical vista, where an expanse of city lights blended up into a dark-purple horizon.

"I can't believe," Mike said, "you actually planned to beat that Crypt Keeper with a metal pipe."

Saying nothing, Eric finished off his can and snapped off another.

"And I'm shocked," Mike went on, "because you don't strike me as the type."

Eric cracked open the new can and took a drink. "That's because I'm not the type."

"Tonight, you could've fooled me."

"I almost fooled myself. But it turns out, we can't stray too far from our true selves, even in virtual reality, which sucks."

"Why?"

Eric breathed in the earthy air. "Because I wanted to make that fucker pay for what he did."

"Wouldn't that make you evil... like me?"

Eric softly smirked and turned back. "You really consider yourself evil?"

"Yeah. I think my actions morally repugnant. I also don't care."

"Because you have nothing to lose?"

Mike shook this off. "Because I'm a necessary evil."

"Don't give me that shit. Don't pretend like you're some superhero vigilante out to night-stick wrongdoers for the greater good."

"You really think that murdering scum is wrong?"

"In a civilized society, yes."

"Tell that to the girl who just got knifed to death."

Eric bit his lip and lowered his eyes. After a moment, he stepped towards the hood and sat alongside his robotic partner.

"Look," Mike continued, "you made the right decision tonight."

"Like hell I did."

"I meant for yourself. Obviously, that girl would disagree, but your decision aligned with who you are, making it the right choice for you."

Eric swigged while considering this. "I agree with you, but that still doesn't alleviate the pain."

"It wasn't supposed to. It was supposed to provide you with some perspective."

"What do you mean?"

"I mean that I've been watching you, reading you, and with more precision than you realize. And believe me when I say that your actions tonight resonated with who you are. So not only did you stay true to yourself, you did so in the face of extreme pressure. That says something."

Eric took another moment to consider this. He also took another swallow, the drink and notion each sinking in. They both felt good. "So if you were me, and you were standing before that Crypt Keeper, would you have hit him?"

"Nope. Because that would've ran counter to who *I* am."

Eric looked over, his face tensed with confusion.

Mike lit another cigarette, and after inhaling, he blew out more silvery vapors. "I would've shot him."

Chuckling, Eric rose from the hood and cascaded the rest of his beer into his mouth. With the can empty, he reared back and winged it down the hillside.

"Fuck me," Mike muttered once more, as the can sailed a pathetic twenty-feet.

Eric turned on woozy legs. "It was empty. I couldn't put much force behind the throw."

"Then here." Mike reached into his jacket and pulled a flat-faced liquor bottle.

Eric took the container, but with it half full, it would be a shame to waste such a large quantity of liquor. He unscrewed the cap, tipped the dark-brown fluids into his mouth, and choked on the stinging bitterness.

Mike muttered more curses.

"Whew," Eric said, his virtual brain now steeped in alcohol. Rearing back once more, he paused and looked over. "Think I can hit the Hollywood sign from here?"

Mike gauged the landmark's distance and shook his head.

"Oh, really?" Eric lined up the landmark in his blurry sights, ran forward and hurled the bottle. He put sufficient force behind the throw, but unfortunately, his boozy vision spoiled his accuracy. The bottle sailed to the right before thumping against the hillside.

"You know…" Mike said.

"You try it, Mr. Robot Overlord!"

Mike eyed him. A moment later, he flicked away his cigarette, snapped off a can and positioned himself. But before throwing, he pulled off his coat and tossed it over.

"Asshole," Eric grumbled while catching the coat.

Mike paid him no mind. Instead, he pulled his pistol, placed it on the Chevy's hood, and repositioned himself. He then ran forward and winged the can into blackened sky.

The can stayed online the entire time and smashed into the *W* in Hollywood. Upon impact, the container exploded, spraying celebratory liquids in all directions.

"You son of a bitch," Eric slurred.

Grinning, Mike turned towards the embittered human. "You see, it's all in the way you—"

"Hold it right there!" shouted a tinny voice. Immediately after, a spotlight blasted to life.

Eric and Mike turned and spotted a bulbous police cruiser parked farther up the hill.

"Shit," Mike hissed. "Come on. Let's get out of here before this gets worse."

Eric *pfft'ed* this off and looked back towards the cruiser. "Fuck you, flatfoot!"

"I said freeze!" came the grainy reply, shouting over a vehicle-mounted megaphone.

"Yeah! Watch me!" Eric darted to the Chevy's hood and grabbed Mike's pistol. He aimed and squeezed the trigger but nothing happened. Face furrowed, he analyzed the gun to figure out what went wrong.

"Get in the car, you moron!" Mike screamed while hustling towards the driver side door.

"Hang on," Eric slurred, poking at the gun to get it operational. It finally discharged. "Goddamn!"

Seconds later, a *crack-crack-crack* rang out from above, followed by zings and pops. Clumps of dirt kicked up as the cop's bullets rained down. With that, Eric figured it was time to flee. He scrambled for the passenger side door and climbed aboard.

Mike already had the 350 fired up, so when his partner spilled inside, he snapped the shifter into reverse and jolted the car backward. All the while, Eric went for another beer, only to drop it when a bullet snapped through the roof and thudded into the upholstery.

"Motherfuckers!" he screamed, incensed over the spilled drink. With the windows still down, he leaned out and fired in the police cruiser's direction.

The .40 cal. discharged relentlessly, releasing deafening bangs and bright flashes. The officers ducked down to avoid the fire, and seeing them hiding, Eric let out triumphant curses. With the pistol's slide locked rearward, he leaned back inside the bullet-riddled Chevy.

Mike looked over with widened eyes. "Just how fucking stupid are you?"

Eric smiled sloppily. How many times would Mike ask him that? Like the first instance, he didn't have an answer, but he did have a question.

"So, were you gonna shoot me outside of that Crypt Keeper's apartment?"

Mike turned once more and answered with a scowl.

Chapter 22

Real Space

Eric smirked as his auto pulled into Sunrise's parking lot. It was like last night never happened. Yesterday evening, after inhaling multiple beers and a little bourbon, he exited net space feeling completely normal. No hangover, no regretful decisions, just a bunch of fun memories. Had the same night occurred in real space, he would need days to recover *and* a plan to free himself from prison. He widened his smirk.

"Good morning, Ann," he said while passing the reception area.

Ann sat up and beamed. "Good morning, Dr. Ryan. You're in a good mood today."

He screeched to a halt. "I was in a good mood...until you called me Dr. Ryan."

Ann slunk in her seat. "I'm so sorry. I can't seem to get that right. Does that mean you're gonna fire me?"

"That depends. What are you hiding underneath your desk?"

Ann sat up once more, eyes wide. "Nothing."

"It doesn't look like nothing."

Red-faced, she lifted a paperback from her lap.

"Thought so. And now, I'm gonna go speak with your supervisor because you deserve a promotion."

Ann twisted her face but quickly relaxed it. "Oh, right. You don't mind if I read books. In fact, you encourage it."

"Hence the promotion. But we'll just keep the reason why to ourselves." He winked and smiled.

"Well," Ann chirped, "in that case, thank you very much, Dr. Ryan."

He wiped away his smile.

Ann slunk once more. "*Now* what did I do?" After a moment, she made a fist and banged it on her desk. "Shoot! I called you that name again, didn't I?"

He brought back his smile. "I'll just leave before this gets any worse."

"That's a good idea. And thank you for *that,* Dr.—Mr.—person—man."

Lips pursed, he simply turned and headed for the elevators.

***

Eric walked into the third-floor lobby, and while starting for his office, he heard ringing sounds emanating from inside. Someone was trying to establish a connection, but who? Hopefully it wasn't Arvin, phoning to say he couldn't show. But he never gave Arvin his work number, only his email address. After gaining access, he hurried behind his desk to check.

The holo-screen read *Dr. William Wright*, which made Eric cover his mouth. Maybe the salvation effort results were in, and Dr. Wright was calling to pass on the verdict.

After taking an optimistic breath, he tapped the display to answer. "Dr. Wright?"

"What, the fuck, is going on?"

Eric gritted his teeth. Dr. Wright found out, but how? To root out the reason, he responded with ignorance. "I'm sorry? What's wrong?"

"You'll need to do better than that. And you better have a good goddamn reason for why you've been sneaking into virtual worlds, along with your robot client, following Chad Vale this whole goddamn time."

Eric mentally cursed. "What do you mean?" he asked while sitting, now hoping to buy some time to favorably spin this.

"Christ, Eric. Don't give me that shit. Everyone knows what you've been up to. What we don't know is why."

Eric jerked back. Everyone? Who the hell was everyone? With his situation deteriorating rapidly, he needed to confess, just not fully. Still unsure about Dr. Wright's total knowledge, he didn't want to dig his grave any deeper than necessary. "Okay. I've been entering a virtual world with Arvin because he told me some off-putting information about Chad Vale. The only way we could verify this was by entering net space and following Chad around."

"What do you mean by off-putting?"

"Have you heard about people snuffing out avatars in V.R.?"

"Yeah."

"Well, Arvin suspects that Chad's one of these people. In truth, I never considered *any* form of online activity noteworthy, until I saw Chad carry out an online killing. It was just about the worst thing I've ever seen. But the killer was an avatar, meaning we weren't sure if it was Chad. So, we decided to find out."

"To what end?"

So Arvin could wipe Chad.

With no intent to say this, Eric kept focusing on pretext. "Arvin is desperate to find out what kind of person Chad is."

"Why?"

"Because he doesn't think Chad is right in the head, and he blames himself for this. Specifically, Arvin thinks that his relationship with Chad's father is what caused the problem."

"You mean the closeness they developed?"

"Exactly. That drove Chad into hating tech, along with him associating with online killers. But again, we weren't sure if Chad was a genuine killer. So when Arvin decided to find out, I said I would help."

Dr. Wright took a deep breath. "Jesus Christ, Eric. Did it ever occur to you that this was, oh, I don't know, a violation of your ethical obligations?"

"I know. And I considered that multiple times. But lately, I've been in a strange place. You know that."

"I do know that. And I understand. But that's no excuse for going on a goddamn virtual adventure when you should've been providing therapy."

Eric nodded. "Agreed. And out of curiosity, how did you find out about this virtual adventure?"

"Because you're not exactly a tier-one covert operative. *They* wouldn't be dumb enough do their online detective work, by logging on through *their* university computer, and with *their* username and password. This is especially true when university computers are monitored for liability purposes, you know, in case anyone with access does something illegal or incredibly stupid."

Eric shut his eyes and rolled his head back.

"Not only did you log in with your own credentials, you went into net space looking like your real space self, which was beyond idiotic given your aims. From that point, we quickly identified the other actors in this little drama, all except for that Alice girl. Who the hell is she?"

"I don't know."

Dr. Wright stayed silent.

"Honestly. I don't know. In real life, I have no idea who she is. Arvin and I think she's Chad's next victim, and that's why she's involved. We were basically tailing her and waiting for Chad to make his move."

Dr. Wright drew another breath. "Unbelievable. I'm just thanking God this wasn't anything illegal. It's plenty damn stupid, but from the sound of it, nothing that'll get you thrown in the can. As for your job, that's up in the air."

"What do you mean?"

"Meaning that like a dumb ass, I met with my superiors and told them how swell things were going between you and the bot, only for them to tell me what's really going on. I tried to pull your ass out of the fire, but you need to see things from their perspective. This was supposed to be a new and fascinating frontier, one where man and machine learned about each other in profound and novel ways... not a goddamn covert op where you turn into a woman and shoot it out with the fucking cops!"

Eric continued sitting there, sweat coating his back.

"Like I said," Dr. Wright continued, "it doesn't seem like you've done anything illegal. All the same, the school wants your ass. I said it was only fair that I get an explanation beforehand, and from what you just said, I might be able to put this in a positive light. But I'm not making any promises."

Eric wanted Dr. Wright to pass on a message to his superiors, telling them exactly what they could do with this job of theirs. He almost hoped they would fire him. That would eliminate the last lingering reason to stay in this world. Then he remembered why he needed them.

"By the way, how did your report go with the higher ups—about Arvin getting onboard with the university?"

"Are you kidding me? You seriously thought they would agree after uncovering the truth? That bot's finished."

Eric closed his eyes.

"Hey," Dr. Wright went on, "I'm sorry about the bot. I really am. I was all for getting him onboard, but there's nothing I can do."

Eric opened his eyes but remained mute.

"So what are you gonna do?"

Still no reply.

"Hey. Ryan."

"What?"

"I said what the hell are you gonna do?"

"What am I going to do about *what?*"

"About trying to save your damn job."

Eric shook his head. Oh, how he hated this world. "I don't know. I guess I'll figure something out."

"Do you even care?"

Eric was certain that he didn't. But he was also disheartened and angered, so perhaps his indifference was a byproduct of resentment. Considering the question once more, this time dispassionately, maybe he did care.

People in this world needed help. While modernity had radically improved the lives of most, some struggled to adjust, and he welcomed the opportunity to assist. What was more, now he could assist better than before because he had glimpsed the positive side of tech. Or rather, he could assist if he could still practice.

"I do care," he finally said. "I do care about my job. And not so much to please UCLA's upper echelon, or even for personal gratification, but for the clients. A lot of them depend on me for assistance and I appreciate being able to help."

"I'm glad you're thinking that way. And not only because it benefits you and me, but because it's the right thing to do."

Eric weakly nodded his agreement. "So what now?"

"Now, I'm gonna go report what I've found and try to save your neck. In the meanwhile, don't you even think about pulling any more sneaky shit. It's just going to land you in more hot water, and you're absolutely terrible at it."

Eric couldn't help but smirk. *Worst spy in the history of the profession.* "Just so you know, I *am* going back into virtual reality, but only to tell Arvin that my role in everything is over. But before I go, I just wanna say thanks for going through all this trouble on my behalf. And I won't say that I owe you because—"

"Because that's so painfully obvious it doesn't need to be said."

He grinned.

"And, Eric..."

"Yeah?"

"Again. Sorry about the bot."

"Me too."

***

Back in L.A. Confidential, Eric walked towards Mike's apartment to deliver the bad news. With the apartment only a few miles away, it wouldn't be long before he came across his robotic partner.

The walk was bittersweet, largely because he would miss all of this. Of course, there was nothing barring him from reentering this world—or entering any world for that matter—but he would need to purchase his own immersion sets, and by then, the mission would be long over.

Still, he planned to reenter in the future, an enticing thought when considering all the worlds Alternate Reality had on offer. And with his love of history, why not continue travelling back in time to scratch this itch? Maybe he could enter 1910's Vienna and visit Sigmund Freud. Or why not enter 1880's Spain and visit his favorite neuroscientist Santiago Ramon y Cajal? Or better yet, why not—

The rumination evaporated when he spotted Mike descending his apartment stairs. He was about to call out but held off. Mike seemed tense and on edge. Or was that anger? Either way, the emotion didn't bode well when Mike readjusted the lapels on his jacket, flashing a glimpse of his nickel-plated semi-auto.

Keeping quiet, he followed Mike who headed off in the opposite direction. He also kept a good ways back to prevent detection.

While passing through the midmorning sunshine, he took note of this city section. The streets looked familiar, but this went beyond the cookie-cutter array of apartments. He had traversed this path before, but when?

He couldn't recall, until fifteen minutes later when Mike crossed the street and approached a novelty store, the same store Eric stopped by last night when he tracked Chad to the wolf pup's apartment. Interestingly enough, Mike stopped outside this very store, which was now open and had people trickling in and out. Adding to the liveliness were the scores of denizens ambling along the sidewalk.

Eric halted across the street and observed Mike who reached into his jacket and pulled out his cigarettes. With the pack opened, he shook out a tube and stuck it between his lips. After returning the pack, he retrieved his chrome-covered butane lighter and torched the cigarette's end. Cigarette lit, Mike closed the lighter and returned it to his jacket. He then casually leaned against the novelty store's glass panel.

Everyone passing by paid him no mind, and Eric would've done the same had he not known who Mike was. But he did know. And what was more, he knew Mike was capable of violence and he stood by the apartments of someone fit for violent retribution. That alone made a toxic combination, but when considering the nickel-plated semi-auto tucked inside Mike's jacket...

Chapter 23

Mike drew another puff from his cigarette then lowered the white tube while exhaling. "Sorry," he quickly called out, waving away the smoke as a young man walked by.

The young man stopped and looked over. "It's cool, Daddio," he said from behind his stylish black glasses. "In fact, you got an extra smoke I can bum off of you?"

Mike nodded, reached into his jacket, and pulled out his pack. He handed it towards the beatnik who wore tight black jeans, a striped long-sleeved t-shirt, and a black beret covering his messy hair.

As the beatnik pulled out a cigarette, Mike retrieved his lighter and sparked a flame. With the flame covered, he brought the fire forward.

The beatnik lit the tip and inhaled, pulled out the cigarette, and exhaled a long trace of silvery smoke. "Smooth, man. You dig it?"

Mike smiled. "Yeah, man. I dig it."

The beatnik handed back the pack. "Well, alright then. Keep it slick, my main man." He stuck out his hand.

Mike likewise extended his palm, thinking the beatnik wanted to shake. He didn't. He made a soft *slap-slap* gesture, then made a hand-shaped gun before strutting off into the sunny afternoon.

Mike stretched out his smile but quickly wiped it away when Victor Vane, together with the young Crypt Keeper, exited the nearby apartment. He took another puff from his cigarette, watching Victor and the wolf pup descend the apartment stairs. The two killers started in the opposite direction, so he flicked his cigarette into the curbside rivulet of dirty water and followed suit.

Minutes later, he trailed the two murderers out of the densely packed apartment area. They emerged in a livelier stretch beset by restaurants, shops, and a car dealership with an enormous cat looming over its sign. A few minutes after that, the wolves ambled into one of the restaurants.

Mike grimaced. He needed to follow them inside but that meant closing considerable distance. Right now, that was fine because they didn't know who he was. But given his mission, he would likely run into them again, and the wolves seeing him twice might raise suspicion. With no other choice, he walked up to the crowded burger shop and entered.

Inside the buzzing restaurant, he studied the layout. The best way to blend in was by ordering something, so he walked to the register where a young girl stood by, beaming in her tacky brown work uniform, complete with a tacky brown visor.

"Hi!" she chirped. "Welcome to Tommy's! What can I get you?"

He looked towards the two wolves who had already placed their orders and were walking deeper inside. He looked back. "This is my first time here, so I don't know what's good. What do you recommend?"

"Everything here is great. Chiliburgers, chili fries, chilidogs—it's all super tasty."

"Chili?"

"Oh, yeah. That's what we're known for. We put chili on everything. It's super tasty."

"I'm not really one to judge because I've never had chili before."

The worker rattled her head, shaking so hard that she needed to readjust her visor. "Are you serious? You've never had chili before?"

"Not once. But if that's what people normally order, I guess I'll have some chili."

"Great. What do you want it on?"

"How about you pick? You seem to know what's good."

The worker perked up. "I'll order you a chiliburger with extra chili. And cheese, lots of cheese. That makes everything even more super tasty. Plus, I'll add some fries that are drowning in chili and cheese. And to drink?"

He shrugged his digital shoulders, surprised the girl didn't offer him a cup filled with chili.

"Coke!" she shot out, before punching her fingers into her noisy machine. "There. Your order's all set. And here's your number. Someone will bring over your food when it's ready."

"Thanks."

He turned and scanned the room. The two wolves sat in a far booth, and while making his way over, he looked for nearby places to sit. Unfortunately, the entire place was packed. To remedy this, he stopped by an adjacent table where a teenage male and female sat, both waiting for their food.

"I can't believe it," he growled, supposedly to himself.

The male looked over. "Can't believe what?"

"I just placed my order, and the server told me they ran out of chili. Now, everything is gonna come out naked."

The male and female jerked back in their seats.

"No chili?" the female said. She looked towards her partner. "Come on. Let's go to Carl's Jr. and get a hotdog."

"Yeah," the male responded. "What's the point of Tommy's when there's no chili?"

"That," the female said as they rose, "and I heard Carl's Jr. is gonna start serving burgers. Let's take advantage before they make the biggest mistake of their lives."

With the irate couple stomping towards the exit, Mike slipped into the now open booth and oriented his ear.

"So it was over in no time," Victor said, "wasn't it?"

"Yup," the wolf pup responded. "After the first couple of stabs, she started fighting back. Then she remembered she was in virtual reality and simply took off her immersion sets."

Victor chuckled. "That almost always happens—the targets forgetting they're in net space. But hell. That's why we carry out these operations, to remind people why they shouldn't lose themselves in these fake realities."

"But does it work? I mean, do the victims ever come out of these murders seeing things from our side?"

"They don't join the Keepers, if that's what you're asking. However, they do adopt a different understanding of virtual reality. They realize that V.R. isn't simply a digital drug for uninterrupted bliss. They realize that it has negative aspects."

"So in a way," the pup responded, "we give them a bad drug trip."

"Mm-hmm. And what happens when drug users experience a horrific trip?"

"They question the reasonableness of using in the first place."

"Exactly. We serve as the wake-up call for these people who are inadvertently ruining their lives."

The pup leaned back and took a deep breath.

"What's wrong?" Victor asked.

"Nothing's wrong. I just... Well, can't we simply explain that what they're doing is negative? Do we have to murder them to prove our point?"

"I wish that were so, but when people undergo bliss, they tend to discount reason. And virtual reality is some serious bliss. To illustrate, just think back to the last time you got laid. While in the throes of passion, were your reasoning centers in control, or did they take a backseat to your animalistic urges?"

"Actually, I've never had sex before."

Now Victor leaned back.

"What you see," the wolf pup said, "is what you get. In real space, I'm only sixteen."

Mike looked over and tightened his lips. With him planning to murder the youngster, those revelations weren't helping.

"Well," Victor went on, "take it from me. When pleasure abounds, people don't wanna hear about the pleasure's negative effects. They just want their fix. That's why we have to rip people out of this state."

A young waitress came over to their table, tray in hand. "Hi, there. Here's your two vanilla shakes." After setting down the weighty drinks, she turned to head off.

"Excuse me," Victor called out, continuing after she turned. "My friend and I have a little bet going on. Are you a computer program?"

The young woman laughed. "With me working at a fast food joint, I can see why you would think that. But no. I'm human."

"Then why do you work here?" Victor asked.

"Because I'm young in real space, and these jobs are part of the growing experience. And with these jobs nonexistent in real space, here I am."

"So," Victor said while taking stock of her, "what we see is what we get?"

The girl bounced on her toes. "This is me."

Mike heard nothing else, so he looked over once more and found Victor smiling at the wolf pup.

"Well," the pup said while turning to the girl, "what do you think about your time in virtual reality?"

"Oh, man. It is so awesome. This is like my tenth job, and all my others jobs have taken place in different eras. I'm not kidding. Each one has been a complete blast."

"Um," the pup went on, "I'm glad you're having such a great time."

"Same here. And I swear, I wish I was a bot so I could stay in these places forever."

The pup looked to Victor, and Victor stretched out his smile.

"I can't blame you," the pup said while turning back. "Oh, and I'm young in real space too. So maybe sometime you can tell me about all the places you've been, and how much fun you've been having."

She nodded. "Yeah. That sounds cool. Stop by at 4:30 when my shift ends."

"Great. See you here."

The girl turned up her makeup-free lips, turned and headed off.

Mike averted his gaze as she passed.

"See?" Victor said. "While real space rots from neglect, people are in here experiencing unprecedented pleasure. Last night's target was the same, this girl is the same, and the more work you do with us, the more you'll realize how many other zombies populate these worlds. Now come on. We'll finish discussing this later. *I* gotta get ready to wake another sleeper."

With that, the duo stood and started for the exit. Mike again averted his gaze. After the wolves stepped into the afternoon sunshine, he likewise rose and headed for the door.

"Excuse me," the same waitress said, holding another tray, this one covered in brown cheesy slop. "Here's your meal, sir."

"I'm sorry," Mike said. "But an emergency came up and I have to go."

The girl waved off the apology. "No problem, sir. It's not like anything will go to waste." She winked.

He grinned and resumed his route. And though he wanted to warn the girl about the wolf pup, he figured it didn't matter, not when considering what would become of the beast.

***

Outside of the restaurant, Mike followed Victor and the wolf pup like before. Some ten minutes later, they neared the pup's apartment. The two wolves stopped, shook hands, and parted company. Victor headed towards his residence while the pup started for his apartment, sucking at his shake while strolling along.

With the pup alone, Mike closed in with long strides. Now ten feet away, he cast around cautious looks, scanning for people and places to spill the pup's digital blood. Half a minute later, the perfect location arrived.

"Excuse me," he called out as they passed an alleyway.

The pup stopped and turned. "Me?"

"Yeah," Mike said, halting a few feet away. "Sorry to bother, but I saw you in Tommy's right now talking to that server. Do you by chance know her?"

"Not really. I just met her right now. Why?"

"There's something you need to know about her."

"What's that?"

Mike cast another furtive look about, stepped into the alley, and conspiratorially waved the pup over. The pup made a funny face and followed him in.

"That girl," Mike whispered, "isn't a computer program. She's an actual person."

"Yeah, I know. When she stopped by me and my friend's table, she told us that."

"No, no. I mean she's an actual human being. She thinks, she feels, she has a past and a future, probably friends and family—all of that stuff."

The pup smirked. "Again, man, I know."

"See, I don't think you do. If you did, you would appreciate these aspects of her humanity."

"Huh?"

"Here. Let me exemplify the mistake you're making, thereby ensuring that you *do* appreciate these aspects of other people." Mike reached into his jacket.

Chapter 24

Eric edged around the alleyway where Mike and the wolf pup had stopped some fifteen feet inside. The two had exchanged words but he couldn't make anything out, not with Mike and the pup speaking in hushed tones. Still, he assumed the worst as Mike not only harbored a seething hatred towards the pup, but also carried a way to express this hatred. Then Mike reached into his jacket for this ultimate expression of ire.

Eric darted into the alleyway, and while hurtling towards the two men, they both spun. He reached out and grabbed Mike's arm, which was pulling out his semi-auto.

"What the fuck!" the pup shouted, stepping back from the sudden commotion.

Eric continued clamping Mike's arm, trying to keep the weapon aimed in a safe direction. The move proved prescient as seconds later the weapon discharged, sending a thunderous blast through the alley. In nearly the same instant, a spark flashed off the nearby concrete wall, along with an errant *ping* as the round ricocheted in a random direction. The wolf pup dropped his milkshake and took off running.

Eric struggled more than before, because with the wolf pup fleeing, Mike violently tried to wrench free. When the pup exited the alleyway, Eric finally let go, but that wasn't the end of the scene. Mike tried to skirt around him, but he shifted sideways to block his path. With Mike's face a furnace, he leveled his pistol at his partner.

"Do it!" Eric shouted while stepping forward. "Shoot me! It doesn't seem like you're capable of anything else!"

Mike eyed him for a few seconds, his gun hand trembling. "Fuck!" he roared while stabbing the weapon towards the ground. Now pacing back and forth, he stopped and looked back. "What the fuck is your problem?"

Eric took another step forward. "You're seriously asking me that? What the fuck is yours? Are you out to murder everyone who's ever done anything wrong, virtual reality or not? What kind of sick vigilante are you?"

"It's justice, you dumb shit!"

"Justice. This is justice. Luring someone into a darkened alleyway so you can gun them down in cold blood. Yeah. That's really fair and impartial."

"That's less than what his victim got. Or have you forgotten her screams?"

"No, but that's not the point. The point is we can't—"

"You can't!" Mike interjected while likewise stepping forward. "I can! I can do what you're incapable of. I can make these hard decisions and live with them."

Eric slowly shook his head. "You're no better than Chad Vale."

Mike stepped back and raised his gun once more.

"Yeah," Eric went on, opening his hands. "Go ahead and make my point."

Mike let a moment pass before finally lowering his pistol and looking away. After a headshake of his own, he looked back. "What are you doing here?"

"First off, I'm not here to spy on you, even though that's what it seems like."

"Then?"

"I came here to tell you it's over."

"What's over?"

Eric took a deep breath.

***

"And that's what happened," Eric said, recapping his story about the school finding him out.

"Holy shit," Mike replied. "You have to be the worst spy in the history of the profession."

Eric smirked while taking another sip from his beer.

Here on the Sixth Street Viaduct Bridge, he and Mike observed the trains rumbling in and out of Union Station. And like at the Hollywood Hills, they made the most of this vista with cold beers.

"Well," Eric responded, "my abysmal spy performance shouldn't surprise you at this point. Even though I'm educated, none of that applies to clandestine operations."

Mike sipped from his own bottle. "That's not the problem. It's your morals. That's what keeps getting in the way. Hell. That's why your quick update turned into a struggle over my pistol."

Eric smiled but his joy quickly dissipated. "You know, this mission update isn't the only reason why I entered."

"Oh?"

"Yeah. In addition to this, I entered to say that your lifesaving plan fell through. Dr. Wright pitched the idea to his chain of command and they didn't go for it."

Mike looked down and rolled his jaw. "Well, that sucks." He looked up and sipped. "But like we said before, even if the salvation effort fails, we're right back to where we started. That's why we decided to proceed as normal."

Eric tightened his free hand around the concrete railing. He knew what proceeding as normal meant—Victor Vane stabbing Alice to death.

Mike looked over. "You still don't want her murdered, do you?"

Eric sipped without answering.

"So let me ask you once more. How much of an emotional attachment do you have to this woman?"

Eric slapped the railing. "I can't tell you, okay? I don't know. I can't peg my attachment to Alice on a scale from one to ten, if that's what you want. Intuitively, I just know this isn't right. Letting her go through that shit when we can stop it isn't right." He took a breath. "I know you feel differently, okay? And I respect that. But I simply can't stand by and let it happen. I hope you can respect the way *I* feel."

"Eric, we discussed this already. While we both agree that the librarian's fate is tragic, we also agreed to reinstate the original plan should the new one fail, and it did."

Again, Eric didn't respond.

"Thursday," Mike said, looking back towards the vista.

Eric knew what that meant. "That's your day, isn't it?"

Mike took a drink and nodded. "Thursday is when I go off to play the harp in robot heaven."

Eric stayed mute once more. In six days, Arvin would be dead. There wasn't much to say about that.

"Ms. Vale," Mike continued, "informed me that Thursday morning, I would be shipped back to the Powerdyne Robotics factory where I would undergo repurposing. All the necessary paperwork is complete, and the Vales were even refunded some of their expenses because I'm still in good working condition."

"When did she tell you this?"

"A week ago."

Eric furrowed his brow. "You've known for a week? Then why did we go through the charade of trying to save your life?"

"There wasn't any harm in trying. That, and I didn't want to burden you with this information."

Eric tightened his face some more. *Didn't want to burden you?* What the hell did that mean—that he was so fragile he needed protection from burdensome information? "You should've told me. This isn't something to keep quiet until the very end."

"Would it have made a difference?"

"Of course."

"How?"

Eric was upset, but he forced himself to calm down and think through the question.

With Arvin's death assured, what might have changed? Perhaps he would've been more accommodating with Arvin, thereby making his remaining time easier. But hell. What kind of trouble would *that* have gotten him into?

He likewise looked out across the vista. "Maybe it *would've* made a difference."

"And why's that?"

"Because of how much your situation sucked."

Mike nodded. "Had you known, I fear you would've acted in ways that differed from who you are. I fear you would've done something you disagreed with. And for this, *I* would've been responsible."

"So you wanted to keep me from making decisions I'll later regret?"

"Exactly. Why compromise your values when doing so isn't necessary?"

Eric rubbed his digital chin. "I'm glad you're looking out for me, but I'm not sure you're doing me any favors."

"How so?"

"Because maybe a person's values need to be violated from time to time, or at least threatened. That way, the person would realize why their values exist in the first place. I mean, how could we ever appreciate our values if we're never in situations that make their importance known?"

Mike slowly nodded. "Fair point. And maybe you've been doing that ever since joining my endeavor—identifying where your values lie and defending them. And while for me this can be... frustrating... your ceaseless drive shows strong character. So in retrospect, I'm rather glad that you're so dedicated to ruining my plans."

"I'm just trying to preserve *my* humanity. Although if I'm the voice of moral reason in all this, that's not saying much."

"On the contrary. When considering the defense of human morality, you're doing a smashing job."

Eric chuckled. "So, what now?"

"I'm going to continue forward. For me, nothing has changed. And you?"

Eric took another sip. *Good goddamn question.*

"And just so you know," Mike added, "I hope you don't involve yourself any further. You've already implicated yourself enough and there's no need for more. From this point, I can complete the mission on my own. And I don't have to worry about any consequences because I won't be around to suffer them. But you have many years to live, so why make them unnecessarily difficult?"

Eric nodded. Good points all around. "Well, then I guess I'm done."

Mike nodded back. "Perhaps that's for the best."

Eric agreed, but withdrawal bothered him nonetheless. He wanted to see how everything played out, especially with the end drawing near. That, and he rather enjoyed spy work despite his operative hopelessness.

***

Eric removed his immersion sets and stared at the ceiling. Ever so gradually, a brooding sense of failure took hold, but what did he fail at?

He considered the past week to spot this problem but couldn't. After all, he met with Arvin as instructed, and with their sessions drawing near, it was clear they derived something positive from the experience. He also progressed with Kim by better understanding their situation. He even stopped despising tech and now appreciated its vast potential. All in all, his life had significantly improved, so where was the monumental failure?

Alice.

He wanted to prevent Victor from brutally murdering her and he failed. Or did he? The murder hadn't occurred yet. He could still intervene. But how? With his cover blown, he couldn't reenter L.A. Confidential without the university knowing. Or rather, they would know if he used a school computer, and reentering didn't require this. Alternate Reality only required immersion sets and a good Internet connection.

He brought the sets back over his eyes and initiated a voice connection. A moment later, Kim came on the line.

"Eric?" she greeted. "Hey. What's up?"

"Kim, are you home?"

"Yeah, I'm here."

"You have some immersion sets, right? Ones that are good for entering virtual worlds?"

"Of course. More than one set."

"And do you have some avatars on standby, ones created for use in Alternate Reality?"

Kim laughed. "Are you kidding? I have enough characters to populate a small city. Why do you ask?"

He smiled. "Because I need to borrow one."

Chapter 25

Five minutes ago, Eric returned home from UCLA. Five seconds ago, he finished updating Kim on everything.

Kim responded with two raised hands. "Wait, wait, wait. You did *what?*"

He held nothing back in his retelling, but he figured he had to be forthcoming. He intended to borrow one of Kim's avatars and make a final attempt to save Alice, so explaining why he needed it was only fair. Plus, he planned to update her anyhow, thereby shedding some light on his recent behavior. Still, he never imagined updating her to this extent.

Kim, sitting on the long living room couch while he stood nearby, started pumping her raised hands. "Hang on. Hang on, hang on, hang on." She lowered her hands. "You mean to tell me that you've been sneaking around a v-world as a chick? A chick named Lana?"

He walked to the love seat and planted himself. "Well, yeah. But like I said, that was for a reason. It's not like I had some fetish thing going on."

Kim smiled. "Of course not. And even if you *were* satisfying a fetish, there's nothing wrong with that. People are free to express themselves however they like."

He cleared his throat. "My decision served a practical purpose. I needed to close in on my target and I figured that becoming female would help. Turns out, I was right."

Kim shrugged. "I suppose that makes sense. And actually, pretty smart move. So," she continued, her smile back in place, "what did you think?"

"About closing in on my target or about living inside a woman's body?"

"What do you think I'm curious about?"

He roughly rubbed his chin. Right now, Victor was probably whistling some creepy tune while sharpening his blade, so this wasn't the time to reminisce over net space ventures. But again, he owed Kim all the explanation she wanted.

"Actually," he went on, "it was rather interesting being in her body, though at first it shocked the hell out of me. I mean, I opened my eyes, looked down, and saw..."

"Female parts?"

"Exactly. So after cursing at the sight of my boobs, I calmed down and followed my routine of moving around. That always helped with net space acclimation. In Lana, acclimation took a little longer, but only because of her unfamiliar female form. The um, hip-to-waist ratio is a little different."

"So I've noticed."

"Yup. And wearing female attire certainly didn't help, like heeled shoes."

Kim arched her brow. "Heels, huh?"

"Tall ones. But not all the time. Normally I just wore two-inchers. But one evening, while getting ready for a fancy dinner, I put on some pumps from hell."

Kim laughed, and he couldn't blame her. After all, it was him describing these ventures in tech.

"But most interesting of all," he went on, "was how much I became Lana, and correspondingly, how much Eric Ryan disappeared."

"That tends to happen. But you're right. It *is* strange how much people become their characters. But anyway, back to you being a woman."

"Like I said, it was interesting, especially the perspective I got from the other side of the gender divide. It helped me understand what females go through, partly at least."

"Like?"

"Like when weirdoes on the street check you out, and make you feel uncomfortable as hell."

Kim laughed. "That also happens."

"So guys really make it that obvious, huh?"

"Sometimes. How do you think I knew *you* were interested in *me?*"

His face grew hot with embarrassment. "Oh, and there's something else. I kinda used my looks to land a job."

"Really?"

He nodded. "The soon-to-be victim works at a library so I tried to land a job there. That meant speaking with the manager. While doing so, I quickly noted his penchant for attractive young women, so I completely batted my eyes and teased my hair."

"And?"

"And nothing. It worked. I ended up getting the position. But I don't know. Something about that bothered me."

Kim smirked. "I hate to break it to you, but I don't have a definitive answer for what you should've done. Being female is too complicated to have one universally correct procedure for every scenario. A lot of times, you just have to use your female instinct."

"Yeah, it's complicated alright. And with only a few days' worth of female instinct, I probably won't get very far, at least not without assistance, like from Alice."

"Alice?"

"The librarian. The one I'm trying to save. I told her what happened and it helped."

Kim nodded. "Nice girl?"

"Pretty nice. Like I said, I initially just needed her for mission intel, but we ended up conversing a few times. We even went out a few times. That's when I concluded she was a good person."

Kim stared for a notable moment. "You like this girl."

"Oh, come on. The perp's about to chop her up and I don't want that to happen. That doesn't mean we're lovers."

"I didn't say *like* as in romantic like. Just friendship like. You two are regular old girlfriends."

He huffed a breath. "Fine. We're friends. We shared some moments if that's what you wanna hear. But that doesn't mean we're gonna run off into the sunset together. I need to maintain objectivity. Keep things professional."

Kim tilted her head. "With all due respect, professional pulled out of the station a long time ago. You know, back when you embarked on this little covert op."

"Maybe you're right. But it's all in the name of justice."

Kim pinched her lips and shook her head.

"You don't agree?"

"I absolutely agree. I'm just thinking about that virtual murderer and how much justice he deserves. I'm telling you. You have no idea how many people would love to get back at these online killers."

"What's stopping them?"

"Nobody knows who they are. And like most online groups, the Crypt Keepers have a net space home, but everyone steers clear of it because it happens to be The Catacombs."

"The Catacombs?"

Kim grinned. "Imagine London during Jack the Ripper's era but always held in perpetual darkness. Big blood-orange moon overhead, eerie mist on the ground, screams heard throughout the city—not exactly an island paradise."

"Damn. Have you ever been there?"

"Sorta. There's bars on the outskirts, and it's cool to say you've had a drink in The Cats, but nobody ventures deeper inside."

He unfocused his eyes. "Well, maybe if I—"

"Don't even think about it. Don't you even think about going there. You've only been to one world, and given your description, it's a real peach. But don't forget. People create these worlds, and people come in all shapes, sizes, and mental states. And the people who created this world are violent murdering sadists who won't think twice about killing you."

"And net space murder isn't illegal."

Kim lifted helpless hands.

"Do you think laws will ever be passed against online violence?"

"That's already in the works, but as you can imagine, it's complicated. After all, when you exist in a digital world, who's being harmed and where is the harmful act occurring?"

"I don't know. But after spending some time in net space, I know that harm *is* occurring, or at least in every way that matters."

"And to some people, it matters so much, they're gonna use a net space killing as justification for a real space killing."

Eric lifted his own helpless hands.

"And why's your friend so dead-set on homicide anyway?"

"He feels it's right. But if he pulls it off, people are going to freak out and scream for bot genocide. And that's completely uncalled for when one bot does something stupid. Bots should be judged individually for whatever they're individually responsible for."

Kim smiled wide.

"What?"

"Oh, nothing. I just think it's crazy that *you* see bots this way."

He returned her gesture. "I just needed the right person to alter my perspective."

"Apparently. And I'm glad for it." She took a breath and went on. "So, what's the plan?"

"Go back in and save Alice. And speaking of which, what avatars do you have?"

"A wide variety. You said vintage L.A., right? 1950's?"

"That's right."

Kim looked up. "Bonnie and Clyde? Nah. Too early. James and Mary? Hmm. That might work."

"As in James Dean and Mary Tyler Moore?"

"That would be them."

He considered this and nodded. "Yeah. That just about fits the bill. I'll go ahead and take James."

"Good. I'll be Mary."

"Wait. What?"

"What do you mean *what?* I'm going with you."

"Listen, I appreciate it but—"

"But you need my help."

He hesitated.

"How long have you been using Alternate Reality?" Kim followed.

"About four days."

"I've been using it about four years. Plus, you're going up against a killer from the Keepers, and a bot with murder on his mind and nothing to lose. And you, my dearest of friends, are the genius who embarked on this mission by using a university computer and your goddamn username and password."

Eric ground his real space teeth. He needed to start a new life in a new world, if only to never hear about that colossal blunder again.

"And," Kim continued, "we're using my avatars. So, yeah. I'm coming with you. And one more thing. Try not to get us killed."

He chuckled. "You know, I don't think James Dean would've put up with this kind of treatment."

"Yeah, well, these are the updated versions. The original Mary Tyler Moore didn't slay monsters in online death battles either. This one does." Kim stood. "So, come on. Let's go rescue your damsel in distress."

He nodded. "Alright then. Let's do it."

Kim walked back to their room, and half a minute later, she reemerged with two pairs of glossy black immersion sets. He took a pair, and while they looked stylish enough, they lacked the seriousness of bulkier equipment.

"These don't look like anything special," he said, turning over the one in his hand.

"Sugar pie, relax. These babies are Vertech 6100s. They'll give you all the immersion you can handle and then some."

He reexamined the gear. "You have *Vertech* immersion sets? How can you afford these?"

"I can't. But my university can." Kim grinned. "And I need these for school... and stuff." Still grinning, she started back towards their room. "Send me your apartment address in L.A. Confidential and I'll plug us in."

He put on the glasses and nodded, doing so at the stunning graphical fidelity and lightning fast response. He logged into Alternate Reality and sent Kim his apartment address in a private message. Five seconds later, a pop-up appeared.

Kim-odo Dragon has sent you an avatar invite. Would you like to accept?

He clicked *yes* and his world went black.

Chapter 26

L.A. Confidential

Eric opened his eyes and found himself standing inside his 1950's L.A. apartment. When his vision focused, he took in the now familiar setting but immediately noted his foreign body. It wasn't awkward, just different, a bit taller and slightly thicker.

He lifted his hands and examined their unfamiliar features. With a small smile, he lightly touched his equally unacquainted facial features, then moved his digits up and over his hair. He stretched out his smile after finding a thick mop brimming with stylish volume.

His new character couldn't be smoother or more attractive, something he knew despite not having seen himself. But that wasn't necessary. He was now James Dean, an iconic figure in American cultural history. And apparently, someone else was equally impressed.

An endearing whistle blew behind him, and after turning, he spotted none other than Mary Tyler Moore. Mary wore a cream-white one-piece dress, white shoes, and a white headband that nestled into her puff of rounding hair. She also wore pink lipstick and eye shadow, both of which played perfectly with her rosy cheeks. All in all, she beamed style and elegance.

"Hey, good looking," she greeted in a soft and sultry voice.

James didn't waste time becoming his character. He donned an arrogant look of boredom and popped the lapels on his leather jacket, producing a satisfying *snap*. Next, he settled the lapels onto his white t-shirt, fussed unnecessarily with his God-like hair, and causally eyed his dark denim jeans and black boots. "This is even better than Lana!"

Eyes widened, he looked up at the sound of his unfamiliar voice.

Mary smirked. "Keep it together, Mr. Dean." She approached and evaluated him. "Yup. Someone loves tech."

"Can you blame me?"

"I'm blaming you for not joining the party sooner." With a satisfied nod, she focused on his movie star face. "Should we get going?"

"Yeah, but give me a second." James looked around the apartment, considering what to bring. After recalling his knives, he started for the kitchen.

"Hey," Mary called out, "you might want this."

He stopped and turned back.

Mary produced a pistol from her purse and extended it. He took the piece and examined the weapon. It was beautiful, light and compact with a black finish and black handle. It reminded him of the signature weapon James Bond carried.

The perfect gift for a spy.

He slipped the firearm into his jacket pocket and looked up.

Mary furrowed her face. "James, dear. Do you know how to use that?"

His face grew warm. "Not exactly."

Mary cast some reassurance. "It's loaded but not ready to fire. You need to chamber a round first. Here, do this."

Now actually glad that Mary came along, he followed her instructions, first by pinching the pistol's back end and pulling the frame rearward. This exposed the firearm's inner workings, along with live rounds held by a magazine. With the slide all the way back, he released it, letting the compressed spring slam the frame forward. This made the all too familiar *click-clack* as the weapon cycled through its action sequence. He looked up.

"Check the safety."

He flipped the weapon and found the thumb-latch safety switch. While working the switch up and down, he noted a red dot appear when lowered. "Red means ready?"

"Red means ready."

Nodding, he placed the weapon on safe, slipped it back into his jacket, and looked up once more. "What about you?"

Mary grinned while tapping the side of her purse.

They exited the apartment, and while standing on the second story walkway, Mary walked to the metal railing.

"Very nice," she said, using her nail to scrape the bar. "Lots of detail here. Whoever made this world put in lots of effort."

"You've never been here before?"

"Not this world, no."

"Then why these avatars?"

She looked over. "You know that old movie *Grease*?"

"Yeah."

"There's a world for that."

He chuckled.

As they descended the stairs and started down the street, Mary glanced over. "So what's our strategy?"

"Head to the library and see if Alice is there. If she is, I'll tell her what's going on and we'll jump out."

"And if she's not?"

"Try her apartment. I just hope she's at either location because our last option is paying Victor a visit."

"You know where he stays?"

James nodded. "Victor gave me and Alice his address when he invited us over for wine, dinner, and a double homicide."

"What?"

"He also wanted to kill Lana, thereby outdoing himself by having two victims in one sitting."

Mary narrowed her eyes. "Oh, fucking hell, how I *wish* he would try that with me."

He looked over.

"Sorry. I just..."

"It's cool. I feel the same way."

Mary drew in air and continued. "Alright, so if we come across Alice, what are you gonna say?"

"I told you. I'm gonna tell her what's going on."

"Wait. You mean everything, everything?"

"Well, yeah. Alice has to believe me, and giving her all the story details is the only way that'll happen. It won't be enough to simply say she's in danger and to stay hidden until it's safe to come out."

Mary hesitated. "So you're even gonna tell her about your real space self?"

"Why not? I don't have anything to hide. Besides, telling her who Lana really is, and why she came to meet her, is a key part of the story." After a moment with no response, he continued. "Should I not tell her who I am?"

"From my experience, exposing your real self usually doesn't go over very well."

"Why not?"

"Because when someone finds out that the truth is radically different from what they originally thought, it can make them feel deceived."

"Okay, this is virtual reality and everyone here is an avatar. So as far as truth goes..."

"Right, but what you see is important. I mean, imagine finding out that Alice is a heavy-set male."

He jerked his head backward. "Oh. Now I see your point."

"Yeah. It's kind of the unwritten rule that you're supposed to stay in character. So if Alice finds out that Lana is a man—one that's been using her for an ulterior motive—she might not be happy about that."

"True, but if Alice isn't murdered because of this, she shouldn't be quite as pissed."

"Trust me. She still has plenty of reason to be pissed. If *I* were used as live bait to lure out the big bad wolf, I sure as hell would be."

"That's one way of putting it."

Mary shot him a look.

"Alright. That's a very accurate way of putting it. But that's why I'm here—to make things right. Or at least try."

Mary gave him a friendly elbow. "I know." Some steps later, she gestured with her digital chin. "Is that the library?"

"That's it. Wait for me outside?"

"I'll be right here."

They stopped at the library's steps, where he took a deep breath and patted his jacket for the pistol.

"Hey," Mary said. "Would you relax? You look like you're getting ready to rob the damn place."

He looked over and nodded. Then after clearing his throat, he started up the steps.

Once inside, he scanned for Alice but only spotted Mr. Miller. That wasn't who he wanted, but maybe the library supervisor could save him some time.

"Excuse me?" he called out, approaching the stocky librarian.

Miller turned on his stumpy leg. "Yes, sir? How can I help you?"

"I was looking for an employee—Alice. Have you by chance seen her?"

Miller's lower lip started quivering. "Alice? Um. I saw her leave a short while ago... with someone. I'd say you missed her by about half an hour."

He mentally cursed. "Would you happen to know with who?"

"I'm so sorry, but I'm not entirely sure."

Why was Miller so nervous? In an attempt to reassure the librarian, James put on a friendly face. "If she left with another man, that's perfectly okay. More than likely it's my friend Victor. We work together at the metal factory."

Miller flushed with relief. "I'm so sorry. I wasn't sure who you were and I didn't want to implicate Alice in anything."

James waved away any need for an apology.

"To tell you the truth," Miller continued, "I believe it *was* Victor. But again, he was in and out really quick so I didn't get a good look."

"No problem. I know where to meet them. Thanks for your time."

"Sure thing."

James turned and started for the exit.

"Well?" Mary asked him outside.

He shook his head while descending the library steps. "Bad news. She's gone. I spoke with the supervisor and he said Alice left with somebody. He didn't say who, but I'm guessing it was Victor."

"Shit. So are we bypassing her apartment?"

He hesitated for a second. "Yeah. Let's go see the wolf."

***

James took a breath as they rounded onto Bishop St, hoping to calm his nerves. He only partially succeeded.

"Alright," Mary said. "How do you wanna play this?"

"Knock on his door, I guess."

She looked over. "Are you kidding?"

"You have any better ideas?"

"Nothing concrete, but whatever we come up with, it shouldn't include letting Victor know we're here. Knocking on his door kinda goes against that."

He considered this. "You're right. Other than befriending his targets, Victor keeps to himself, so two strangers knocking on his door will look suspicious." After a few steps he continued. "Okay, his place is just up the street. When we get there, we'll casually look around to establish their presence, and *then* we'll come up with a plan."

"That'll work."

They reached the Paradise Apartments, both grateful to find the area mostly deserted. Some people milled around in the park across the street, but other than that, nothing.

"Okay," he said, stopping at the apartment stairs. "Stay here and keep an eye out. I'll head up. If anything happens, cough a few times. That'll be my signal to get out of there."

Mary nodded, and he started up the stairs.

"Hey!" she whispered.

Pausing, he looked back.

"Don't forget about your safety!" Mary pointed towards the pistol in his jacket.

"I know," he replied before resuming his route, now truly thankful that Mary came along, as he already forgot about that damn safety switch.

Cresting the stairs, he started down the walkway and slowed after nearing the destination.

Room 213. There it is.

He spotted an outward facing window and made sure to stay clear of it. Now at the door, he placed his ear against the faded brown wood and listened.

Nothing.

Moving his head back, he tried to glance through the outward facing window.

Nothing.

With the blinds shut, seeing inside was impossible. After some muttering, he spun and started back towards the stairs. As he descended the steps, Mary turned and put up both hands, silently asking for an explanation. He held up one finger, silently asking for time. She nodded and turned back towards the street.

He wanted to sweep the area so he worked his way between the Paradise Apartments and the adjacent complex. Not long after, he exited into a parking lot where he found a few classic cars but no sign of his targets.

"Shit."

He started back towards the main street, stopping midway down the corridor where he looked up towards Victor's room. Could he break inside? If he could just sneak in there and gather some clues, he could—

Click.

He froze. It was the all too familiar sound, the hammer moving back on a pistol, readying it to fire. He then spotted a shadowy figure in his periphery, but he didn't turn towards the person. Instead, he slowly raised both hands.

"You better tell me who the fuck you are," the shadow growled.

James recognized the voice. "Mike," he responded, still not turning to prevent startling him. "Mike, put your goddamn gun down."

The shadow readjusted his grip on his weapon. "What the fuck did you just call me?"

"Relax," James said. "Okay? Relax."

He slowly turned, and like the first time they met in this world, Mike bore his pistol on his chest. But unlike that encounter, Mike now had a pistol aimed at him, one held by Mary Tyler Moore, and Mike didn't realize this. With Mike's hyper-focus on him, he never noticed Mary sneak up from behind.

"I said," Mike repeated, "what the fuck did you just call me?"

Mary kept her muzzle inches from Mike's head, but she didn't look down her sights. She stared at him. Why? Then when she shrugged her shoulders, James parted his lips. Mary was asking if she should fire a bullet into this person's skull. To answer, he quickly shook his head.

Mike narrowed his eyes, likely as he caught on that someone stood behind him. When he slowly looked over, he faced the ominous black hole of a massive .45-caliber handgun.

"Arvin," James said. "Arvin, it's me. It's Eric Ryan."

Mike looked back, lifted a shaky hand off his gun, and pointed at Mary. "And her?"

"That's my girlfriend, Kim."

Mary snapped back her .45's hammer. "You wanna lower your pistol away from my James Dean, sport?"

Mike slowly nodded and lowered his weapon. Mary followed suit by moving her gun's hammer forward and lowering it as well. Mike then placed a hand over his heaving chest, turned towards James, and tried to speak without success.

James noticed his struggles, so he lifted a calming hand and turned to Mary. "Kim, this is Mike, the avatar of Arvin, my bot client." He looked to Mike. "Mike, this is Mary Tyler Moore, the avatar of Kim, my girlfriend."

Mike turned to her. "Well, Eric's mentioned you before. It's so nice to finally meet you in person."

Mary smiled. "He mentioned you as well. And believe me, the pleasure's all mine."

With introductions out of the way, James figured it was time to explain why they all stood here, guns drawn.

"Well, boys," Mary said before he could open his mouth. "I don't know about you, but I could use a drink."

James looked to Mike and shrugged.

Mike took a deep breath, slipped his pistol into his holster, and turned to Mary. "I know of a good Irish pub. It's just around the corner."

Chapter 27

Back at The Clover, James, Mary, and Mike waited for their drinks—James and Mary on one side of their booth, and the robot on the other.

"So," Mike said, "what brings you two around here?"

"We're here to warn Alice," James responded. "Or more to the point, I'm here to warn Alice. Mary came along because she offered to help."

Mike nodded.

"I know you didn't want that," James continued. "And I'm sorry if that pisses you off. But I have to do this irrespective of the consequences."

Mike turned to Mary. "You know, when he really wants something, it's amazing how stubborn he can be."

Mary grinned. "You have no idea."

Mike grinned back and turned to James. "So how successful were you?"

"Not very. We stopped by the library to warn Alice but she wasn't there. The supervisor said I missed her by thirty minutes, and that she left with some man. I figured it was Victor so we went over to his place. That's when we came across you."

"And to what lengths are you willing to go in order to stop me?"

James paused for effect. "Whatever it takes."

"That serious, huh?"

James nodded. "I can't let it happen, Mike. I can't let Victor knife Alice to death and plaster that shit on the net, adding ridicule to an already horrific experience. And if you think I lost objectivity because I got too close to the target, you're right. But what's also true is that Alice isn't just some goddamn target. She's a human being, like *you* and *me*."

Mary perked up at this.

"Well," Mike responded, "I can't say this surprises me. And like we talked about earlier, your dedication is actually something positive. It makes you a lot less like Chad Vale, and a lot more like the Eric Ryan we all know and love."

James and Mary smiled.

"You know what," James went on, "there's something I don't understand. If you didn't want me involved in this, why did you tell me about your suspicions about Chad?"

"I was thinking ahead. After I completed the final act, I knew you would search around for explanations to my actions. I wanted to assist by providing some context." Mike softly laughed. "I never thought you would get so knee-deep in this. Hell. I never thought I would actually see you here." He shook his head. "I couldn't believe it when I did—seeing you walk up to Victor's apartment in that ridiculous avatar of—"

"Alright," the waitress interrupted. "Here we are. Two pints of Guinness for the gentlemen, and an Annie's Irish Red for the lady. If you all need anything else, jus' let me know." She beamed some cheer and headed off.

Mary grabbed her long-necked bottle and turned to the bot. "So, Mike, have you given any thought to what's gonna happen afterwards? And I'm not just talking about tonight, but after your *final act*."

"Of course."

"And you think people will understand your motives if you provide them with context?"

Mike nodded.

"Well, I hate to break it to you, but you don't stand a snowball's chance in hell of succeeding."

Mike smirked. "And why not?"

"Because you're a bot."

Still smirking, Mike shrugged.

"You're a bot," she repeated, doing so with some force. "You are *not* human."

Mike didn't shrug this off. Suddenly, things became tense. And James, fearing these two might again pull their pistols, was about to raise calming hands.

"You're not," Mary said while leaning in. "You're more than human—more advanced. You don't warrant the human title because that title isn't good enough for you. That would be like calling us—" she gestured towards her and James— "primates. Are we technically primates? Sure. For matters of taxonomy, fine. But in practice, fuck no. That's an insult. We're light-years beyond our primate relatives just like you're light-years beyond us."

Mike listened intently, sipping his drink.

"Humans are at their end," she continued. "We're at the end of our leg on the evolutionary relay race and *you* take the baton from here. That said, you really think that humans, who are still running the show, will hear you out if you kill one of their own? They're too scared for that. And *why* are they scared? Because bots are supplanting them as the Earth's dominant species." She leaned in farther, placing both elbows on the table. "But you already know this, don't you? Tell me, how often do you conceal your abilities in real space? Are you one of those bots who secretly grumbles because they have to act human-like? You know, use baby talk with us?"

James narrowed his eyes. "It's true," he told Mike, "isn't it? You don't think and operate like humans, even though that's what it looks like." With no response coming, he continued. "So how do you operate? How powerful is that neural chip of yours?"

Mike took another sip. "Let's just say that if I wanted to tell someone like me everything we did over the past week, I could tell them in a few seconds."

James jerked back. "Holy shit." He turned to Mary. "You know, I did find him strange at times, like when he read an entire page of text in half a second."

Mary arched her brow. "Really? That's pretty good." She turned back towards the bot. "So what else can you do?"

"I can mop a floor like nobody's business. And wiping down dusty shelves? Forget about it. Oh, and when I'm done cleaning, I moonlight as a justice-seeking vigilante."

James and Mary chuckled.

"C'mon, Mike," Mary continued. "People won't see your murder as pretty good, all things considered. They're gonna see it as an existential threat and fight back. However, you *can* make Chad pay without taking such drastic measures."

"How?"

"By using what you have. By using what's never existed before—one of these murdering bastards' identities." Mary went on. "Everyone knows that net space murders aren't illegal, but there's a reason why net space murderers keep their identities hidden. In short, they want to avoid the shit storm of retribution they would face if found out. Trust me. If you disclose this creep's identity, his suffering would be unreal."

Mike worked his jaw. "How could we pull this off?"

Mary turned to James. "By filming the murder ourselves."

James turned to her. "Excuse me?"

"Look," Mary told him. "In reality, every murder video on Crypt Keeper could be fake. However, there's a way we can record this murder, say who's behind it, and verify the footage as real. That's by filming the murder ourselves and including authenticators."

"Authenticators?" Mike asked.

"Because faking vids is so easy," she explained, "people developed what're known as authenticators. Essentially, they're codes embedded into video files that serve as seals of approval. If we stamp our footage with them, that's all the credibility we need."

"Goddammit," James interjected. "So we're right back to where we started?"

"No," Mary told him. "We are *not* back to where we started. The original plan ended in a real space murder. But if this is the new plan, that murder is off the table because this plan requires letting the perp live so he can suffer." She turned to Mike. "Right? If we implement this plan, nobody gets real space wiped?"

Mike let a long moment pass and finally nodded. "Okay. I'm good with that. So what did you have in mind?"

"Alright, with the hit scheduled for tonight, I need to set up recorders in the perp's apartment. Because he's probably still out, now's the perfect time. As for the victim, we need to make sure she walks into the trap, because we probably won't get another shot at this."

"Why not?" Mike asked.

"Because I'm gonna stick cameras all over the place. And while the cameras are small, they're not *that* small."

Mike nodded. "So the longer she's in there without being killed, the more time Victor has to stumble across your gear."

"Exactly. And I do have to put the cameras everywhere because we don't know where in the apartment it's gonna happen."

James looked away and shook his head.

"We need to find Victor and Alice," Mike went on, "and keep tabs on them while you're setting up your cameras."

"Good idea," Mary responded. "You two split up, head to opposite ends of the city, and work your way back to his apartment. Unless—" she turned to James— "unless you already know where to look."

He pursed his lips. Just how was he back to facilitating Alice's grisly demise?

"James," Mary prodded. "You with us? We don't have a lot of time here."

"Dominique's," he growled, looking back but facing the table.

"The Italian joint you told me about?"

"Yeah. They go there all the time."

Mary nodded. "Alright, you two head there. I'll go back to his apartment and start prepping."

She and Mike got up to leave.

"And what about Alice?" James shot out. After Mary and Mike reseated themselves, he continued. "Obviously, she doesn't get a say in this, right? She's just a pawn after all." He shot looks between them. "Right? We're all in agreement about that? That we're just using her? That we're gonna let that sick fucking maniac murder her? That she's gonna be stabbed to death for the greater good?"

"You want me to sit in for her?" Mary asked. "I can copy her avatar and take her place. It won't be hard. I just need to see her in person."

James again looked away.

"He really told you everything," Mike said, "didn't he?"

"Everything?" Mary asked.

"Eric volunteered to take the murder on Alice's behalf. He was going to have his Lana character killed so Alice wouldn't endure this."

Mary turned to James but spoke to Mike. "No. He failed to mention that part." She focused all her attention on her friend. "Look, this is a shitty situation all around. Nothing good will come from it. In an ideal world, we wouldn't even be here. But this isn't an ideal world. In the world we live in, assholes like that murdering psycho exist, so we have to do what we can, when we can. And right here, right now, we can do something. We can show these creeps that they aren't safe—that we can find them out. And when we do, there's gonna be hell to pay. But we can't do that unless... unless an innocent gets hurt in the process."

Mary and Mike polished off their drinks. James took a long pull from his glass and nodded to himself. Mary was right. Nothing good would come from this. A deep breath later, he finished his drink and was the first of their group to stand.

Outside of The Clover, James and the group verbally repeated their assignments. With their efforts synchronized, Mary opened a chat box with James to establish a communication line. She started for Victor's apartment but stopped after a few steps and turned.

"Hey," she called to James.

He looked over and found her standing there, a small smile creasing her face.

"Don't forget about your safety."

He smiled back.

His decision to reenter hadn't turned out as intended, but Mary made this easier. That wasn't surprising because she had always been a source of comfort when things grew difficult. She also kept him focused, which was equally important, since he again forgot about that damn safety switch.

Chapter 28

James walked with Mike towards Domonique's, and like many times before, he took in the setting sun as it painted orange streaks across the digital skyline.

"Don't forget about your safety?" Mike asked.

James looked over. "In case you haven't noticed, I'm not exactly a highly trained covert operative. Mary surmised this after handing me this pistol—" he patted his jacket— "and she realized I had no damn clue how to use it."

"So she taught you?"

"Pretty much. I haven't fired it, but as I understand it, I just need to flip the safety switch and pull the trigger. That's why she told me don't forget about your safety."

Mike nodded. "That's good that she showed you. Who knows? We might come to need it."

"You still have yours. And I know this because you pulled it on me. *Again.*"

Mike grinned. "Sorry about that. Greeting you with that thing is becoming a habit."

James shook his head. "I don't know why you pack heat in the first place. When it comes to violence, you should pay tribute to your roots and crush-kill-destroy."

Mike chuckled.

"So," James went on, "what did you think of what Mary said—about you being more than human?"

"She's dead right."

James gave another headshake.

"Alright. I'm joking, but not entirely. In a lot of ways, she *is* right. I can register information that humans can't, process information much faster, and do both with ease. But at the same time, I'm not some God-like creature walking amongst mere mortals. What I can do is actually normal."

"Normal for your kind, right?"

"Exactly. Look, what I'm trying to say is that I'm not unique. To illustrate, I think her human-to-primate comparison works well. I mean, do humans get all high and mighty around chimps and consider themselves master race deities? Of course not. They just understand that humans and chimps are different and go on about their business."

James nodded. "That makes sense. And when you put it like that, it also makes bots seem benign, like they wouldn't go to war with humans because why bother? Just like humans would consider it a waste of time waging war on chimps."

"And that's how robots want humans to see things, though that's easier said than done."

"What do you expect? We humans are an arrogant bunch. Stubborn as hell, too."

"The blessing and the curse." After some steps, Mike likewise looked across the orangey cityscape. "It may be hard for you to comprehend how bots think and operate, but in time, you will."

"What do you mean?"

"Humans will have our abilities soon enough, if you want them, of course. This might not happen for another few decades, but certainly within this century."

"What makes you so sure?"

Mike let a moment pass. "Because we're going to give them to you."

James snapped sideways.

"Oh, don't look so surprised," Mike said, meeting his gaze. "This has been happening for a while now—humans infusing electrical components into themselves. It's going to continue but at a much faster rate. And how fast depends on how much we decide to assist."

James stopped walking, making Mike do the same. "Hang on. So machines have the info but refuse to cough it up?"

Mike stepped close. "That's right. And I'll even tell you why. Because humans scare the shit out of us." He crossed his arms. "Do you know why humans have always been so scared of A.I.? It's because they imagine A.I. acting out in human ways. Funny, that's what scares *us*. And speaking of humans that are cause for worry..." He gestured towards the road.

James turned and spotted Dominque's in the distance. They resumed walking, and a minute later, they reached the entrance.

At the front door, Mike grasped the wooden handle but didn't open it just yet. "James. Whatever happens tonight... don't forget about your safety." He pulled open the door.

James stared for a second, then walked inside muttering curses on behalf of his species.

***

A short distance away, Mary curled up her lips while walking down Bishop St. With this mission unfolding in a tech-free world, breaking into Victor's apartment should be easy as digital pie. A few minutes later, she reached her destination but didn't move in just yet. She first sent James a message.

Mary:
Hey. I'm outside of Victor's place, but I'd rather hold tight until you confirm their whereabouts. Any sign of them?

James:
Mike and I just got to the restaurant. We're sitting down now.

Mary:
Okay. I'll stay put until you confirm.

James:
That was easy. They're both here and in the middle of dinner. You should be good on time.

Mary:
Got it. I'll get to work. Message me if anything happens.

James:
Hey, wait.

Mary:
Yeah?

She received a picture from James, one taken from his and Mike's table, and which showed Victor and Alice at their table.

Mary:
That's them, huh? Good thinking!

James:
You know me!

Mary twisted her lips. No doubt it was the bot's idea, but she decided against accusing James of plagiarism. Instead, she minimized the screen and cautiously ascended the stairs.

She slowed while approaching room 213, and after reaching the weathered door, she glanced around to verify seclusion. With nobody present, she knelt and examined the lock.

Too easy.

She brought up her online inventory, pulled a few metal picks, and inserted her tools. A couple twists and prods later, her pick came to rest on the locking latch. She cranked over the latch until it clicked open, stood and slipped inside.

She stayed just within the apartment, refraining from moving in. First, she retrieved a camera from her inventory and started snapping pictures, intending to do so in every room. She would have to disturb items while setting up her recorders, so she needed to reposition everything as before, hence these photographic templates. With every room photographed, she put away the camera and returned to the living room.

She scanned above for hiding spots, knowing that elevated positions would cover larger areas.

"Air vents. Perfect."

She slid a chair towards the first of three vents, climbed atop and pulled a screwdriver. But while unwinding the screws, she looked up and froze.

"Son of a bitch," she growled, darting away from the camera already placed inside.

Climbing down from the chair, she went to her purse and retrieved a mirror compact. After clambering back up, she flipped open the compact and slowly moved it in front of the vent. She assessed the camera through the mirror and found the recorder non-operational. Then a *ping* alerted her of an incoming message.

James:
Are you done? Victor just called over the waiter. He might be ordering desert or asking for the check.

Mary:
I'm still setting up my gear. But shit. This bastard has cameras stashed in all the good spots. I need more time.

James:
Dammit. How much... wait.

James:
Ah, hell. Whatever you need to do, do it fast. Victor and Alice are getting up to leave. I don't know if they're going back to his apartment but just assume they are. That said, you have a few minutes at best.

Mary:
Got it. I'm on it.

No question, she dared not place her recorders alongside Victor's. There was too great a possibility he would check his gear before the show started. So, she planned to hide her equipment in plain sight, inside of ordinary items that didn't warrant special attention. Hopefully, neither Victor nor Alice would examine these commonplace objects with unusual levels of scrutiny.

She embedded her cameras inside the television set, the clocks, the radios and picture frames, anything that exuded normality and blended quietly into the background. As she worked, another *ping* rang in her ear.

James:
They just got into a taxi. They'll be there any minute. Just make sure each room has one camera and get out!

She didn't respond despite having placed her last recorder. She still needed to ensure their operability, so she activated the cameras and breathed immense relief. Every feed came through strong. However, she again didn't respond because she still had to embed the authenticators into the camera feeds.

She started the authentication process, and while watching the progress update screen, she bit her virtual nails. On the screen, an empty meter filled with blue fluid at excruciating speeds. She looked underneath the meter at text describing the progress, but that only drove her closer to digital delirium.

Authenticating data feeds. Please wait...

Authenticating data feeds. Please wait...

"Oh, for fuck's sake!"

Authenticating data feeds. Please wait...

Data feeds authenticated.

She bolted through the apartment, looking around to ensure she repositioned everything. She also scanned for her gear to prevent leaving anything behind. The check was messy but there was no time for thoroughness, a notion that reasserted itself with another *ping*.

James:
Hey! You there?? Did you get my last message???

Mary:
I'm done. I'm out.

She exited Victor's apartment, closed the door and checked the knob. With the door secure, she started hustling downstairs, but almost immediately slowed. A taxicab just halted along the sidewalk, and Alice and Victor exited, both looking in her direction. She mentally cursed as her only available route led directly by them. Outwardly, however, she smiled politely while reminding herself that Alice and Victor didn't know her. That didn't ease her pulsing nerves, not with Alice and Victor staring so intently.

She wanted to quicken her pace but that would raise suspicion. Instead, she smiled wider and nonchalantly moved her hand into her purse, wrapping it around her semi-auto.

Alice pointed. "Wait! Mary Tyler Moore, right?"

"Yeah, yeah," Victor chimed in. "Mary Tyler Moore, right?"

Mary giggled, lifted her hand off her .45, and pushed up her volume-filled hair. "Very good eye."

Merriment all around, Alice and Victor continued past her, and she started across the street, cursing under her breath. When she reached the other side of the divide, two men materialized in the park, both jogging in her direction. The men quickly morphed into James and Mike, and she raised her hand, halting them just inside the park.

"Look over my shoulder," she said while approaching. "Did they go up upstairs?"

James leaned sideways. "They're outside of Victor's room. Now he's opening the door. Now they're in."

She stopped and faced the grass. "Alright. I'm accessing the cameras." As James and Mike stared holes into her, she wanted to offer them an update. Instead, she jerked up and started walking. "Shit! Let's go. *Let's go!*"

"What happened?" James whispered as they started moving.

"Nothing happened. They're coming out."

"What do you mean nothing happened?"

"They just went inside to get overcoats. I'm turning off the recorders."

As the three of them pushed deeper into the park, trees began obscuring Victor's apartment.

Mike took a final glance backwards. "Yeah. Alice and Victor are out. And with the taxicab gone, they're heading to their destination on foot."

Mary stopped. "Alright. You two follow them and keep me posted. I'm pulling out. They already saw me once, and if I run into them again, that'll be odd. I'll work the cameras from real space. Cool?"

Both men nodded, and she raised her hands towards her temples.

***

Kim removed her Vertechs and blinked a few times, watching as the ceiling came into focus. Now back in reality, she eased herself off the bed and started for the living room.

She voice-activated her computer while entering, veered to the kitchen, and opened the refrigerator. Grabbing a bottle of green tea, she entered the living room and nestled herself onto the couch, her computer screen powered and waiting.

She grabbed the bluish window, brought up the camera feeds, and moved the images off screen. After increasing their sizes, she pasted the images against the far wall and analyzed the feeds. Everything looked good. The cameras covered every room inside Victor's apartment and dead space was nearly nonexistent. With that, she retrieved her screen and brought up her chat window with James.

Kim-odo Dragon:
Talk to me, Goose.

James:
Mike and I are back at The Clover and we're observing Victor and Alice from across the room. I guess we'll just nurse drinks until they're done.

Kim-odo Dragon:
Got it. I'm in the living room with the camera feeds against the wall. And the whole apartment is covered, so if anything happens, we'll get it. And what's the asshole's name again?

James:
Chad Vale. Why?

Kim-odo Dragon:
You remember how our plan is to publicly tar and feather the bastard? Well since I'm just sitting here, I might as well get started.

James:
Don't pull any punches.

Kim-odo Dragon:
I won't. And one more thing. Have Mike send me a link to his bot data file, and tell him I need full access to everything, not just public information. And if there's firewalls, encryption, anything like that, tell him to disable it.

James:
I just told him. Mike said he doesn't have a problem with that, but he would like to know why you want it.

Kim-odo Dragon:
To save his life.

Chapter 29

L.A. Confidential

James tightened his lips while staring at Victor. Here at The Clover, Victor sat in a distant booth with Alice, the murderer laughing it up. After Victor gave another raucous chortle, James considered pulling his pistol, strolling over there, and—

"You okay?" Mike asked.

James shifted his stare towards his friend. Mike stifled amusement.

"Mary said he has cameras everywhere," James followed, his vision losing focus. "...stashed in all the good hiding spots. Why do you think that is?" He looked back towards Victor. "It's because he's gonna kill her tonight... and we're gonna *fucking* let him."

"We're gonna let him because that's part of our plan."

"I know," James fired back, immediately regretting his delivery. He took a breath. "Look, I'm not going to sabotage our new plan. I'm just a little pissed right now, and I'm sure you can guess why." Leaning back, he kept his fingers coiled around his drink, which he still hadn't sipped. "I just can't believe this. I can't believe I'm back in the same goddamn position, orchestrating Alice's death."

Mike sipped his half-full glass. "If you want to leave, that shouldn't be a problem."

James looked up without responding.

"Really. Our plan no longer requires you being here. The recorders are ready and we've identified the targets. The only thing left is tailing them back to Victor's apartment, which I can do on my own. When they get close, I'll send Kim a warning and she has it from there."

James looked down towards his drink. Mike was right. He didn't have to stay. But should he leave? Should he head back to real space and wait this all out? The thought initially tempted him but it quickly soured. Maybe he needed to watch Victor murder Alice. Maybe he needed to suffer through this, so that way, he could say Alice didn't suffer alone.

"I'm staying," he finally answered. "I need to be involved in this... to the end."

Mike nodded.

James finally lifted his glass and sipped, the cool thick liquids not having their usual effect. He took another swallow all the same. "And how are *you* doing?"

"Fine. Why do you ask?"

"You're fine? With your original plan scrapped, I figured you would be pulling your hair out. After all, I know how set you were on—" James jerked his head towards Victor's table and ran a finger across his throat.

Mike chuckled. "Chad's final farewell. Oh, how I wanted to attend that going away party."

"You know, I tried numerous times to change your mind about that, and you put up a fight that would've made Patton proud. And now with your plan reversed, you're not upset?"

"Not after considering what Mary said. She helped me realize what would happen if I actually went through with it. She made me realize that my actions would extend far beyond the Vale Estate." Mike took a sip. "I just wanted payback so bad I could taste it, gustatory cortex or not. But I'm glad Mary came along. I needed someone to point out that my actions were..."

"Blindingly stupid?"

Mike eyed him. "Overly ambitious."

James turned up his lips. "You're flawed, Mike. Flawed. So who knows? Maybe you're more human than anything after all."

Mike raised his glass in salute. "And this new plan *is* a decent substitute, all things considered."

"Yeah. After we expose Victor, I imagine scores of victims looking for revenge. But what if that doesn't happen? What if the outcome falls short of our expectations?"

Mike jerked his head towards Victor's table and ran a finger across his throat.

James smirked. "For what it's worth, I'm glad you changed your mind about that. It must be hard not seeing Chad get his due, but you're sacrificing this for the sake of others. I mean, how many bots will owe you their lives for you not going through with it? It's just too bad they'll never know what you sacrificed because you sacrificed a lot."

Mike nodded, sipped, and eased his glass down. "You know what's so peculiar about all this? How pissed Dr. Vale would be for me doing any of it. And deep down, I'm not happy with it either."

"Cognitive dissonance?"

"Human," Mike corrected. "Although, I'm starting to think the terms are interchangeable. Hell. Maybe self-deception *is* the key human ingredient."

"You might be right about that. Case in point, right now I wanna pull out my pistol, walk over to Victor's table, and fire a bullet into his skull. And who can stop me? Nobody. So why aren't I doing this?"

"Because you're stopping yourself. And let me guess. You're doing so with self-deception, half-baked justifications, and cognitive distortions?"

Now James raised *his* glass. "To being human."

They clinked glasses and took long swallows. With their drinks on the table, they eased back and soaked in the humming atmosphere.

As James did so, he concluded to stay in this world, where oddly enough, humans could exist in ways organic to their original design. But why? Why did he possess this desire to begin with? Was he searching for something? Perhaps he wanted a deeper understanding of what being human meant. If so, what better place than here? After all, how many truths had virtual reality exposed about himself? And what was more, he had only been here for a week. So what might he learn in a month, a year, a lifetime? What would he learn as he—

"James," Mike said.

Snapped from his reverie, James refocused on Mike who was eyeing Victor. He looked in the same direction and spotted the couple getting up to leave. "Damn, that was a quick outing."

"Quick or not, let's get ready to move."

James did exactly that by polishing off his drink. All the while, he kept an eye on the couple, watching as they ambled towards the exit. However, they stopped just short of the door.

Alice broke off towards the rear of the pub, perhaps to go powder her digital nose. Victor halted by the bar.

James kept observing Victor, focusing on his hands that fidgeted in odd ways. After a moment, he figured out why. Victor was typing on a virtual keyboard. When Victor finished, he looked up and continued waiting, a devilish grin sneaked across his face. This prompted James to bring out his own keyboard.

James:
Kim, you there?

Kim-odo Dragon:
I'm here. What's up?

He sent Kim his Crypt Keeper username and password, and asked her to access the message boards to see if Hanging Chad posted anything.

Kim-odo Dragon:
Damn. He just put posted a global message, telling everyone to stay tuned because the wolf was out tonight. Well, that's not exactly what he said, but pretty close. Where are you?

After reading the message, James cursed under his breath. In his response, he said that he and Mike just left The Clover and were walking forty feet behind Alice and Victor. He also said that if the targets didn't make any unforeseen stops, it would be about ten minutes before they reached Victor's apartment.

Kim replied saying she was ready.

He and Mike cut through the park, hoping to decrease their chances of detection. True, the park had scores of streetlights, but they provided little illumination. Furthermore, the lights dotted along the cobblestone walkways where James and Mike stayed clear. Instead, they kept on the grass, cloaked in nightfall, and they halted in these shadows after reaching an ideal vantage point of the apartment.

As James observed the murderer and his soon-to-be victim, he narrowed his eyes. It was cold, bitingly cold. Where had summer disappeared to? He didn't know, but a shivering chill filled the vacuum, one that worked up his spine.

He tried to steady his nerves by taking deep breaths. The effort had a negligible effect as Alice moved ever closer to the gates of hell. Now with her just about there, he alerted Kim who quickly acknowledged. With that, he crept toward the apartment.

"Where're you going?" Mike whispered.

"I'm moving in closer."

"For what? Nothing requires you to move in closer. The recorders have it from here. And speaking of which..."

"Kim knows. She's ready."

"Good. Now stay put."

James stopped by a tree and continued observing the apartment, where Alice and Victor eased up the stairs and started down the second-floor walkway. After reaching the front door, Victor opened it and they went inside.

With the couple out of view, he tapped an anxious fist against the tree, stopping after Kim messaged him. He read the missive and turned back to Mike. "Kim sees them. She's recording."

"Good. Now just hang back."

He refocused on the apartment, wondering what was unfolding inside? But did he really want to know? Kim offered him the option by sending the bedroom camera feed where Alice and Victor now were. Grimacing, he opened the feed and linked it to Mike. Now, all three were watching in real time.

In Victor's bedroom, Alice sat on his bed, her arms extended behind her, her palms on the cream-white cover. She faced Victor who casually leaned against a dresser drawer, his right elbow resting on top. With both Alice and Victor calmly conversing, everything seemed uneventful. Then the inevitable happened. As Alice kept talking, Victor slowly turned towards the dresser, and just as slowly, he opened the top drawer. Alice didn't know what this signified, but James did, and it parted his lips.

Victor pulled out an object, one obscured by the shadow cast from his body. To James, that didn't matter because he knew what Victor clutched. Then when the wolf turned, James' lips started quivering.

"Oh, Christ!" he hissed, spotting the same hideous blade from the murder video, its serrated edge like bared teeth.

"James," Mike whispered. "James."

As Victor kept turning, his grip kept tightening around the blade's handle. That was all James could take. He bolted from his position and ran towards the apartment, Mike yelling from behind. All the while, the vid feed projected to his visual field, so when he reached the apartment stairs, he realized he wouldn't make it.

Victor lunged towards Alice, catching her completely unaware. He pinned her down by straddling atop her, and kept her there by clutching her neck. With Alice trapped, he lifted the knife, held it for a half-second, and plunged it into her chest. He repeated the blows, stabbing hard and fast. As he flashed away, Alice tried to scream, but she couldn't with her throat clamped shut. Instead, she whipped around her appendages.

Alice clawed and kicked with all her strength, but that didn't stop the knife from driving into her, so she tried to wriggle out from underneath. When that didn't work, she tried to buck Victor off. Both moves were useless, as Victor was too heavy, too strong, and she was taking massive damage.

The knife continued ramming into her chest, into her stomach, and across arms that hopelessly tried to block the blows. With her body pouring out red fluid, her peach-colored dress turned a ghastly crimson, as blood also arced upward with each successive stab.

James remained at the base of the stairs, white-knuckling the railing. He stood there paralyzed, watching Alice fail to remove her immersion sets in time. Her hands were weakly patting at her temples when her eyes rolled back into her skull and her body went limp. Her avatar experienced full death. She experienced the murder all the way to its gruesome end.

James went supernova with rage. He drew his pistol and bounded up the steps, clearing three at a time. After streaking to room 213, he reared back, kicked the door in, and ran towards the room where Alice just lost her virtual life. He shoulder smashed the bedroom door, bringing up his gun while storming through. Inside, he found Victor kneeling on the bed, covered in blood, confusion and gore streaked across his face.

James stared at Victor, and Victor stared right back. Then Victor brought a hand to his temple. In response, James aimed and pulled the trigger, but nothing happened. The goddamn safety. He rapidly switched it off, aimed once more, and fired.

A deafening *bang* split the room but it was too late. In the time James switched off the safety, Victor removed his sets, resulting in a metal projectile zipping through empty air and punching a harmless hole into the far wall.

"Fuck!" James screamed.

He kept screaming the word as no other descriptor would suffice. After shouting his vocal chords raw, he wanted nothing more than to break everything in this evil, horrid apartment.

He needed to rip the appliances from the walls and shatter them on the floor. He needed to pour gasoline over everything, burn this goddamn place to the ground, and then piss on the ashes. To begin, he stomped towards the living room, planning to ram his foot through the television. But after entering, he halted.

Mike stood there, pistol by his side.

James shook his head, his face full of ache. But he stopped as something was off. Mike wasn't displaying any emotion. He simply stood there, eyes vacant as if nothing existed behind them.

"Mike?" he asked. "Mike."

Nothing.

Mike continued standing there, looking every bit a zombie, when out of nowhere, he disappeared.

"Oh, fuck," James slowly told the silence.

Mike had just returned to real space, where Chad Vale was now located. In all likelihood, Mike returned to hunt down Chad.

Chapter 30

James continued standing inside of Victor Vane's apartment, his troubling notion deepening. Mike returned to real space to rip Chad limb from human limb. That was worrying enough, but then terror shot through when his shoulder suddenly moved. Unable to account for the alien body syndrome, he grunted in frustration while aiming his pistol about. After convulsing again, he slipped his finger over the trigger, ready to empty the magazine in all directions. He held off when a voice called from the heavens.

"Hey!" Kim said. "James!"

***

Eric ripped off his immersion sets and found Kim hovering over him, her hand on his shoulder.

"Where the hell did your friend go?" she asked.

"Shit!" he responded while bolting upright, head spinning from the abrupt change in realities. "I don't know. He jumped out without saying anything."

"Yeah. That's what I saw."

He tried to stand but lost his balance while getting up on rubbery legs.

"Easy!" Kim said, reaching out and lowering him back onto the couch.

As fluids refilled his veins, he spotted the vid feeds pasted along the wall. "Did you see it?"

"All of it. Pretty goddamned sickening."

He nodded. "Did you record it?"

"All of it."

He drew in air, unsure if he was grateful for their success. This was especially true with the bedroom vid feed showing a blood-soaked bed. That made him want to destroy everything— the film, the perpetrator, his memory of the event, everything. But if a time ever existed where emotions needed checking, this was it. One person on their team had already gone off the reservation, and reeling him in would require clear-headedness.

With his senses back online, he took a final breath and stood. "I need to go to the Vale's."

"You can't contact the bot from here?" Kim asked, her fingers drumming on her computer.

"I'm gonna try," he replied, hustling towards the kitchen. "But judging by Arvin's look, something tells me he's offline right now and isn't checking his messages. If so, I need to see him in person."

"Well, I'm done here. So whenever—" Kim cut herself off after glancing over. "You gotta be kidding me."

Eric looked up from the massive knife he clutched. Nodding, he put away the knife and grabbed a meat mallet. With the tenderizer in hand, he looked up and nodded with additional vigor.

Kim twisted her face.

"What?" he asked. "You saw what that sick maniac did to Alice. You think I'm going over there empty-handed?"

"Oh," she responded, her face unwinding into a smile. "I thought you were getting ready for a showdown with the bot."

He rolled his eyes.

"Well," she continued, "I'm done here, so whenever you're ready, let's head out."

He froze while walking around the kitchen counter. "You're coming along?"

Kim stood. "Yes, I'm coming along. Because while you needed my help in net space, you especially need it now. And not only so I can watch your back, but because the bot's life-saving plan is a go, and I need to explain this to him."

He parted his lips. "It is? What does this plan consist of?"

Kim opened her hands. "Eric, you want me to explain everything while the bot rips that asshole into chunks of meat? We need to stop him at all cost. If your friend kills that guy, I can't do shit for him. Let's get going, and I'll fill you in when we have a chance to breathe."

He nodded, and with the meat mallet in hand, he and Kim headed towards the door.

***

Inside his auto, Eric directed the vehicle towards the Vale residence. "Well," he told Kim, checking the time estimation, "it won't be long before we get there. Just twenty minutes."

"What do you think will happen once we arrive?"

"Worst-case scenario, we find Chad in a pile of smashed remains. But maybe we'll get lucky and catch Arvin on route to Chad's room, cracking his metallic knuckles."

"And if that plays out?"

"Try intervening. The only question is with verbal pleas or the meat mallet?"

"What are the odds of either working?"

He shrugged. "I'm not sure. Arvin might be so hell-bent on revenge he won't care what we say or do."

"Damn. But do you think he'll injure us to complete his mission?"

"I doubt it, but even rational people can act irrationally when placed in difficult situations."

"Trust me, I know. Your life went a little south, and you bypassed your ethical obligations to become a digital detective, complete with a female cover, high heels, and a pistol."

He smirked. "Everyone deals with difficult situations differently."

Kim grinned and looked over. "I agree. But, Eric." She waited for him to turn. "I'm glad you finally have some vitality back. Admittedly, I wish you would've directed this vitality towards something more principled, but the spark is there nevertheless, and that's what matters."

He nodded. "I'm glad too. And to think, all it took was a murderous robot."

***

Eighteen minutes later, the auto reached the Vale residence. As it approached, Eric spotted the death bot, so he directed the auto to park farther down the street. That would give him time to hide the meat mallet, as showing up at this hour was odd enough, but strolling up clutching a meat tenderizer...

He and Kim exited into the cool night air. They closed their doors and approached the security post, its death machine eyeing Eric all the while.

"Good evening, Dr. Ryan," said the gravelly voiced hulk. "Shall I call on Ms. Vale, or is she expecting you?"

He smiled to mask his nerves. "She's expecting me, and I'm sorry to say I'm a little late!"

"Understood. Please proceed. I will message the residence of your arrival."

Eric didn't want his arrival announced, but he decided not to argue. With the bot granting him access, there was no need to press his luck for more.

While walking towards the front door, he and Kim halted when the door unlocked and cracked opened. Feet frozen, he kept his eyes glued to the elegant wooden panel, waiting for someone to emerge. No one did. He turned back towards the checkpoint. Had the metallic menace opened the door or someone from inside? Unsure, but not wanting to ask the death machine, he turned back towards the door and cautiously approached.

Peeking through the crack, he found mostly darkness, which didn't ease his tensing nerves. Shaking this off, he pushed open the door, turned back, and nodded Kim along. After they entered, he eased the door shut and they stood there straining to detect signs of life. There wasn't much, just a barely audible voice coming from upstairs.

"Chad," he guessed. "When I was here, he came down from upstairs, so maybe his room is on the second story."

"And the bot?"

"I don't know. Arvin mentioned something about staying in basement quarters, but I have no clue where that is."

"In that case, we should split up. You head upstairs and check on Chad, and I'll go in search of the bot."

"Alright. Good idea."

"Okay. And be careful."

"You too."

With that, Kim headed off into the darkness, while he started for the rounding staircase.

Halfway up the ascent, he pulled out the meat mallet. He also shook his head. Why in the hell had he brought this damn thing along? How would he explain it to anyone here? For that matter, how would he explain being here? Then he recalled the murder, and how Chad slaughtered Alice with such unremitting violence. Now nearing the perpetrator, he readjusted his grip on the makeshift club.

He inched along the second-floor hallway, stepping heel-to-toe, when the voice droned once more. Chad. His room was a couple doors down, and he was inside talking to someone. Eric glared at this. He had hoped to come across a lone wolf. Now at the beast's lair, he would simply have to see how things played out.

He cautiously cranked over the knob and eased back the door, but only enough to peek inside. Chad was alone. He sat at his desk talking to blurry holo-images. Eric, still at the entrance, tried to make out the speakers. While he couldn't, Chad's words promptly placed their identities.

"...I fucking hate it," Chad went on, "that they die so quickly. You only have like, ten seconds to do them and that's it. Once they realize what's going on, jumping out's the easiest thing in the world."

Inaudible voices responded.

"Well," Chad replied, "it's impossible to keep them *in* the world. They have full control over that. That's why torture won't work. Believe me, it would be nice, but we can't stop them from escaping."

More muffled voices responded. Clearly, Chad was discussing tonight's events with his cohort of lunatics.

"What?" Chad playfully asked. "You wanna compete to see how long we can draw it out? Fine, because for me, that's no competition at all!" His amusement soured. "But first things first. I need to find out who the fuck came into my apartment."

More responses came in.

Chad grew outright heated. "I know that was James Dean, you moron! That's not what I meant! I meant finding out who was controlling James Dean, how they knew where I lived, and how they knew when I would pull off the hit!"

More than ever, Eric regretted not shooting Victor Vane when he had the chance. He had also heard enough. And since he couldn't think of any verbal pleasantries to announce himself, he cleared his throat.

Chad spun in his chair and narrowed his eyes. "What the fuck are you doing here?"

Eric smirked. *Good goddamn question.*

Chapter 31

Kim padded into the darkness, looking for something that hinted at basement quarters. With the house so shadowy, it was hard to make out much of anything. Luckily, she had tech that could assist. She mentally activated her net-enabled contacts and eye-tracked through the blue-colored menu options. After stopping at the environmental enhancers, she activated the light amplifier. Seconds later, the home's shadowy hues glowed greenish-brown.

She continued rooting around the estate, now with a cat-like perspective of the darkness. She spotted various corridors and doorways, but after briefly checking each, she found them leading into elegant rooms, kitchens and closets, but not quarters where the home's robots stayed.

She came across another rounding stairway, one with a door positioned just underneath. Testing the knob, she found the door locked. However, the door's modern presentation made her think of something.

Guessing the lock was digitally controlled, she activated her contact's scanner and analyzed the system. Sure enough, the lock was networked into the home's security system and controlled just the same.

She went back into her menu and brought up a hidden subfolder, one storing off-the-books options such as hacking programs. She knelt and used her onboard computer to trigger the locking switch. After a few cautious looks around, she opened the door and slipped inside.

She entered what seemed like a storage room, but the boxes along the shelves didn't feel right. After walking up to boxes and rifling through them, she saw that they contained medical supplies, and a home possessing a hospital's worth of stores didn't make sense. Nevertheless, she kept looking over the boxes, trying to find a theme within the stash. Unfortunately, the box's medical jargon was hieroglyphics. Good thing her onboard system could assist here as well.

She activated her data reader and rescanned the boxes, now with the aid of the Internet. Just beside the scanned boxes were digital data projections, the information detailing what the containers held.

"Opioid-based pain killers?" she murmured.

Were the Vales running an illegal drug ring out of their home? But Eric and Arvin mentioned something about murder, so that couldn't be right. She kept reading the data projections and paused once more.

"Incapacitation anesthetics?"

She picked up a box labeled Mivacurium Chloride, and learned that hospital staff used this neuro-muscular blocking agent to numb people into paralysis while leaving their mental faculties intact. That by itself didn't seem nefarious, but in the hands of someone aiming to commit murder, it was a different story.

Opening the box, she found a couple Mivacurium bottles inside, with one bottle half full. That meant someone had used this, but when? Uncertain, she replaced the box and continued down the aisle, only to freeze once more. Stopped at another container, she prayed this one's contents were full.

"Potassium chloride."

She knew the purpose of this substance, but her still-active scanner explained nonetheless. It stated that prison authorities used this drug to stop the heart of those being executed.

Opening the box, she pinched her lips after finding another partially drained bottle. So far, none of this was direct evidence for the commission of a crime, but it sure as hell didn't look good. To ensure the authorities had this information, she activated her onboard recorder and captured what was here.

With the footage saved, she sent the file to her personal account, but the message never went through. Unsure what accounted for this, she checked the strength of her Internet connection. The bars lit up five out of five. What the hell was going on?

She ran a diagnostics and learned the connection was fine, but the file wasn't leaving the confines of the house. Something here was preventing data transmission, perhaps a blocker. To bypass this, she turned and started for the door, only to freeze once more. In the doorway stood a woman, one looking about lower forties, and staring at her with hooded eyes. Kim made this out thanks to her light amplifier. She also made out a box in the woman's hands. The woman had likely retrieved the box from this room, but which one?

Kim was about to say something, but she held off when the woman stepped back and reached for the door. Kim knew why, so she darted forward to reach the door before the woman shut it. She didn't succeed. The woman closed the door and turned the lock. But Kim had bypassed this before, so she again brought up her hacking program. Like last time, the program successfully opened the lock, but when she grabbed the knob and pulled, no luck. The woman had slid across a deadbolt, a primitive security measure whose low-grade technology would evade her onboard system.

"Fuck," she uttered. The exit was useless.

After a quick dash around the room, she paused. There was no other escape. She again brought up her online messaging system, this time to send a panic call to the authorities. But as before, the transmission failed to get beyond the home. But could she message someone *inside* the home—someone who was similarly equipped to receive electronic data?

***

Eric continued standing outside of Chad's room. How should he answer Chad's question? Why was he here? In truth, he arrived to protect Chad from an unhinged robot. But after realizing who sat before him, he decided to pursue a different course.

"Did you kill your father?"

Chad hesitated for a moment. He then turned towards his screens, closed the windows, and turned back. "I'm sorry?" he asked, a grin edging into his face. "Did I what?"

"Did you kill your father?"

"My father died from a heart attack."

Eric furrowed his brow. "How stupid do you think people are? Everyone knows that dying from natural causes is astronomically unlikely. And you want people to believe that your father dropped dead, and nobody saw it coming?"

"Rare, but it happens."

"It also happens that you have medical training, and probably access to equipment that can stage a murder as something else."

Chad crossed his arms, his grin firmly planted. "Even if what you're saying is true—that my father died under mysterious circumstances—what makes you think I had anything to do with it?"

"You had motive."

"What motive?"

"You hated him. And it's not even hard to pinpoint when the hatred started. It started when your father became more interested in Arvin than you."

Chad's grin evaporated.

"You told me yourself," Eric went on, "that your father put distance between you and him. That he developed a meaningful relationship with Arvin, and he was more concerned with this than with you. *Some people love their work more than anything else.* That's what you told me. I guess that included you, right? How did *that* feel?"

Chad didn't respond.

"Like I said, you hated him. But you couldn't keep this hatred inside. No. Someone had to pay for this. But first, you needed to figure out who was at fault, and thereby figure out who would pay. Tech. It was tech's fault. So, tell me. Is that why you kill people who embrace tech? Why you murder their online avatars?"

Chad leaned forward and squinted his eyes. "James Dean?"

Now Eric kept quiet.

"Jesus Christ. That was *you?* How the fuck did you find me? How did you even know— The bot. The fucking bot!" Chad started to rise.

Eric moved aside, bringing the meat mallet into view. Chad stopped, grinned once more, and reseated himself.

"Killing people in virtual worlds," Eric continued. "That's pretty sick. It's not illegal but sick. And when you couple that with all the other circumstantial evidence, it doesn't look good for you. And what might people find if they investigate further? What if the police get involved and conduct a real probe? Hell. I'm just a psychologist with a hunch, and look what I came across?"

"So," Chad said, now struggling to mask his ire, "what exactly did the bot tell you?"

"Stuff. Mainly filling in what I wanted to know or confirming what I already suspected. But Arvin did help me piece together this puzzle. I'm curious. Is that why your family is getting a new bot? I mean, if Arvin gets wiped, no more suspicion, right?"

Out of nowhere, Chad's cheer returned, and brighter than before. Eric wondered what elicited this when something stung his neck. He cupped the puncture point while spinning, and there stood Ms. Vale, syringe in hand. Dropping the mallet, he whipped out his phone to call for help. He had to act before the substance took effect.

"I wouldn't do that," Ms. Vale cautioned. "Not if you want your girlfriend to live."

Eric froze with his thumb over the call button. Shit. Hit the button or no?

"It won't matter either way," Chad said, standing from his chair. "Our home's security system prevents unregistered data from entering or exiting."

Eric snapped back to Chad. Was that true? It *didn't* matter either way, though not because of Chad's stated reason.

Eric's legs buckled and he crashed onto the floor, his phone clattering alongside. Reality blurred, and he couldn't tell if that was from the injected substance or his head smacking onto the floor. Whatever the reason, reality would soon fade to black. And when it did, he doubted he would ever see its light again.

But the world didn't slip into darkness. It approached the precipice but stopped short of going over. The injected substance paralyzed him but left his awareness intact. And while he appreciated maintaining his wits, the sensation chilled him, as if his body had disappeared and only his ghost remained. In a way, that made him desire unconsciousness, but awake he remained. He was even awake enough to make out the room's voices.

"He's done," Chad said.

"Get him out of the goddamn hallway," Ms. Vale responded.

Seconds later, hands shimmied underneath his armpits and dragged him into Chad's room. He felt nothing as this happened, save for some weak sensations in his face. For all he knew, his back could've been broken. As for movement, his head simply wobbled while carried, then it wobbled once more when Chad gripped his shirt and flipped him over. Now on his back, he could make out most of the room, including Ms. Vale locking the door from inside.

She walked over and stared down. "Is he fully immobile?"

Chad similarly approached and used his shoe nudge the lump of meat. "Yeah. He's out. He's awake but he can't feel or move." He knelt and examined Eric with thoroughness that could only come from training. "How much did you give him?"

"Just one dose. And only the paralyzing agent."

"One dose of Mivacurium," Chad reflected. He pinched Eric's chin and shifted it around. After a few seconds, he let go but kept on appraising. "Ten minutes. With him probably weighing one-seventy, he'll be like this for ten minutes." He took a breath. "So what now?"

"What do you think?"

It was an answer, not a question, and judging by Ms. Vale's delivery, he was in trouble. This didn't surprise him given her personality, but oddly enough, the decision seemed to freeze Chad.

"It's not going to be as easy," Chad finally said, speaking absentmindedly, "as it was with... with Dad."

That was even more interesting. Clearly, Chad wasn't comfortable with this. What was more, Chad seemed to regret that something similar happened in the past. Unfortunately, Eric couldn't exploit the occurrence. He also couldn't stop Chad from swallowing his emotions and summoning anger.

"Suicide," Chad suggested, spinning towards his mother. "Won't that work?"

"You tell me. Will people even believe that?"

"Of course, they will. This guy hates his life, he hates society, he hates having lost his old job..."

"But where? Here?"

Chad shook this off. "His place. We'll take care of this there. I'll scope it out, and if we're lucky, he lives alone and we can do it tonight. If not, I'll check the patterns of the people staying there."

Ms. Vale tightened her thin lips. "And if you have to *check the patterns of the people staying there,* how long will that take?"

"That depends on who's there and what their schedules are like. I don't know. A couple of days?"

Now she crossed her thin arms. "A couple of days? What are we supposed to do with him for a couple of days?"

"That's the worst-case scenario. Either way, he'll be asleep the entire time. I still have tons of sedatives, so we'll move him somewhere quiet and you won't even know he's here."

Ms. Vale cast her hawkish stare towards the prisoner. "Fine. Hide him and keep him sedated. The sooner you take care of this, the better." She turned back towards her son. "And Chad." She waited for him to look up. "Don't forget why we're in this situation to begin with. Don't forget that when people hurt you, they lose the right to fair treatment. And don't forget about the person who hurt you the most, and how this person hurt me just the same." She paused. "And don't even think about injecting the final substance. As with your father, you leave that to me. Is that clear?"

Chad hesitated for a long while before slowly nodding.

"Now," Ms. Vale said. "I need to go see his girlfriend." She turned, started for the door, and extended her hand towards the knob. The door ended up exploding into the room, sending her flying backwards.

Eric's mind electrified as he hoped a special tactics police team just breeched the room. But how did they know he was in trouble? Seconds later, a figure slowly moved into view. It wasn't the police.

Chapter 32

Arvin slowly clomped into Chad's room, stopping a few feet inside where he surveyed the room's occupants one-by-one. Through his optic receptors, he kept track of everyone here while mentally messaging Kim, the data sent to her net contacts.

Kim, I'm inside Chad's room. I also gave Eric a cursory scan. He's not in immediate danger. Did you get outside and alert the authorities?

Yeah, Kim messaged back. *Cops and medics are on their way. I'm coming back inside.*

No, you're not.

What do you mean no? I'm coming inside and heading upstairs. And speaking of that, where on the second floor is Chad's room?

A moment later, she sent another message. *Hey! Arvin! Open the front door!*

Banging came from downstairs.

Arvin! Kim continued sending. *Open the goddamn—*

Arvin clipped off the communication line and calmly stepped towards Ms. Vale, now struggling to stand. Taking a knee, he grabbed her elegant black shirt, stood, and lifted her off the floor. She probably didn't weigh much, but the effort didn't register in the slightest. He didn't even react when she started kicking his metallic body as she clamped onto his crane-like arm.

With Ms. Vale thrashing, Arvin turned his attention to Chad who had retreated to the room's far end. Without ceremony, he slowly moved in.

Chad spun towards his desk, rapidly looked around, and picked up a classic finger-punch type keyboard. He spun back and hurled the device. The keyboard struck Arvin square in his face, its plastic frame cracking in half. As keys spilled onto the floor, Arvin didn't flinch or break his stride.

Chad's color drained from his face and he rapidly looked around some more, apparently for an escape route. He lunged towards the door, but Arvin not only possessed superhuman strength, but superhuman speed. He darted sideways and snatched Chad by the throat, then lifted him off the floor and pinned him against the wall. Chad's terror increased when the robotic grim reaper tightened his alloy hand.

Ms. Vale and Chad now flailed helplessly, both gouging, kicking, and slapping at him. Arvin didn't blink a mechanical eye. From the moment he kicked in the door, to the moment he snatched up the two most hated people, his facial expression hadn't changed. That induced a horrifically chilling effect.

Chad jerked his fingers towards Arvin's grip and started digging, but this was pointless. Arvin locked in his hold with mechanical strength. Maybe Chad realized this, maybe he didn't, but either way, his fight wound down and his eyes began to shut.

"Arvin!" Ms. Vale pleaded.

Arvin paid her no mind.

"Arvin!" she shouted once more. "Dr. Ryan!"

This got his attention. He turned towards Eric who was slowly regaining his strength, the notion evident in Eric's raised and trembling hand.

Eric still couldn't speak, but that didn't matter. Arvin never needed to hear his words to understand him. Eric must've realized this, which was why he beamed out specific data. *We're the same. There's no difference between us. You and I are the same.*

Arvin knew what that meant. With them identical, and with Eric wanting to avoid completing the mission to preserve his humanity, mission completion would destroy his own humanity. How could he let this happen? How could he willingly give away what was so important?

He didn't understand humanity perfectly, but he knew it was fragile, knew it could be lost. And losing it over Chad Vale—the most inhuman person he ever met—wasn't worth it. No, he wasn't about to destroy his most valued possession over the likes of that goddamn machine.

Arvin loosened his grip, and Chad took deep desperate breaths. At this, Eric lowered his hand, relief streaking across his face.

Arvin turned to Chad. "What did your mother give Dr. Ryan?" He slammed Chad backwards to hasten an answer.

"A sed... a sedative! It's not... it's not lethal!"

"That's lucky for you, because Dr. Ryan is the only reason why you're still alive."

With that, Arvin readied two data files. The first was his scan of Eric that he would give to the paramedics. The second, which was for the police, was his recording of Chad's room where Chad and his mother admitted to murdering Dr. Benjamin Vale.

Epilogue

Eric walked down the street in L.A. Confidential, quite literally back to his old self. He was inside his original avatar, the spitting image of his real space body, and the character strolled along with his head held high.

He beamed despite the mission not turning out as planned, because in lieu of exposure, Chad and his mother were incarcerated and facing murder charges. They would surely hire the best lawyers money could buy, but the case was solid. Not only did Ms. Vale admit to the murder on film, Eric pointed out her and Chad's forensic footprints to the officers now investigating the case. But while real space moved swiftly against its wrongdoers, net space was a different story.

Online killers were still on the loose. The Crypt Keepers were only down one member, and knowing them, they would probably step up their murderous efforts just to show everyone the consequences of targeting their own. But on the bright side, L.A. Confidential was free of the wolf that stalked its streets. Furthermore, the wolf only claimed one victim before his banishment. Still, this probably didn't console the person who suffered his wrath.

Eric often thought of Alice. He even considered reaching out to her, mostly because he wanted to apologize. Unfortunately, he didn't have her contact information, and given what happened, she was likely off the grid. He would still make an attempt but not now. The first order of business was meeting Mike at The Clover, which was the only person he could meet because Arvin was dead.

When the story's dust settled, Arvin had his memories wiped, something Eric tried to halt by arguing that Arvin never killed anyone. But Arvin's role in the story was unacceptable to those deciding his fate, something Kim saw coming. Before his wipe, she contacted friends who illegally copied bots, and they successfully transferred his data into net space.

Eric smirked while considering this. It was him who yearned for a virtual existence. He still planned on doing as much, but he would have to make frequent returns to real space, because by some miracle, Dr. Wright pulled him from the fire yet again, when UCLA wanted to terminate him yet again.

But Mike was free to roam net space as he pleased, and when he arrived for the start of his stay, he invited Eric to their favorite Irish pub.

***

Mike leaned back in his booth and smiled. With folksy Irish music and chattering voices swirling around him, he urged to inform Eric of his plans to visit historical worlds with one purpose: obtaining a deeper understanding of who he was. Because he stemmed from humans, he figured that investigating their history meant investigating his own. And now, he had a boundless opportunity to do so.

He could now venture back in time and learn of his ancestors by living their lives, and by seeing what they saw. Wholly unchained, and with an indefinite future ahead of him, he was now free to learn the human story—free to learn *his* story.

Made in the USA
San Bernardino, CA
16 January 2020